For information on other books by this author, visit Jessahme Wren online at
https://jessahmewren.com

Paperback ISBN 979-8-9921943-5-7

For all of us looking for our place in the world.

FOREWORD

I set out to write the kind of story I'd always wanted to read. That's the way most writing endeavors start out, after all. You're fulfilling a need that would otherwise go unfulfilled. All my life, I've loved plucky protagonists…powerful females I could look up to. As a child, I read about real-life heroes—Alabama First Lady Lurleen Wallace and Amelia Earhart. I dove into the chaotic and caring world of Red Cross founder Clara Barton, imagining myself making those decisions and affecting those lives.

Then I found fiction. *Ramona and Beezus* and others. I loved how real they felt. I swam in the sultry worlds of Ray Bradbury, luxuriating in how human his characters were and how his worlds breathed.

When I started writing Terra Firma, it was the summer of 2023. I wrote longhand with cheap pens that bled through the paper, filling palm-sized notebooks until the pages tenderized and curled at the edges. Sev and Phoenix had different names then, but the story was there. And at the heart of the story was a wise-beyond-her-years 12-year-old looking for her place in the world.

There were surprises along the way. Sev was older in earlier drafts, but I quickly realized I needed to contrast her youthful innocence with a world gone rotten. Her wide-eyed wonder tempered with the sharp focus of her wisdom, would contrast perfectly with Phoenix's roguish naivete, and later, his redemption.

Phoenix was another matter altogether. Originally, he lost his arm on Terra Firma, and he spent the first two chapters of the book with four whole limbs. I realized, however, that he needed the gravitas of having a disability early on…something to temper his bravado. A mirror reflecting the cruelty of the world he lives in.

I soon realized Phoenix needed a counterpart—an equal, and it couldn't be Sev. He needed an opposing answer to his question, someone to show him the sort of kindness he believed the world lacked. Enter Pearla. I never intended for Pearla to be a major character, and in Terra Firma, she isn't. She is integral to the Terra universe, however. As essential as breathing. Early beta readers did not take kindly to Pearla. They felt she took the focus off Phoenix and Sev's relationship. They felt she was in the way. I advocated for her, though. Her kind spirit and loving nature won me over as an author, and I knew she had a lot to offer Terra. Truthfully, I see so much of myself in Pearla, and maybe that's why I knew she was here to stay. It was up to me then to convince my readers.

Phoenix and Sev's relationship is, to me, the purest representation of platonic love. They need each other, but they're not codependent. They fill in the blank spaces in each other's lives. Phoenix is looking for a soft place to fall. He's looking to start over. Phoenix finds a fresh start in a bright-eyed, rough-edged little girl who inadvertently becomes his to care for. He didn't ask for it, but there she is all the same. Unexpected, but not unwelcome.

Sev, similarly, is left bereft…fatherless and directionless, but not helpless. She is never helpless. Sev takes care of herself. She takes care of an injured Phoenix. She aids him in escaping Terra Firma, even in the strange circumstances of their unexpected and unconventional partnership. This partnership, born of necessity, grows into something pure and surprising. Sev needs a father. Phoenix needs a new start. The universe provides both in each other.

I hope you enjoy spending time in Terra as I have. I hope these characters touch your life as they have touched mine, and may you see yourself in their triumphs and struggles, both.

–Jessahme Wren

CHAPTER 1

S ev watched her shoes, doing her best to dodge the fetid puddles that dotted the pockmarked streets of Central City. She had her hands stuffed into the pockets of her flight suit. The air was hazy and foul…the distant noise of transports landing and taking off buzzed in her ears.

Her father Del was a few paces ahead; he walked quickly, trudging through the puddles with no regard for the mess or the stench. Some detritus from his careless strides splashed Sev on the leg, and she recoiled, a deep frown on her face.

Del glanced back at his daughter and muttered something, ordering her to walk faster. Sev ignored him. Ahead, one of the last transports to Terra Firma shook into the sky, its boxy, silver hull crawling upward at a surprising speed. Sev stopped and looked up, watching it climb into the heavens and disappear into the endless black.

When she continued walking, it was at a slower pace. No need to rush, she thought. They'd never make the calcet harvest in time, now.

Del seemed to sense this, too. He regarded his daughter, a rueful scowl on his face as if he blamed her for missing the transport.

Sometimes Sev wondered if he wished she'd never been born.

She followed her father as the streets narrowed and the sky darkened. Her stomach protested, and she realized she didn't know the last time she'd eaten.

"I'm hungry," Sev said to no one. She flushed, unbelieving that she'd said it aloud.

1

Del turned to look at her, and his face was softer. He allowed her to pull up even with him, and he placed a tentative hand on her shoulder. "We'll get something at the Terminal," he assured her.

But Sev knew they wouldn't. If they ate anything, it would be ration packs. The credits had run out two systems ago. They had stolen and bartered their way to Central City…their last-ditch effort to make some bank so they could rent their own transport and be able to take on more jobs, only to run out of credits and do it all over again.

Sev was tired. She was twelve years old, but she felt ancient. Her father had pulled her halfway across the galaxy ever since her mother died, a woman Sev couldn't even remember. She couldn't remember a home, or a school, or even childhood friends. There was only her father and the work and the empty vastness of space travel.

Del checked his chrono and shook his head. It would be nighttime before they made the Terminal. The next transport would be a day, maybe more. They didn't have the resources for that type of stay. They needed credits.

When they reached the Terminal in the crushing dark, he didn't say a word. Sev hadn't mentioned her hunger again, but that was hours ago, and he knew she must be famished. Del sold his chrono to the first peddler who approached him, all sharp teeth and predatory smile. He bought three expired ration packs and gave Sev two of them. He stuffed the extra in his pack to keep for later.

They settled on the dirty carpeted floor in one corner of the Terminal. There were no chairs in that area; there were nutrition stations and a few trash receptacles and a single window. People and beings from all over the galaxy passed by them without a glance; they were all on their way out of Central City, while she and Del were stuck.

The Terminal was Central City's only spaceport. The barges there were huge, rectangular ships that went back and forth between star systems every couple of days. If you were lucky and had credits, you sought lodging and waited for your transport. If you didn't, you stayed at the Terminal.

The pale light of a distant moon sifted through the window above them, its ghostly pall the only light shining in the tiny alcove.

Sev chewed bitterly on the ration bar. They weren't her favorite, but she never complained. She paused, broke the bar into two pieces, and handed one half to her father.

Del took it without comment, chewing on it unenthusiastically, suffering the dry, chalky ration bar for the sake of nourishment rather than taste.

"It's just a layover," Del said around a mouthful of ration. "We won't be here more than a day. Maybe less."

Sev doubted that. They'd be stuck in the Terminal at least two days; it took twenty hours to get to Terra Firma and even longer to get back. She unzipped her pack and pulled out her well-loved notebook.

Del had finished his portion of the ration bar and was looking out the window. Sev began to write, the soft scratch of her pen on the paper loud in the space between them.

"You really shouldn't waste resources like that," Del said. Sev stopped momentarily, but never lifted her pen from the paper. "We could sell the pens for credits. Drek knows we need them."

She frowned. Her father did not respect her writing; he saw it as frivolous and useless. Writing was Sev's favorite thing, aside from listening to her music. The worlds she created were the only thing that kept her sane most days.

Sev glanced up at her father, who was staring out the window with dull eyes. He was thin with the pasty complexion of someone who'd spent too much time in the black depths of space. He relied on stim sticks to keep him working, phials to help him sleep. She saw him glance at where his chrono would be. She did not miss the brief expression of regret when he remembered he'd sold it for rations.

"Tell me about mom," Sev said. She was still writing, the pen moving smoothly across the lined pages of her notebook.

Del sighed. It was a story he had told many times, but despite the repetition, Sev never tired of hearing it.

"She was beautiful," Del began. "She had this long blonde hair…wheat-colored hair. Her eyes were a light green, almost blue. She loved water. She loved it when I took her to Dobani, to the beaches there. I took her when she was pregnant with you. And she loved music. She was like you in that way. She

3

loved holographs, especially the celebrity ones. I would take her whenever I could."

Hearing she was like her mother in at least one way never failed to make her cheeks warm. Sev imagined her mother going to the holographs. She had never been to one…Del never had the money to take her, even as inexpensive as it was. On the rare occasion she'd met other children, they'd spoken of the holographs they'd seen with their parents, and Sev had been sick with envy.

Sev briefly wondered how different her life might have unfolded if her mother had lived to raise her with her father. Would her father be the twitchy, desperate man who worked her to the bone alongside him? Or would he be sensitive…protective? A twinge of longing pulled at her chest, and she tucked those thoughts away.

Del appeared wistful, as he usually did whenever he spoke of Sev's mother. He wiped a hand over his face. "She had a hard pregnancy…she was sick a lot. She craved Rafa fruit the whole time, and it was hard to afford." He looked at Sev, sadness coloring his eyes. "She asked for it the night you were born. I've never hated myself more than when I couldn't give her what she wanted."

He cleared his throat, straightening his legs out where he was sitting on the floor. He withdrew a phial, opened it, and swallowed the contents. Del closed his eyes, head reclining against the wall. She observed her father for the few moments it took him to fall into a shallow, drug-induced sleep.

Sev had stopped writing. She was now picturing a beautiful woman with light hair like hers. Green eyes like hers. She wished she could embrace her. She imagined what the wind would feel like on her mother's face. Sev imagined she was the wind, free to go anywhere, to be anything she wanted.

She read over what she had written, listening to the arrivals and departures in the cavernous Terminal. Del slept fitfully, his head lolled against his shoulder. Sev had written a story about meeting her mother on Dobani, holding her hand and wading into the jewel-colored water.

Del awoke some hours later; the stiffness in his neck evident by how gingerly he moved it. He peered at the chrono on the wall and realized how late it was. "Let's try to get some work," he said.

Sev stretched, putting away her journal and pen and zipping up her pack. Her stomach grumbled; the rations she'd eaten hours ago were already long gone.

She said nothing, though. She knew they were out of credits; even though Del never shared their finances, she wasn't stupid. They were running out of things to sell. They needed to work.

Del approached the job counter and pulled a ticket off the board. "This one's right here in the Terminal, Sev." The job was hustling leaflets for some sort of cult, a half credit each. Sev took the pamphlets in her hand and took up a position at the entrance to the Terminal. People were more likely to take pamphlets from a kid, and she knew it. As if on cue, her stomach growled again.

Sev and Del worked a few hours until most of the pamphlets were gone. By the time they'd received their pay, Sev was exhausted. She could mine all day under a solar rain, sweat pouring from her, but talking to people and conniving her way into their good graces was not something she was good at.

They waited in the Terminal. They worked some more, they slept, they nibbled on rations. Sev did not write more, having lost the urge to do anything but work and rest. When their number was finally called, Sev sat back in the passenger seat of the transport barge and closed her eyes. The engine roared, and the craft lurched forward, digging into the sky on its way to Terra Firma.

CHAPTER 2

"That's two draws. What else you got?"

The burly, unkempt man stubbed his stim stick out on the table, grinding it until it was black with ash and bent in the middle. He stared at Phoenix with open disdain, glancing between him and the hand of numbered tokens he held.

Phoenix checked his hand. He was four short, but he wouldn't let Gar know that. He'd won the last two hands on bluffs. This one should be no different.

"All in," Phoenix said with a confident smile. He pushed his pile of credits to the middle of the dirty table. It was cold in the back office of the slaughterhouse, with a flimsy plastic curtain separating the men in the back from the carnage of the refrigerated warehouse. "I would be obliged to see that hand of yours, if you don't mind."

Gar scowled. He drew three tokens, then turned to one of the other men there and gave him a greasy smile. "We'll be eating good tonight, boys." He laid his tokens down. "Three and eight. Doesn't get much better."

The small gathering roared, cheering and clapping for their imminent good fortune. Phoenix suffered it all in stride, all the while internalizing his panic at Gar's excellent hand as any good token player would have. He shuffled the tokens in his hand before slipping his fingers under the edge of the table to retrieve a hidden one. To the untrained eye, it was an insignificant tick, but to the very paranoid or to the outright cheating scoundrel, it was a certain tell.

Phoenix cleared his throat and presented his tokens with a flourish. "Three and three. A perfect run."

The room went deadly silent. Gar sneered, spittle flying from his mouth as he cursed him in his native language. His cronies stepped forward, but before they could seize him, Phoenix smiled bashfully and pulled the pile of credits across the table toward him.

"Cheater!" one man accused, a thin, willowy man with bluish skin. "I saw'r him me'self. He reached under the table, he did."

Phoenix swallowed, stuffing the credits into his bag as hastily as possible. He needed to get out while he could before things got ugly.

Gar stood, his bulbous body bumping the table and almost tipping it over. The blue-skinned man pushed Phoenix out of the way with a strength that belied his size and finished flipping the table on its side. With the table upended, Gar could see the small compartment where Phoenix had hidden the extra token.

Phoenix dropped his credits, hoping to diffuse the situation with a little bribery. The slaughterhouse boys had a strict code against cheating, and he'd just broken it.

"Now gentle beings," Phoenix began, holding his hands up in acquiescence. "I am sure we can all come to a satisfactory conclusion. Everyone can walk out of here none the worse for wear and a little richer to boot."

Gar snarled. Someone grabbed Phoenix from behind. He tried to fight them off, but there were too many. Gar glanced at his compatriots, men who were hungry for blood. "Take his arm," he ordered. "Make him bleed."

The men dragged him through the plastic curtain and onto the slaughterhouse floor. Slabs of meat hung salted and curing in the frigid air. Phoenix's heart roared in his ears, adrenaline making him shaky and faint. He'd cheated the wrong people, and they were going to make him pay.

They stretched his arm across the butcher block and lashed it there with a leather strap. With a flip of the switch, the table saw whirred to life, and Phoenix watched in horror as it blurred into motion.

He screamed. There was a spray of red, a high-pitched stuttering sound, then darkness.

Phoenix woke up alone on the floor of the slaughterhouse. There was the smell of iron and burned flesh. Someone had tied a leather tourniquet above the elbow of his right arm. Or where his arm should be. The arm was gone, the stump cauterized crudely to stop him from bleeding out.

He looked down at the stump and wiggled his phantom fingers. "For Drek's sake," he said to himself, in shock over losing his dominant arm.

His stump was screaming with pain by the time he made it to his flat in Central City. He had no credits for a medic; the slaughterhouse boys had taken all he had and more. He stumbled into the kitchenette, flipping open cabinets until he found his stash of elixirs. The one he preferred was brown and sweet; he flopped down into his raggedy living room chair and pulled the cork out with his teeth.

Phoenix took a swig, and then another. He drank until the throbbing had lessened to a dull ache, something he could push into the background of his mind.

He took off the tourniquet and tested the burned flesh of his stump. It was not bleeding, for now. Phoenix laid his head back against the chair and closed his eyes.

The calcet rush on Terra Firma was in a few days, and his harvesting hand was gone. He would have to harvest one handed, and with the lesser of the two. He frowned, regretting having agreed to that token game with the slaughterhouse boys. It was foolish, trying to cheat them. And now his arm was gone.

Phoenix drained the bottle and set it on the table near his chair. Light diffused inside the empty vessel, as dull as the contents had been. His mind became pleasantly fuzzed, and his stump no longer hurt.

Terra Firma would be a new start, he thought as he drifted. He would harvest enough calcet to move out of Central City for good. He could get a little house somewhere sunny, harvest when he wanted, and not just when he was hungry. Maybe he would quit swindling…or just quit being caught. He'd be back on his feet. Things would be good again. Tomorrow was a new day.

When he eventually fell asleep, he did not dream.

Morning came with a crushing headache and a sour taste in his mouth. The numbing effects of elixir and sleep had worn off, and his stump was on fire with a searing pain. Phoenix blinked; it was nearly midday, and he was due at the hangar by noon.

He stood stiffly, grunting with the effort it took to right himself after drinking the entire bottle and then passing out in his living room. It wasn't the first time he'd done so, and he doubted it would be the last.

Phoenix took off his shirt and tossed it onto the floor. It was bloody from the amputation and stank of sweat and burned flesh. He stripped the rest of the way to the bathroom, finally stumbling into the shower and turning on the water.

The cold spray almost took his breath. Hot water was for the wealthy; besides, the chilly shower would help him wake up.

He scrutinized where his right arm should be, tears springing to his eyes.

The excess flap of skin puckered grotesquely, covering up the remaining bone. Whatever they'd used to cauterize the wound had done the job. Any attention they'd paid to his wound was purely performative, he knew…Phoenix was no good to them dead. Leaving him alive and maimed sent a message to everyone who saw him…there's a price to pay for cheating in the Outer Edges.

Phoenix stood under the frigid water, gooseflesh pebbling his skin. He could barely wash with one hand; he hadn't a clue how he would harvest.

Phoenix shut the shower down and hastily toweled off. The sun was coming through the grimy window of his flat, staining the floor with its murky light. He rummaged through his dresser, looking for something to wear under his suit.

The suit was another matter altogether.

The sleeve would need to be tied up well. He couldn't risk it not being airtight. Phoenix examined it where it lay spread over his bed, rubbing his chin with his remaining hand.

He got dressed and got to work, cutting the sleeve and sealing it against the elements.

When he arrived at the hangar, Taz was waiting for him near the ship. Phoenix's appearance surprised him, his eyes fixed on his missing arm. He held out the card with the launch codes, a sympathetic expression on his face.

"Rough night?"

Phoenix frowned. "You could say. I've definitely had better."

Taz appeared serious, withdrawing the card before Phoenix could take it. "This makes us even, you understand?"

Phoenix inclined his head. "I do appreciate you lending me your fine ship," he said. "I shall treat it as my own."

Taz frowned. "Don't bother. You can't even keep all your appendages."

Phoenix quirked his mouth in a regretful sort of smile, but said nothing.

"How are you going to harvest, Phoenix, with one hand, and the left one at that?"

Phoenix quirked his mouth, his eyes hard. "Now, I believe the condition of your debt to me does not include questioning my actions." Phoenix grabbed the card and pocketed it. "So, if you'll just step aside, I'll be on my way."

Taz huffed but stepped out of the way for Phoenix to board the ship. He struggled at first, but Taz offered no help, and Phoenix didn't ask for any.

The hangar roof opened just as he fired the thrusters. With one last look at the dismal hangar in Central City, Phoenix punched in the coordinates and shot into the dirty sky on his way to Terra Firma.

CHAPTER 3

Terra Firma was lush, exotic, and dangerous. Sev knew this from the books she'd read...of deadly spores and poisonous air...of exposed flesh rotting away like it was doused with acid, blackened and charred. That's why Del had postponed their participation in the annual calcet harvest until they were well and truly desperate. That's how she knew things were as bad as they were.

It was a perilous place, and although Del was not the best father by any stretch of the imagination, he wouldn't put her at risk unless it was necessary for their survival.

Sev adjusted her suit; she had changed on the barge. There were other harvesters there...people and beings going to seek their fortune. Their suits were shinier, newer, nicer than hers and Del's. Either this was their first time on Terra Firma, or they had credits that she and Del didn't. She caught someone looking at her, and she quickly averted her gaze. She was the only child on the transport.

The stranger huffed a laugh, vaporous and distorted through their helmet's modulator. "Didn't know they made suits that small."

Sev blushed, then shot them a scornful glance. The stranger turned their attention to Del. "Terra Firma is no place for children. You know that, right?"

Del ignored them. He was extra twitchy today...probably too many stim sticks and no breakfast. "Sev can handle herself," he groused. He placed a hand on his air gun, a not-so-subtle flex. "We both can."

Sev rolled her eyes. Her father was not as strong as he would have people believe, and sometimes his bravado got them in more trouble than was necessary.

The barge lurched, then shook violently as it entered the volatile atmosphere of Terra Firma. Sev braced herself, tightening her pack and checking her air filter for what was likely the twelfth time in the past hour. It was half full…not new, but it would do. The barge settled down onto the dreadfully beautiful landscape, and the harvesters on board the barge started jockeying for the hatch. Sev took a breath, steeling herself. Her father motioned her faster, and they followed the others out onto the surface of Terra Firma. They would have to walk to the calcet pit from here, a half-day's journey.

The private transport Phoenix borrowed from Taz saved him from the notoriously slow transport barges others relied on to take them to Terra Firma. The one on the way to the planet was the last barge that would run the route, or so he heard. Future harvesters would need private transports like the one he'd taken or not go at all. They were faster than a barge, and as a result, he was one of the first harvesters at the Pit.

He would need the head start. This was the first time he'd harvested with one hand, and he was still reeling from losing it.

He settled at the Pit, his kit beside him. The Pit was a large cavity, maybe fifty feet across and about five feet deep. It belched and undulated with the half-alive membranes that contained the precious gems.

The other harvesters considered him warily, dubious of the one-armed harvester with the curious white patch in his hair. They stayed mostly to themselves; it was an unspoken rule…you didn't get too close to other harvesters, and you minded your business at the Pit.

Harvesting gems was as much a physical process as it was a chemical one. First the harvester extracted the bulb, then the membrane had to be cut. Cut too deeply, and the acid sack surrounding the gem would burst, and the gem would melt. Don't cut deeply enough, and the gem would die inside the

14

membrane, clouding its clarity and diminishing its worth. With two hands, Phoenix was skilled at it; now with just the one, he found himself challenged.

But he had never backed down from a challenge. It took some effort, but he had several gems already, and it was hours before sunset.

By the time Del and Sev arrived at the Pit, there was hardly any room at the edge. Harvesters from all over the system competed for a position around the rim. They climbed in and out of the Pit, stepping over one another and tripping on their own air hoses.

Del pushed Sev forward first, maneuvering her roughly between two harvesters. Her job was to retrieve the membranes and carry them back up to her father for the cut. He was skilled with the chemicals needed to flush the acid and free the calcet. Sev knew little about such things, but she could climb. She could do her part. She lowered herself down into the Pit and set to work.

Phoenix, close to being done with his harvesting, observed all this impassively. Who would bring a little girl to Terra Firma, he wondered to himself. Someone greedy. Someone unfit to be a father.

Phoenix averted his eyes, adhering to the golden rule at the Pit.

Hours later, he was walking back to his transport, lost in the fantasy of his new start and happy with his harvest, when he felt the barrel of an air gun press into his back.

Phoenix raised his arm, dropping the calcet gems onto the verdant forest floor. He turned around slowly, arm still raised, only to find the man he'd noticed at the Pit. The one with the little girl in tow.

"Well hello friend," he said with a put-upon smile. "To what do I owe the displeasure of this conflict? Have I wronged you in some way in which I am wholly unaware?"

His eyes fell on the little girl. She was watching with quick green eyes a few steps behind her father. She held an air gun of her own, and she trained it on Phoenix.

Del stepped closer to Phoenix, the gun pointed squarely at his chest. "Give us your gems and the launch code to your transport, and no one has to get hurt."

"Dad—"

"Shut up," he hissed. "This doesn't concern you." He cocked the gun, and it charged with a low hum. "Slide the bag of gems over to us. With your foot."

Phoenix swallowed, weighing his options. He could take him down, but the little girl was close. He didn't want a child getting caught up in a brawl on Terra Firma. Too much could happen. Suits could get torn in the scuffle. One whiff of spores and the lungs burn right out of your chest.

He ultimately obliged, slowly sliding the bag over to Del who grabbed it greedily.

Del stared at him down the barrel of the gun. "Now, the codes."

Phoenix scoffed. "Well, you've confiscated my treasure, and now my transportation too? Did you not travel here to Terra Firma just as I did? Why don't you go back the way you came?"

Del became quiet. His eyes were the empty, soulless eyes of a desperate man. Sev glanced between her father and the one-armed man he held at gunpoint until she finally understood.

"He bought a one-way ticket," she said aloud. "Didn't you, Dad? You didn't have the credits for a round trip. And now you're stuck. We both are."

Phoenix raised his eyebrows, surprised at the girl's deduction. She was a quick one, the little mouse. She had no place being on Terra Firma, where the air kills and the spores poison your flesh.

"I said, SHUT UP," Del gritted out, looking at Sev and lowering the gun briefly. Phoenix took his chance. He rounded on Del, but not before pushing the girl out of the way. She dropped the air gun and fell with a harmless thunk on the forest floor.

Phoenix threw his whole body into him, knocking him to the ground. They tussled; the gun went off between them once, and once more, and Sev was sure her father had killed the one-armed man.

But the man rolled off her father and lay back on the dense vegetation of Terra Firma, gasping for breath. He was bleeding from an air gun wound to the stomach. Sev knew he wouldn't last long; his air filter was compromised, and spores were probably already infesting the wound.

She ran to her father's side. The gunshot had pierced his chest. There was no breath coming from his modulator. Blood bloomed around an ugly hole in his suit, and his eyes were fixed and lifeless.

Del was gone.

Sev stood, trying to catch her breath. The green of Terra Firma spun before her, and she closed her eyes against it. She walked over to the one-armed man; he was wheezing, fogging the inside of his helmet. She hooked him to her filter; her father's air gun had blown his out. Sev took a steady breath, and the air filter rattled. She'd been on Terra Firma too long to be safe, and now her overtaxed filter was struggling to churn out clean air for two. Her vision went dark at the edges, and she sat down on the forest floor before she could black out.

The man stumbled to his feet and stood over her. He was speaking, his one arm clutching his abdomen, blood a steady flow from beneath his hand. "Just catch your breath, little mouse," he was saying. "It'll be alright. Just you see."

It was not alright. Her father was dead. She was alone on a deadly planet. She looked into the eyes of the man who had killed him, and her world went dark.

CHAPTER 4

"We'll stay the night if it's amenable to you," the man said, sweat beading his brow. "Terra Firma does not offer favors lightly. We would be remiss to hand one back unappreciated."

Sev settled on the cot, her eyes on the thin zipper enclosure that separated them from Terra Firma. The man had carried her to an old miner's tent, its air filter still intact. His wounds needed attention, and her overtaxed filter needed time to reset.

"Besides, you're peaked still. The spores did a number on you, girl." He looked at her, deep brown eyes shining. "Take slow, deep breaths."

He was one to talk. He was clearly hurting, both from the wound in his abdomen and the amputation that seemed very recent and very raw from the blood that still seeped into the fabric of his tied-up sleeve. "What's your name?" she rasped.

The man grinned despite the ugly wound in his abdomen. "Phoenix," he said. He stuck out his hand, thoroughly covered in blood. "At your service."

Her mouth twitched at that, but she did not shake his hand. She breathed in, slowly and deeply. The air filtration unit in the old miner's tent was surprisingly true. The air inside was humid but clear of spores.

Phoenix fiddled with a ration bar, struggling to open it with only one hand. He was being surprisingly patient with himself.

"Give it to me," Sev snapped, tired of seeing him struggle.

He handed it over, giving her a lazy smile. When she passed it back to him, his stump twitched, the impulse to grab it with his missing dominant hand causing the muscles to contract.

"I thank you kindly, little mouse." He settled down on the side of the cot, a nasty cough rattling his chest. "I thank you kindly."

Despite her better judgment, she'd patched him up. It was a shoddy job with the poor kit they'd found, but it would hold. She'd felt compelled to help. She was alone without him, after all. Del's death, as new as it was, clung to her like a shroud.

Phoenix was an adult. He could be useful. And she needed a way off the planet. He was no good to her dead.

Sev lay still, looking up at the rust-red of the underside of the tent. She could hear Phoenix's labored breathing, the sound of him making his way through the ration bar, thoroughly dissatisfied. She began to worry, as was her way. Things seemed bleaker than usual.

"What about the transport? What if we can't make it back?"

Phoenix took a shaky breath, a cough on the tail-end of it. He covered his mouth with his remaining fist, a vain attempt to stifle the spasm. He was sweating, the only indication that he was in pain.

"We'll make it back. For now, we could use the rest." He lay back on the cot with a grunt.

She frowned, preferring to leave for the transport sooner rather than later. Sev couldn't deny she felt better, though. She was already feeling the edifying effects of the clean filtered air, the ration bar in her stomach.

Phoenix clutched his abdomen, his brow creased in consternation. "You stitched it up good," he said, his voice strained. "Sealed it proper. Fit for Terra Firma." His voice held a note of awe. "What a talented medic you are."

She gazed over at him, her face softening. The moments stretched between them, punctuated only by the rickety air filter and Phoenix's pained, uneven breathing.

"Why didn't you leave me for dead when you had the chance? Why didn't you shoot me like you shot my father?" Her voice was flat and sounded far away. She wasn't sure why she'd asked, but some part of her knew he would answer truthfully.

He turned on the cot, leaning on his good side to look at her. "I am a lot of things, Drek knows. A killer, as you have had the misfortune to attest, and a scoundrel. But I am not the sort of monster who would harm a little girl."

It settled her. She didn't think she had misjudged Phoenix. In fact, she was sure she hadn't, but perhaps there was just more to him than what was obvious.

Phoenix coughed, ragged and loud in the small space. He got his bearings and took a steadying breath to calm himself. His abdomen was on fire, his stump screamed with pain. It was at once a deep-bone ache, though there was no bone there to suffer so, and a pulsing, throbbing acuteness. "While we are pursuing this particular discourse," he stammered out, "let us chase this line of inquiry to its foregone conclusion. Get to the truth of the matter, as it were." He clutched at his shoulder, trying to relieve some of the agony. "Why did you not run away, little mouse? When you awoke in this tent and had all of Terra Firma to flee too?"

She said nothing at first. The girl was short with her words, but thoughtful. He appreciated that.

"There was nowhere else to go," she admitted.

Phoenix smiled. "Well, I am certainly glad you didn't," Phoenix said. "My wounds needed tending, and you were spore-sick too, although to a lesser degree than I. Seems as though Terra Firma stepped in with providence for the both of us."

They fell into an easy silence. Phoenix, as much as he could with the pain he was dealing with, and Sev, still battling the fatigue brought on by a spent filter. She thought of Del until she couldn't bear it any longer.

"Do you need another phial?" Her voice was smaller than she would've liked, but she was tired, worn from this terrifying planet. They'd found some analgesics in the left-behind field kit, and the one she had given him had most certainly worn off.

"I would be obliged if one were available," he said, his voice little more than a whisper. He patted the wound on his abdomen with his remaining hand. "Your father's bite is but a phantom now, but it still stings."

She got up from the cot and rifled through the field kit. Sev found the phial and brought it to Phoenix where he sat waiting for her.

She pulled the cap and gave it to him to drink. He did so and gasped, his head going back. A full body shudder went through him until the analgesic effects of the phial kicked in. He sighed, seeming to deflate. Then he smiled, hazy and for the first time, relaxed.

"Drek sent," he whispered, and Sev was unsure if he was talking about the phial or about her. The warmth spread through his body, a soothing balm that pushed the pain, which was ever-present, into the background for a time.

He closed his eyes, and Sev thought he might fall asleep sitting there. When he opened them, they were fixed on her. "Why did your father make you harvest the calcet," he asked, "when he was perfectly capable on his own?"

She listened to him, his lilting dialect taking on a simpler affect. "He said I was smaller," she said as she discarded the spent phial and returned to her cot. "Faster. And because I'm young. He thought maybe the other harvesters would let me have first choice."

"Hmm," he hummed. "Too young to be working so," he said to himself. "But such is the Outer Reaches."

She lay back. She thought of the jobs of her tender youth, that summer harvesting Gala eggs, of how hard Del had pushed her. The more eggs she could reach, the more credits they earned only to spend them and do it all over again. The jobs changed, but it was always the same. No destination…no home to call their own. And seemingly no end.

She closed her eyes. "Have you ever been to Dobani?"

He said nothing for a moment. He was drifting, she knew, and somehow it didn't anger her like when Del used the phials for his own purposes…no emergency, no medical need. Just because they made him feel nice.

"Why, I have indeed. Beautiful Dobani." He fell silent for a moment. "Why do you ask, mouse?"

"Tell me what it's like," she said instead.

Phoenix inhaled…even his breathing was better now. It must be the filtration unit, she thought. "Dobani is warm," he said. "With glittering sand beaches and water besides, as far as you can see."

Her eyes were still closed. She imagined standing at the water's edge on Dobani, the place her mother loved.

"What did you do when you were there?" she asked. She knew she was straining him, but he never seemed to tire of her questions, and these were things she'd wanted to know from Del, who had been unwilling to talk or even to listen.

"Oh, trading, mostly. Dobani is as good a place as any to restock your wares, nutrition and field kits and the like. Lots of beings on Dobani from all over." He hummed to himself. "Beauty often attracts an audience."

"You didn't swim?" She wondered if Phoenix could, or if he was like her...land-bound and would sink like a stone.

"Not that time," he said, quieter now. "There are many things to do on Dobani besides."

She opened her eyes. What Phoenix said was the opposite of what Del had told her once. She had assumed it was a water-world, no land in sight. It gave her a renewed sense of hope that Dobani wasn't off-limits.

"I want to go there," she whispered.

Phoenix perked up. "A noble desire," he said. "When we make it to the transport, you'll be able to go anywhere you like."

The thought was sobering rather than inspiring. She was alone now. Phoenix had killed her father. She had no one.

"I'm sorry about you getting shot," she blurted out. It seemed like her fault; after all, she had participated in the robbery attempt, and she felt the guilt acutely.

"It is no matter, little mouse. You couldn't control your father's actions. Drek wills it so, and so it is. Think no more of it."

Sev let the matter drop. Her eyes closed of their own volition, sleep trying to claim her. She started awake at the last moment.

"I'll help you," she said in the darkness. "I'll be your other hand. Until we get back to Central City."

It made Phoenix smile. "Indeed," he said. "With such an able partner, how can we fail?"

"Even split?" She asked, although they had not discussed what would happen to the gems they'd held onto after the skirmish that ended up killing her father.

"Even split," Phoenix confirmed, before slipping off to sleep.

She listened to his even breaths for a long time before closing her eyes again, as well. She dreamed of Dobani, of sand between her toes. And in her dream, Phoenix was there, too.

CHAPTER 5

There were bodies everywhere. When Phoenix and Sev arrived back at the Pit, evidence of a shootout littered the forest. Scorched trees and dead harvesters blemished the otherwise pristine grassy glade where the pit of calcet lay, riddled now from the avarice of too many harvesters down on their luck. Gems lay unclaimed, shining in the bright sun. Blood stained the ground.

The transport was gone.

Someone had overridden the launch codes and taken Phoenix's only way off the planet.

And, as providence would have it, his temporary traveling partner was a child whose father he'd just killed.

The odds were not in his favor, if they had ever been, and Drek had turned her face from him. Things had been bad ever since he'd lost his arm, in fact. He was not a lucky man.

They said nothing as they walked. The girl, whose name he still did not know, had hooked him to her air filter, his long spent. It was a kind gesture, one he did not deserve after making her an orphan. It didn't matter. He guessed they were helping each other now. Things like this happened in the Outer Reaches.

Up ahead, a man lay in the clearing, bleeding onto the forest floor. Other beings lay littered around a makeshift campsite, their twisted bodies lost among the plants and vines. A potbellied ship stood off to the side, looming over the carnage.

Suddenly, someone staggered forth from behind a tree. He had a knife in his hand. In a flash of movement, Phoenix produced his own blade and lunged at him.

Sev crouched behind some tall grasses, trying not to be a target. She witnessed him struggle with the assailant. Phoenix, injured and one-armed, was already at a disadvantage. The man stabbed Phoenix once, twice, before Phoenix got a wild strike in and severed the man's filter hose.

She rushed forward, urging him to his feet. Phoenix was heavy at her side, his broken body unable to fully support its own weight.

The men's ship stood in the clearing. It was a bulbous, rattle-trap thing, but a ship was a ship. They climbed into it with great difficulty, and Phoenix collapsed on the floor in a shuddering heap.

"Let me look," Sev breathed, winded from shouldering him and shaky with adrenaline.

The wound in his abdomen gaped alongside the gunshot. Rot had already started, black and festering. This is a mortal wound, she thought. He may never make it back to Central City alive.

She left him for a moment to punch in the coordinates of Central City's Terminal. If they were going to get off Terra Firma in one piece, they had to leave now. She leaned over the instrument panel, the only thing the previous owners hadn't stripped to make weight. The inside of the skiff was bare bones. Two seats, an instrument panel, and paper-thin walls she doubted would clear the atmosphere without taking on too much heat. The thrusters engaged, and with an ear-splitting rattle, the entire ship shook into the night sky.

Sev turned to look at where Phoenix lay on the floor. His hand shook where it clutched at his abdomen, a vain attempt to staunch the blood. He was ashen, his eyes slammed shut against the pain.

She stripped off his helmet. Flames licked the view panes of the shaky skiff as they broke through the atmosphere. Phoenix groaned, cursing in a language she didn't understand. His fever was already climbing; she could feel the heat from his skin even through his suit.

She fumbled with the skiff's field kit. It, too, was bare bones. There was a needle, catgut, and a few painkillers…some fever-reducing tablets. They had no hydration packs; he'd have to swallow them dry. And there was a scalpel.

"Excise it," Phoenix grunted, as if reading her mind. "I can't do it weak-armed; I'll cut too much."

Sev cut the suit and the old stitching away from the wound, revealing the pink, angry flesh. She frowned at him. "It's deep," she said, her voice strained with concern. She put the blade to his skin, just a touch, and he howled in pain. She instantly recoiled, fear seizing in her chest.

It must've been writ on her face. "Don't you worry, mouse," Phoenix stammered out. "We do what we must out here in the Outer Reaches." He paused, catching his breath. Then he grabbed her wrist with his bloodied hand. She hadn't realized it, but she was trembling.

"The black rot spreads…your steady blade can staunch the flow." He looked up at her, brown eyes shining with fever. "Get to it, girl."

Sev leaned over him, scalpel in hand. She took a few centering breaths, eyeing the black rot deep in Phoenix's abdomen. She held the scalpel in sure fingers and set to work.

The second cut and Phoenix jerked, his remaining hand fisting the air beside him, beating the floor of the skiff. He tried to keep still, to breathe through the pain. It reminded her of their night in the miner's tent, when Phoenix had been in agony despite the phials.

She'd give anything for one now.

She cut again, and he swore, voice strained and raspy. "You're doing good, mouse. Don't stop. Just keep going." His breath was coming in rapid pants, the fingers of his left hand clawing at the remains of his suit. She made a vicious cut, black rot bleeding into healthy red flesh, and Phoenix gasped, his eyes rolling back. "Drek be damned," he cursed at the end of a breath and finally passed out.

His unconsciousness was a welcome relief. It allowed her to focus, to finish the task. She made the last cut, leaving pink, bloodied flesh behind, and Phoenix came to.

"I had the strangest dream," he slurred. "You and I were on Terra Firma, but the air was clean…no spores. We took off our helmets, and it began to rain. In all my time on Terra Firma, I never saw the rain."

She took some gauze from the kit and pressed it to the wound. There was fresh blood now; it would need sealing. Phoenix propped up on his elbow and inspected her work.

"Beautiful job, little mouse. No medic in Central City could've done any better." He lay back, an exhausted smile on his face. "Stitch it up good; it'll do until we get to the Terminal."

Sev threaded the needle. There was little to no medical care at the Terminal. Phoenix knew that. Her excision was going to have to do.

She pressed her lips together, concern clouding her features. "Take these," she ordered. She handed him a handful of fever tablets and a few painkillers from the field kit. If she had botched the excision, Phoenix would die. If the thread didn't seal, Phoenix would die. *Drek*, she thought, *he might die anyway*.

Phoenix swallowed the tablets and laid back against the floor of the skiff. His face twisted from the pinched, agonized expression he'd worn since boarding the skiff into a facsimile of peace. Even if it was a medically induced peace, it made her feel better.

They existed in silence for a few moments. Sev stayed by his side, watching him warily. Phoenix's breathing regulated, and she thought he might be asleep.

"I do apologize for that," he said weakly. "That's ugly work for a little girl." He frowned, then opened his eyes to look at her. They were soft, very unlike the way Del had ever looked at her. It made her feel strangely seen.

"It's ok," she assured him. She remembered the way he had saved her life, taking her back to the miner's tent when he could've easily left her to die alongside her father. "You would do it for me."

He huffed a breathy little laugh and closed his eyes again. "Indeed I would," he agreed. "What are partners for, after all?"

The way back to Central City lay along the dark side of Terra Firma. What was usually a twenty-hour trip took three to four days, at least. Another day passed and Phoenix stood, finally, on shaky legs. He stubbornly refused Sev's attempt to help him, a hard-headed and useless exercise in pride. Sev took it as a good sign. He might pull through after all.

Phoenix made it to the command chair, and Sev settled in the navigator's seat adjacent. He was still clutching his wound, still in obvious pain, but his color was better…his hand on the controls steadier. Sev had called ahead to the Terminal, requesting medical assistance. She had received no answer.

"We'll get no help out here," Phoenix had informed her. "Think nothing of it, little mouse. Your hand was true. I can feel it."

Sev did not share his confidence.

On the third day, they entered the path to intercept. When they docked at the Terminal, Phoenix was walking without her help, even without clutching the hastily stitched wound. He assured her it hurt less. Sev was not sure she believed him.

They stood at the boards, Sev staring blankly at the various drop zones. She was alone, she realized. She had nowhere to go.

Maybe she could stay at the Terminal, she thought. Somewhere familiar…somewhere she could find work. Yes, she thought miserably, that was her best option.

In that moment, an entire lifetime of working junk jobs like her father, earning credits just to spend them on transports, and eventual hopelessness stretched out in front of her. It was a bleak prospect. Her eyes watered. It was all she knew.

"For Dobani," she heard Phoenix say. "Two to transport." She stood numbly as the man punched Phoenix's card, handing it back to him. Phoenix shouldered his pack, then favored her with a soft smile. "Let's go, little mouse. We've trading to do."

And just like that, he'd decided for her. She was not alone…wouldn't be alone. Something inside her shifted.

Phoenix sold the calcet at the exchange office at the Terminal while waiting on their transport. It was the gems her father had tried to steal…his treasure, he had called it. He took the credits and bought another field kit for the skiff, some hydration packs and nutrition.

"This'll hold us over for a while," he said, but all Sev could hear was *us.* They were together now, their hastily forged partnership on Terra Firma had carried over into the Black. They sat in the skiff, waiting for their drop.

"When's the last time you had some proper food?" Phoenix asked. He honestly appeared better; maybe the excision had been good after all.

Sev didn't answer. Ration bars and nutrition packs were all she knew. She couldn't remember the last time she'd shared a meal with her father, not in a place where food was served. Had she ever?

Phoenix handed her a nutrition pack, newly purchased with his earned credits. "When we get to Dobani…oh, mouse, we'll eat at a fine place. You've never seen the likes of it, I assure you."

When we get to Dobani. It seemed like a dream to her, actually seeing it. She couldn't remember the last time Del had taken her somewhere without the intent to work. Would they work on Dobani? She didn't care. Maybe that's what Phoenix was doing, setting up the next job. It didn't matter to her. She would see it, and somehow that was enough.

"My name is Sev," she said. She opened her pack; this one was not as stale as the ones she was used to eating. She realized then how hungry she was.

Phoenix smiled. "It's a pleasure to know you, Sev," he said. She liked how he said her name…like it was a rare and precious thing.

They finished their packs and settled into their seats. Phoenix certainly seemed better; maybe things would work out.

The Terminal dock groaned, and a comm flashed. The impassive voice informed them to expect departure to Dobani momentarily. Unbidden, a little thrill went through her.

Satisfied, she pulled out her notebook. It was the first time in a long time that she had wanted to write, so she penned a few sentences, the soft scratch of her pen loud in the small space.

"What is that you're writing?"

Sev had thought he was asleep, the way he'd leaned his head back, eyes closed. He had seemed so peaceful. She reflexively held the notebook to her chest. "Just a story," she evaded, suddenly shy.

Phoenix smiled. "Something I've heard of?"

Sev's eyes brightened, and she shook her head. "No. Something of mine."

They strapped in, and the Terminal launched them on a path to Dobani. Phoenix tapped the console with his one hand. "I would be honored to read, if you were so inclined to allow it." His eyes twinkled. "I have always been a great purveyor of the arts, scoundrel that I am."

Sev's brows creased. "I don't think you're that bad," she admitted, her voice thick. Indeed, she knew Phoenix had done bad things. He had killed her father in self-defense. But did that make him a bad person? Del would have thought so. Now, it didn't seem so cut and dried.

"Drek knows and so do you, little mouse. I am rotten to the core." He gave her a lopsided smile. "I would be remiss to let that rub off on you, as good as you plainly are."

She unclutched the notebook then and handed it to him. He looked at her, startled, his mouth gone soft. It spread into a smile. "Why thank you, Sev. I shall treat it with tender hands."

Not *mouse* or *little mouse*, but *Sev*. The gesture struck her deeply. It was the first time in them knowing each other that he had used her name.

She nodded and closed her eyes. He read her story all the way to Dobani. She dreamed of water, spread far and wide, and the sun on her face.

Dobani was warm, just like Phoenix had described. But it was also *full*, brimming with sights and sounds and more beings than Sev had ever seen in one place. After they had cleared the immigration office, Phoenix had walked her out into the bright sun, the whole world open to them.

Phoenix made good on his word; despite her wanting to see the ocean first (and she could see it, just a silver thread on the horizon), he took her to get something to eat.

The place wasn't fancy, but it was *nice*. It was clean and rife with the aromas of various foods. They sat in a booth across from each other, and Phoenix handed her a card with the names of different dishes on it.

"Pick what you like, little mouse. We're celebratin'. Drek has blessed us with another day, and for having been stabbed and shot on Terra Firma, that is no small gift."

None of the food was familiar. She realized, then, that she had never had this experience…that this was something entirely other than what she was used to. She glanced up at him, overwhelmed.

"Can you help me?" she asked, her voice small. It made her feel younger than she was.

Phoenix brightened. "Why, of course," he enthused. He launched into an explanation of each dish, how they would taste, and Sev found it extremely helpful, even calming.

She settled on something not dissimilar to what Phoenix had ordered, but with a side of fresh fruit. Phoenix insisted, saying "No growing girl can thrive without it," but Sev had never had fresh food, let alone fruit, and she begged to differ.

"So," she began, her voice quaking with nerves. "What did you think?"

Phoenix blinked, and she could see him ciphering her words, unwilling to plead ignorance. "About my story," she said, and she saw his eyes light.

"I believe, and Drek knows, I am in the presence of true talent, the likes of which I have never seen." He chewed his food thoughtfully, blotting his mouth with the corner of the napkin he had spread in his lap. It was strange to see him behave so. She wondered if this was really who Phoenix was when he wasn't on Terra Firma.

"And I may be mistaken–and if my literary analysis fails me, then do let me know–but isn't the protagonist of this fine tale yourself, little mouse? She seems awfully familiar."

Sev couldn't stifle the smile. "I was trying to write it like my favorite book, but it ended up being more about me."

Phoenix gestured to her as if trying to make a point. "And I hazard that it is all the better for it. I can't thank you enough for letting me read. For that and for any future tales, count me a willing and eager audience."

She smiled again…she had done that a lot lately…and her face grew warm. It was a strange sensation. She bit into the fruit, flavor bursting on her tongue, and closed her eyes against the taste. Phoenix watched her eat, satisfied.

He had cautioned her of the sand, how hot it would be and how it would get in her shoes. "Take them off…walk barefoot into the water," he'd instructed. So, she did so, leaving her shoes and socks near the boarded walkway and taking off across the hot sand.

It bit into her toes, the grit and heat, until she splashed knee-deep into the foam. Space was cold, but Dobani was a place of contrasting textures, tastes, and sensations…the scalding sand, the cool blue-green waters. She peered out over the undulating surface, the sun glancing off it like gems in the sunlight, thinking she'd never seen anything so beautiful.

She saw behind her that Phoenix was watching her from the dunes. He had his hand in his pocket, a soft smile on his face. The wind blew the blond patch in his hair away from his forehead until it stood upright in a comical sort of cowlick. He was already browning in the sun, she could tell, his forearm and face sun-kissed and glowing with a light sheen of sweat. She took a few more steps into the water, feeling the tide pull her toward the deep.

"Not too far now, mouse," Phoenix called to her, his voice nearly lost on the wind. She braced herself against the waves; pants soaked to the thigh, her feet sinking deeply into the wet sand beneath.

Phoenix made his way through the sand; he'd stripped his suit back on the skiff and now wore what lay underneath–light white pants and a black short-sleeve T-shirt. His stump was on display, cauterized and sealed against the elements.

He pointed out over the water; predator birds swooped down from the sky to snatch up creatures in hungry beaks. "You remind me of those, little mouse," he murmured. "Persistent and strong."

It was the type of thing she would say about a character in *Nautica*, her favorite book, not about herself. Did Phoenix really think of her that way? She looked at Phoenix, the sun beating down on them, the birds calling to each other over mouthfuls of food. "I don't want to go back," she admitted to him. "To the Black."

Space had taken, taken, taken, and they had got nothing in return. They'd barely escaped Terra Firma with their lives, and her father was dead. She realized, standing there on the beach with Phoenix, that she didn't want him to die. It was a fierce and desperate thought.

"We don't have to," he assured her. "We'll make do." He pulled her back a little from the water where the tide had drawn her further in, a warm, calloused hand on her back. "Don't fret it."

She observed him, her eyes fixed on the blond patch that blew willy-nilly over his tanned forehead in the cool breeze off the water. Del would've never left the Pit on Terra Firma full of gems. Phoenix had given it up in favor of their escape. They were not the same.

"Ok," she breathed, noticeably relieved. Together, they stood looking out over the water and watching the birds as they plucked their meals from the unrelenting sea.

CHAPTER 6

Sev had never felt a close kinship with her father. Truth be told, he was more of a work partner than anything else. But grief puts people into a softer focus. Del looked out for her…maybe even appreciated her, in his own way. Sev knew she had been a liability to him; it was no easy thing, dragging a child around the Outer Reaches. He never said as much, though, and that was a kindness she was grateful for now that he was gone.

But she was alone, more than anything, and she felt that acutely. Del's loss filled the space between her and Phoenix, a large and tangible thing.

Phoenix was a conundrum. With every passing day, she wondered more about him.

From what she had experienced, Phoenix was kind. He was patient. Phoenix was considerate in a way that she was not used to. Phoenix never rushed her, unlike her father. He never pushed her to make decisions, small or large. She wondered mostly what his plans were past their present situation. He didn't seem pressed at all, satisfied with how they'd found themselves. Life now with Phoenix was a day-to-day revelation.

The two of them had a little room on Dobani. It was not in Dobani Proper, which would have been cheaper, but it was just outside it, and to Sev's delight, it was near the beach…close enough for her to hear the waves crash ashore each night.

Phoenix had not asked Sev about the room, and she hadn't minded. It was the same way he didn't ask when she opted for nutrition packs over going back to the restaurant, or when he lost her and she was standing at the shore at night, watching the moon glow over the surface of the water. Phoenix had a quiet understanding about him, and as much as he liked to talk, he let her have agency. He gave her space.

It was something they both needed. After being thrust together in an uneasy alliance and then later (and now) a partnership, Sev needed time to sort things out. She suspected Phoenix did, too.

One conclusion she had made in her quiet ruminations was that they were almost out of credits. Phoenix never said as much, but he didn't have to. They weren't spending a lot, but they were living without working, and if there's one thing she had learned in the Outer Reaches (and from Del) was that living was expensive.

Phoenix seemed, for lack of a better word, content. He slept, still recovering from his injuries, both his missing arm and those he incurred on Terra Firma, and Sev wrote.

She wrote more than she ever had. It reminded her of the time they were in the Black, her and Del, and she'd had a little stability. The memory made her smile; it was getting easier to think of him now.

She wrote curled up in her chair by the window, listening to the waves, while Phoenix slept on one of the small beds in the apartment. Sometimes he snored, and that too sounded like the waves. Sev had almost forgotten what someone looked like when they slept without help, what they sounded like. And when he awoke, he was the same Phoenix as when he'd gone to bed. Not like her father at all.

"I suppose it's time we settle our accounts, being that we are partners," he declared one day. He'd pulled a chair up to hers, flipped it around backwards, and sat astride it. Sev eyed him curiously, putting her notebook down and fiddling with the edges of the paper.

To her surprise, he had his own notebook, a small ledger, which he pulled from his pocket. The white patch in his hair shined under the bare bulb hanging from the ceiling, a stark contrast to his brown skin. A few weeks in the Dobani sun and you would have never known Phoenix spent so much time in the Black, where skin goes sallow and eyes lose their luster.

He handed her the ledger, and there, in his careful glyphs, were the figures. "That's all of it, little mouse. Every credit accounted for, including expenses accrued during our time here on Dobani."

She scanned the paper, eyes roving over Phoenix's writing. He'd made notes in the margins like "ate here today. Sev liked the sweet cream best," and then the cost of their meal. It made her cheeks heat.

She looked up, and Phoenix had his arm over the back of the chair. "Why are you showing me this?"

He smiled then, and it was bright and soft at the same time. "Because communication is the key to a successful partnership, little mouse, and I would be remiss if I were not forthcoming on our financials, such as they are."

She teased her lip with her teeth, thinking. "We'll need to work soon," she said. They weren't in dire straits. Phoenix had been smart with their money, but the little cushion they'd arrived with from the sale of Phoenix's calcet was practically gone.

He wiped his hand over his mouth once, lips twitching. "This briny air has been good for my lungs…and you as well, little mouse. You've colored a touch too. And so to say, if you will follow my line of discourse to its rightful conclusion, I ask, do you want to stay here on Dobani, and strike out, or would you like to move on?"

Sev pursed her lips, eyes glancing from the ledger to Phoenix and back again. She knew what Phoenix was asking in that roundabout way of his. To "strike out" meant to look for employment. They had to work, whether on Dobani or elsewhere.

"I like it here," she began, careful and slow. "But if you want to move on—"

"I have no such inclination," Phoenix interrupted her, his hand out in a placating gesture. "Seeing as you are our navigator, and an accomplished one at that, I was merely garnering your opinion as to what our next moves should be." He smiled then, and it made him look younger. "Make no mistake, mouse. If you're happy here, then so am I."

She nodded numbly, still gripping the ledger in her hands. She was unaccustomed to being consulted as to her immediate future. It was a foreign but welcome thing, having input in this way. "What kind of work is there on Dobani?"

Phoenix shrugged, his stump twitching with the motion. "For a one-armed cheat and a little girl? Why, industry mostly. The shipyards, perhaps. Loading and unloading. Manufacturing, maybe."

Her eyes narrowed. She had not thought about what the future might look like if they didn't go back to Terra Firma. Harvesting was dangerous work, but the pay-off was handsome. Terra Firma didn't care how many arms you had or how young you were. It would try to kill you just the same.

"Where do we go, to Dobani Proper?" Sev was used to job boards and drop pods and long cycles in the Black. She was used to life in the Outer Reaches, not whatever they'd started here.

Phoenix nodded. "Dobani Proper. Take the chute in to the employment office there. See what they've got for a dried-up old husk like me." He grinned wryly before running his hand through his hair.

"And me," Sev added. "I can work. I've always worked." A little jolt of anxiety went through her at not being able to contribute to their partnership. When she was with Del, she'd often finished her job and his too, when it wasn't harvesting. He'd be out of his mind on stim sticks or in one of his moods, and she would step in and take up the slack.

Phoenix seemed to collect himself, his brown eyes dark and serious. "I know you have, little mouse, and you're an excellent partner. But they may not let you do that here. There are rules on Dobani and other worlds against such things."

Sev flushed. "What rules?"

Phoenix stood, his hand on his hip. "About children in the workforce and work besides. Drek, they may not even have me, half a man that I am now."

Sev frowned. "Maybe we should go back to the Terminal. Stick to the Outer Reaches." Her eyes flashed up at him. "It's what we know."

Phoenix shook his head. "It's what we know, true, but there's more to life than that." He made no further comment and stood stock-still for several seconds. Then he sighed. "Come along, little mouse. Let's see what they have to say."

The chute took them far from the beach, into the clean but crowded depths of Dobani Proper. Sev lay her head against the view pane, watching the kaleidoscope of Dobani blur past in a myriad of flashes.

The employment office was a dingy blot on an otherwise spotless vista of steel and white, its cramped quarters and bright orange wallpaper glaring, dated, and gaudy in the fluorescent light. There was one woman in the office manning a computer terminal with a perpetually bored look on her face. Phoenix approached her, his one hand extended.

The woman shook Phoenix's hand, then followed her eyes to the shirt sleeve tied up over Phoenix's stump. "What can I do for you both?" she asked a little cautiously, eyes flitting from Phoenix's stump to what Sev approximated to be the white patch of hair just above Phoenix's forehead. Finally, she saw Sev.

"To speak plainly, we need a job," Phoenix began, "preferably one together as we work best that way." Phoenix waggled his stump, causing the woman to frown. "Sev here is my literal right hand."

The woman made a little noise, then keyed some info into the computer. "How old is the girl?" she inquired, her voice flat. Sev had already decided that she did not like her much.

Phoenix snorted. "Old enough to work. If you had anything at the docks—"

Her eyebrows raised. "You can load and unload with one arm?"

Phoenix humored her with a lopsided smile. It was a clever way to hide his intelligence, she knew. "As I said," he repeated, his voice a little lower, "Sev here is my right hand." He withdrew his punch card and slid it across the desk, stopping just before he reached the terminal's interface.

She inspected the card, and then she shot a glance at Phoenix. "Are you attempting a bribe, sir? I'll have you know we don't do things like that he—"

"And I would never presume," Phoenix segued smoothly, his hand gesturing graciously. "Just merely a business offer. One that you should be inclined to take." He pointed to the card. "There are two credits there at your disposal. And if it eases the way for us, then the rest is just paperwork," he said with an amiable smile.

The woman huffed, then delicately picked up the punch card. She slid it into a drawer on her right and said nothing else before returning her attention to the terminal once more.

Sev observed this with great interest. Phoenix had a finesse about him that her father did not possess. It was why that bit of nastiness on Terra Firma had gone so badly between them. Del was a blunt object...thick-headed and unyielding. Sometimes in life, you needed to *bend*.

The woman handed them their work orders, a slight smile on her face. "Good luck," she murmured as they left the office behind them and melded into the crowded Dobani sidewalk.

Phoenix handed Sev the papers for her inspection. Relief flooded through her as she compared the work assignments. The employment office had not separated them. Sev noted with some interest that he had given them the same last name.

So, that was the story then. They were related.

Sev followed where he walked a little ahead of her, shouldering his way through the crowd. He was broad, even without his arm, and as strong as he looked. He'd taken down that man on Terra Firma, injured and sick as he was, with little problem. Sev clutched the papers to her chest, falling in step behind him. Maybe things would be ok.

That afternoon, they went to the beach. Phoenix led her into the deep, coaxing her forward and grabbing her hand when she lost her footing. She sputtered and coughed, flailing in the dying sun.

"Easy now, little mouse," Phoenix soothed. His hair was wet, and he'd slicked it back over his head. "Floatin' is half of swimming. If you know how to float, you can learn how to swim."

She nodded quickly, treading water with one hand and clinging to Phoenix's with the other. His hand was calloused and warm, even in the cool water.

"Lay back...relax your breathing. Let your arms go out to the side...legs too." He had his arm under her back so she wouldn't sink, and Sev closed her eyes.

"Imagine there's invisible strings pulling on your arms and legs, holding them up out of the water. Let the wind tug on those strings and your body will do the rest."

Sev imagined, just as Phoenix had instructed. She thought of her mother, who had waded in these very waters while Sev was still in the womb. Sev had floated then, too, in the waters off Dobani.

Sev slowed her breathing and waggled her fingers in the water. "You can take your hand away, Phoenix," she murmured as the current buoyed her. "I want to try it by myself."

Phoenix huffed a little laugh and held up his hand. "You've been doing it on your own for a while, little mouse." He grinned, a note of wonder in his eyes. "By Drek, I think you've got it."

Sev smiled back, relaxing into the water. It was as natural to her as breathing.

That night, after they had scrubbed themselves clean of saltwater, their bellies full and in their own beds, Sev turned to where Phoenix lay across from her.

"What will tomorrow be like?" She was worrying her thumb with her fingernail under the blanket, a habit from when she used to hide the fidgeting from Del.

Phoenix sighed. "Lots of people…the glint of the sun off the salt that they pack the fish in. Gulls squawking at us for scraps. It will be a time, sweet mouse. It will be a time."

Sev settled. She could always count on Phoenix to be descriptive if not plain-spoken, something that soothed her frayed nerves. Del often told her as little as possible and shot down her questions. After a while, she stopped asking them.

She listened to the sound of the waves, realizing that she would miss them if she could no longer hear their soothing rhythm. "Will we need to give up the room?"

Phoenix looked over at where he knew she was. "Now why would we do that, after we've gone and gotten comfortable here all these days?"

She blinked in the dark. "Can we still afford it, though?"

Phoenix clicked his tongue. "We are paid through the next few weeks, don't you worry. We'll make the credits for the rest." He let the matter settle between them. "Get some sleep, little mouse. We've an early rise tomorrow."

Sev closed her eyes, all her questions answered for the moment, and let the sound of the waves carry her to sleep.

The docks were on the water, but closer to Dobani Proper than their room was. This was not the touristy part of Dobani, Phoenix had explained, this was the business part. It was a little grungier than the pristine beaches down the road from their room, but Sev still found it pretty if only because it was something entirely other than the Black or Terra Firma.

They lined up to get their cards punched. Phoenix had purchased them overalls and work gloves, and they were still stiff and new here at the beginning of their shift. Sev stood behind Phoenix, following his lead. She had helped him cut and tie up the sleeve of his right arm just that morning.

The foreman explained the job to the assembled crowd there. It was simple, from what Sev could gather. They were moving fish from one area of the dock to another. There was an assortment of seedy-looking characters working their shift too, and they were all cobbled together in a half-circle with Sev and Phoenix.

More than once, she caught one of them staring at her.

She unconsciously moved closer to Phoenix, though if he noticed, he did not show it. It was easier to forget once they started working. The sun was relentless, and the fish had to be moved before spoiling. Crates of salt glinted in the sun, just like Phoenix said it would, and sure enough gulls called to them from the pilings, begging for a meal.

The fish were enormous creatures with three eyes, longer and bigger around than Sev's entire body. It took the two of them working together to maneuver them onto the pallets to be loaded onto the trucks. Phoenix was patient with her, showing her how to grab them by the gills, showing her how to leverage her body to keep the fish from swinging wide and trapping them beneath it.

By midday, Sev's back was aching, and she was sweaty and filthy. An assemblage of workers had loosely formed in the shade; they were on break and some men were eating lunch. Phoenix stood chatting with a man with one eye. They'd brought no lunch, but Phoenix had water, which he'd shared with Sev.

She was turning around for a drink when someone brushed past her. The contact felt purposeful and *wrong*. The person did it again, slower this time, and she saw that it was the man from before, the one who was looking at her.

Sev set her jaw, lowering the canteen and gripping it tightly in her hand. She held it defensively in front of her. The man leered.

"What is a fair-haired little flower like you doing here on the docks?" He reached and brushed a strand of hair away from her face, causing her to stiffen and recoil. "Yet here you are, ripe for the plucking."

She spat at him, and before she realized it, she had taken the canteen and hit him across the face with it. He howled in anger, grabbing her roughly. She screamed then, and Phoenix was there in two long strides.

She saw the fury in his eyes, brown almost gone to black. He spared no glance at Sev; he had his eyes fixed entirely on the man in front of her. Phoenix grabbed the man by the front of his shirt and smashed him against a nearby piling.

"You so much as look at her ever again, and I'll kill you." The knife must've been in his hand already, because the blade unsheathed, keen and bright, and Phoenix pressed it against the man's neck. A thin line of blood trickled down his collar, soaking the fabric there.

The workers had crowded around, intrigued by the spectacle. Phoenix had him pinned, and the man let out a low groan.

"She yours then?" the man panted, but Phoenix didn't answer. He let the edge dig in a little deeper, and the cut grew wide and red.

Phoenix released him just as the blade slipped beneath the man's skin, leaving a deep gouge. There was a gout of blood in its wake, and the man clutched at his neck, stumbling forward. Phoenix held his head up so he could look at him, then drew back and punched the man in the face, knocking him out cold.

Phoenix rounded on the rest, making eye contact with the onlookers. "Same for you. You so much as look at her, and I'll kill every person standing."

He was vibrating with rage. Sev could see it in his body, drawn tight as a bowstring. The small knife in his hand still dripped with blood. He had not drawn a mortal wound, but it would be enough. The crowd murmured, then drifted apart.

Sev blinked, processing how fearsome he looked. She had never seen Phoenix this way...not even when he had killed her father back on Terra Firma, a planet that brings out violence in the gentlest of beings.

He was nothing to fear, she reminded herself. She walked up to him and slipped her hand in his, pulling him into the shade.

Later, after they had showered and changed, Phoenix took Sev out to eat. It was the place with the sweet cream dessert, she remembered, and she smiled to herself when she thought of the note in Phoenix's ledger. Perhaps he was self-conscious about his actions at the docks. He shouldn't be.

She was used to the wayward eyes of the occasional ill-intentioned stranger. If Del had ever noticed, he never told her. When she was younger, she would have nightmares of being sold to slavers. If Del could've made enough money to warrant the loss of her as a work partner, he might've done it. That realization used to frighten her. It no longer did.

Phoenix was biting hardily into a sandwich of some kind. Sev didn't recognize the protein. He was doing well for one arm. She thought of the credits they were earning, of what Phoenix had said about how there was more to life than the Outer Reaches.

She took a sip of her water. "Would you ever wear a prosthetic?"

Phoenix chewed for a moment, then put the sandwich down and blotted his mouth with the napkin in that careful way of his. "They're expensive," he finally settled on. He regarded her with brown eyes full of humor. "Are you tired of eyeing this stump already, girl?"

Sev shook her head. Her agency had never extended to credits...Del dealt with that. What they earned went to drop ships and nutrition packs, and there never seemed to be extra for what Phoenix considered living. Like eating out occasionally. "We could save our credits," Sev suggested. "With both of us working, it wouldn't take long."

He drummed his fingers on the table, then dropped his hand to his lap. "Ah now, mouse, we can't be spending our credits on such frivolous matters as replacing a missing arm," he began. "Especially since I'm doing just fine without."

She frowned. She didn't know how to tell him about the guilt she still carried, about how she felt responsible for her father shooting him, making him a murderer by proxy.

But she didn't, so she just shrugged. "It's important to have goals," she said instead. "Something to save for."

Phoenix smiled. "Indeed, you are right, little mouse. Which brings us to our next appropriate point of conversation." He gestured to her not unfondly, pointer finger in the air. "Your schooling."

Sev furrowed her brow. "I can't work and go to school both," she reasoned.

It pleased him. "And right you are. So, one must suss out the more important."

Sev stabbed at her protein before taking a bite. "Work, obviously. We need the credits."

Phoenix leaned forward, his chin on his hand. "Not that obvious." He grew serious then, placing his hand on the table between them. "What happened today must never happen again."

Sev stopped eating. In fact, she pushed her plate away. "You're not my father," she said, and to hear it in the open air, it was like an accusation.

Phoenix cleared his throat. "No, I am not. You belong only to yourself, little mouse, and have done so since you were orphaned on Terra Firma. Drek knows, maybe even longer. And orphaned by my own unfortunate hand at that."

She looked away through the window, frustrated tears burning her eyes. "You can't threaten everyone who looks at me," she argued, but it didn't have the bite she'd intended.

Phoenix looked at her, her profile soft in the neon glow of the sign outside. "I can do worse, if need be," he said, his voice dropping low. "As you well know."

She turned to look at him then, and his face had gone soft. He appeared almost sad, sitting there looking at her. "It's what partners do, after all. Look out for one another."

Sev sniffed, wiping at her eyes. "I want to work," she protested.

Phoenix nodded. "I know, Sev."

That night it rained, and Sev could not hear the roar of the ocean above the torrent. Lying in her bed with the rain hitting the roof made her feel small, like she was being tossed about in a boat on a great sea. "Phoenix?" she asked, just as she was falling asleep.

She could hear Phoenix turn on his side, his too small bed creaking with the movement. "What is it, sweet mouse?"

"Are you going to make me go to school?"

Phoenix lay motionless. "Far be it from me to make you do anything, force that you are. I can only make suggestions."

It captured her attention. "What do you suggest, then?"

Phoenix sighed. "With your talent, mouse, and intelligence and will besides, your mind needs cultivatin'. You won't get that slinging fish with me."

She opened her mouth to speak, but he put his hand up to stop her. "Work a while. Let the thought settle on your mind and see how it fits in a few months, hmm? You can do anything you want, sweet mouse. Be anything you want. There's more to living than what we can see right in front of us."

And so she did and soon fell into a dreamless sleep.

CHAPTER 7

S ome days, when the catch was plentiful, and the foreman was feeling generous, he would send Sev and Phoenix home with a little parcel of fish. Phoenix would tuck it under his arm, and they'd take the long way back through what Phoenix called the Farmer's District. Phoenix would ruminate there over the stalls of produce, a finger to his lips, and Sev would tease him for taking so long to choose. Eventually, they would walk away, Sev holding the little bag of vegetables and Phoenix the fish. Sometimes Phoenix would whistle, and Sev would hum along to the tune, yet unknown to her but familiar, all the same.

Phoenix was standing at the stove in their little room, expertly flipping a saucepan to-and-fro to disperse melted butter over the fish within. He had a hand towel tucked into the waistband of his pants, and it was as white as the undershirt he wore. Sev watched, her eyes sharp, as Phoenix flicked his wrist and then set the pan back over the heat.

"Hand me the salt, little mouse. No fish worth their brine can be without it, I assure you."

Sev stopped halfway to the stove, a question on her lips. "Let me?" And Phoenix smiled. He rarely told her no.

"Just a touch," he cautioned her as she shook the grains into the pan. "Salt is a powerful seasoning. It's in the air here on Dobani. It's healed our lungs and closed my wounds." He patted his abdomen, his large palm flat over the scars Sev had only seen glimpses of since she'd treated him on the skiff.

"Do you want me to peel the tubers?" she asked.

He spooned the juices over the fish, her mouth watering. The air in the close kitchen was all smoky-salt and the heady aroma of cooked fish. Phoenix nodded, then began whistling the same tune from before when they had made their way back to the room.

Sev arranged the purple tubers on the cutting board, paring knife in hand. She started by cutting the ends off, then she began spiraling her knife around the tuber in a languid circle, holding it in one hand and cutting with the other. The peeling sloughed off in a pretty curl.

"Who would peel your vegetables if I weren't here?" she asked him. "It would be hard to do with only one hand."

Phoenix hummed. "I suppose, little mouse, I would eat them peelings and all." He glanced at her, a glint in his eye. "But Drek sees fit that I should have help and help me you have. I can't imagine peeling that tuber with only one hand." He nudged her playfully. "Good thing you're here."

She popped a piece of raw tuber into her mouth, crunching loudly. "Good thing," she mumbled around the mouthful of starchy vegetable, and Phoenix couldn't suppress a smile.

When Sev had peeled and sliced the tubers, Phoenix placed them in the pan where the fish had been. They sizzled until they were soft and caramelized, then Phoenix took them off the heat and poured them into a bowl. He portioned out their meal, a piece of fish for each of them, and they sat down to eat.

Sev knew nothing of setting a table; she rarely ate with utensils, opting for the ease and efficiency of nutrition packs. So, Phoenix showed her, in that calm and patient way of his, where the forks should go in relation to the spoons. "It's ceremony, mouse," he'd explained in dulcet tones, "it's what separates man from the animals." Sev had only nodded.

Sev had learned that Phoenix was a man of simple pleasures. When he wasn't in the Black, he did not mind lingering over a meal or a walk home or taking a moment to view the sunset from their window. She thought of how many meals he'd enjoyed on his own or with others, and of how little she still knew of him.

"Where did you learn to cook?" It seemed innocuous enough, the question. She speared a piece of tuber with her fork and bit into it. It was far more delicious cooked like this than when she'd eaten it raw.

Phoenix sighed. "Oh, here and there. A man picks things up along the way." He grew quiet, and he must've realized he hadn't satisfied her curiosity. "You get used to not doing things in the Black. I haven't cooked in, oh…it must be years now."

Sev nodded, still chewing. She took a sip of her water. "I want you to teach me," she said. "How to fillet a fish. How to cook. All of it."

Phoenix stared at her across their little table. His hair had grown out a little, and the white patch stuck out over his tanned forehead, shining bright like a beacon. "Of course, little mouse," he said. "Far be it from me to withhold knowledge from a willing audience." He gestured with his one hand. "Anything you want to know, I'll share."

Sev nodded and began clearing the table.

After the dishes were done and they had stretched out in their beds, Sev listened to the waves come ashore. She often wandered to the beach late at night and waited for the tide to come in. She would not wander tonight, full as she was on fish and sleepy, too.

Her mind was abuzz with thoughts.

She thought of where her mother had stayed on Dobani…if it was close to their room or very far away, in the heart of Dobani Proper. She would like to think her mother stayed near the beach, where she could wade in the cool foam whenever she liked. Sometimes when Sev held her late-night vigils, and the moon hung pregnant in the sky, she wondered if her mother had gazed at that same moon, had thought about her unborn child and what they might look like. Sev wondered if she had thought of her, at all.

"Phoenix?"

She could hear the bed protest under Phoenix's weight, and he groaned slightly as he turned over. "Yes, mouse?"

50

"Do you ever think of going back?"

Phoenix blew out a breath, deliberate and long. "To Terra Firma, little mouse? Ah, I would be a lying man if I said I did not dream of it, at times. All that calcet just ripe for the taking. I wake up and it's right there in front of me, just beyond my grasp."

Sev frowned at the admission, but it wasn't surprising. Sev was a child of the Black. She knew very well its siren call. Phoenix belonged to the Outer Reaches. He was here on Dobani because of her.

"Are you happy, Phoenix?"

Phoenix hummed. "Exceedingly so, Sev. I would say exceedingly so. I have all I could ever need right here. Why do you ask?"

Sev frowned. How could she say that she was worried he would leave her one day? Even though he had never given her any reason to fear it, that she did anyway? She said nothing, letting the silence fall around them.

He sighed. "We are partners, little mouse. Where one goes, the other goes. Why, I assume if you ever get tired of Dobani you'll let it be known, will you not? And then we'll move on, into the Black."

She clasped her hands over her middle, worrying the fingers of her right hand. "Yes, Phoenix," she answered. Neither of them spoke again before she drifted off to sleep.

The next morning, Phoenix was at the stove again. The aroma of fried meat filled the little room; it made her nostalgic, though she had no memories of the smell to draw from. It made her think that she and Phoenix sometimes existed outside of time.

"Rise and shine, sleepyhead," Phoenix said. "It's close to noon, so rather than breakfast, lunch will have to do."

Sev rubbed the sleep from her eyes. Once the fog had cleared, a panicked realization dawned, and she bolted upright. "Noon? What about work?"

Phoenix tutted. "They'll not miss us one day," he assured her. "Come and eat, and I'll tell you of our plans today."

Sev stumbled into the bathroom. She splashed some water on her face, then made her way to the kitchen table. The plate of meat and bread and a bowl of some sort of porridge lay steaming and waiting for her.

She tucked into her meal, realizing belatedly that she was hungrier than she thought. Phoenix watched her eat, a satisfied expression on his face. "Would you like to know where we're going, mouse?"

Sev nodded. The porridge warmed her from within, and the meat was flavorful. She liked when Phoenix cooked the best, better than any nutrition pack or meal out, though she had never told him.

"Where are we going if not to work?"

Phoenix inclined his head. "A place of wondrous delights, little mouse, the likes of which you will not soon forget."

She chewed, considering. "Well, you already taught me to swim. Are we staying on Dobani?"

Phoenix tapped the table. "The very place."

Sev spooned the last of her porridge. "I think I want to be surprised," she decided. Phoenix appeared pleased.

Curiously, Phoenix packed them food, leftover sandwiches and the fish from the night before. He took her to the chute that would take them into Dobani Proper. She remembered it from when they visited the unemployment office, as dreadful as that was. Phoenix settled on the bench seat beside Sev, giving her the place by the window. She leaned her face against it as the world blurred by.

Phoenix led them out of the chute at a stop in Dobani Proper, in front of a shiny glass building that was two stories, maybe three. A sign on the grass out front read "Dobani Museum of Modern Art."

Sev looked at Phoenix in surprise, a smile spreading her face. "You're taking me to a museum?"

Phoenix just nodded. "And a picnic on the grounds after we've looked our fill," he added. Sev hurried to fall in step with him, and then she grabbed his hand.

The interior of the museum was all shiny-bright with newness, and Sev struggled to take it all in at once. She pulled Phoenix to the first exhibit, a light show against a blank canvas. Phoenix showed her how to read the plaque, and he let her stand for as long as she liked before moving on. "After all," he had said, "there's a whole museum at our disposal, little mouse, and only so many hours in the day."

And so it went with Sev and Phoenix working their way through the exhibits, past paintings and sculptures and installations, past bound books and canvases full of glyphs.

"They should put *Nautica* in a museum," Sev said as they were nearing the end of their tour. "It's beautiful enough. Rare enough." She glanced up at Phoenix. "What do you think?"

Phoenix inclined his head. "Well, seeing as I only have your word to go on, little mouse, but knowing your word is true, I would have to agree."

Phoenix stopped at the little gift shop. They'd toured the museum well past the luncheon hour, and as it was, their picnic would be in twilight. Still, there was one stop he had to make.

"Let's go inside," Phoenix prompted her, blinking at the confusion writ on her face. "When you go somewhere new, it's nice to have something to remember it by. Come on, girl."

Sev followed him inside. The gift shop at the museum was full of trinkets like paperweights and snow globes and refrigerator magnets. She did not see the need for them to buy anything...they couldn't spare the credits...but Phoenix had his mind set.

Phoenix disappeared and then reappeared, a beautiful hide-bound journal in his hand. He handed it to Sev. "I think this will more than do the trick and be useful besides."

Sev ran her hands over the fine cover. She had filled her notebook to overflowing; Phoenix must've noticed. He produced a pen, one of the fancy ones that were refillable, and placed it atop the journal.

She said nothing. The cool of the cover leached into her skin; she ruffled the pages, blank with promise, and breathed in the dry scent of new paper.

"Oh, Phoenix," she breathed. "We shouldn't."

Phoenix put a hand to her back, steering her to the attendant there. "And why not? Life is for living, sweet mouse. What good are these credits we earn if they don't buy us a little pleasure now and then?"

Phoenix let her pay, and when the transaction was complete, she clutched the book to her chest. "What now?" she asked, a little starry-eyed. Phoenix just guided her out of the gift shop and onto the lawn of the museum.

There was a picnic table there under a single streetlamp. Phoenix withdrew the bundle he'd wrapped their lunch in and spread it over the table. Sev ate with one hand on her new journal as if it would dematerialize once she removed it.

"Phoenix, why did you never have kids?"

The question surprised him, though he tried to hide it. His cheeks blushed even in the waning light, and he brushed his hair back over his forehead. "Never had occasion to," he mused. "I haven't lived the sort of life fit for a child. Spent half my adult life flitting from job to job...no child should have a father like that."

He hadn't called him by name, but Sev thought of Del, anyway.

They ate in silence. It was the first time they had shared a meal in the open air and so far from their little room by the beach. She couldn't hear the waves from where they were, but there was a discordant white noise here in the heart of Dobani that appealed to her. It sounded like the ocean as much as it did when you put your ear to a shell, as Phoenix had shown her. "You can hear the ocean, little mouse," he'd instructed her one sun-bleached afternoon. "Put your ear up to it and listen to the waves any time you like."

It was dark when they made it back to the chute, and Sev was fading. She still held the journal and pen—the ink would be expensive for it; she would have to be careful. Sev settled in her seat by the window and waited for Phoenix.

With his arm gone, there was no reason she couldn't sit a smidge closer to him, given they had all this room, and so she did. As the chute took off from the stop, Sev dropped her head against Phoenix's shoulder, feeling the heat of his stump through his tied-up sleeve. She thought of a prosthetic, just before falling asleep, and how Phoenix could harvest calcet with two working hands. A prosthetic would never be warm, though, and would never feel this good. She folded her arms over her journal, flush to her chest, and let the chute rock her into oblivion.

"Sev," Phoenix whispered sometime later. "I've only the one arm to carry you, mouse, and unless you want me to sling you over my back like those fish we move, you'd better get up."

Sev laughed, then yawned and stretched. She got up on wobbly legs and exited the chute. Sev could smell the ocean again; she could hear the waves.

"Let's go to the beach, Phoenix."

The moon was high above them. Its pale eye matched the white flag of hair on Phoenix's brow. Curious, she thought, that it grew so white.

Phoenix protested at first, but he conceded. "Only for a time, little mouse, and then you need to sleep."

She grabbed his hand and led him across the street to the dunes. "What about you?"

He hummed. "Me as well." He squeezed her hand. "Did I ever tell you about that time I stayed up all night? All night until the suns rose…all on account of a woman."

Sev laughed, pulling him to the water. "No," she replied, rushing knee-deep into the spray, holding her journal above her head so it wouldn't get wet. "Tell me."

CHAPTER 8

The sun was bright and hot in the sky, but it wasn't the pleasant warmth that baked her skin when she was standing on the shore. Instead, it was a smothering sort of heat that shimmered over the docks, that made her lightheaded and short of breath, that made their usual labor even more intensive.

A bead of sweat rolled down her temple, and she swiped at it with the back of her arm. She and Phoenix stood side-by-side at the rough wooden work bench. They were gutting fish…small ones. It was tedious work for two hands, but Phoenix, with his one, made it look easy. Phoenix held the fish in place, the blade of the knife pressing into its belly. He made the cut, careful not to pierce the interior sac, and fished the whole thing out with a swipe of his finger. It made her think of harvesting calcet, the delicate touch required, and how she'd seen her father botch so many cuts that day in the Pit. He caught Sev looking at him, and he gave her a lopsided grin.

"Bad day to be a fish, I reckon."

He was sweating just as badly as her, but with no spare hand to keep it out of his eyes. She would get him a bandana, she thought to herself. She blotted her brow again. Maybe she would get one, too.

Sev's pile of empty fish was smaller than Phoenix's, and it was hot, strenuous work. She nudged his shoulder, and he turned to her, sweat dripping in his eyes. She reached up and wiped his brow with her clean hand, wicking the moisture on her overalls. "You're better at this than me."

Phoenix quirked his mouth. "Don't you worry mouse; you're doing a fine job. A fine job. Say, did I ever tell you of the time I was a deckhand on a fishing boat? What a time that was!"

Sev settled back into her work, brow furrowed and lips pressed tightly in consternation, taking care not to nick the membrane that held the internal organs and using her small fingers to clean out the body cavity. She let Phoenix's voice flow over her. She remembered when his loquacious tendencies would grate on her nerves. Now, his talkativeness soothed her.

"And that's how I learned I was no hand at seafaring," he finished with a tired chuckle. The whistle blew, and he slung his arm over her shoulders. "Let's get going, little mouse. I've had just about enough of fish guts for one day."

They walked pressed tightly together despite the heat, Sev's fingers cramping against the hard day. She held their lunchbox in one hand, the other arm hanging free. Phoenix squinted ahead, reading a storefront sign.

He stopped, greeting the shop owner with a wide grin. Sev realized how they must look to them, bedraggled and sweaty and covered in fish slime. Phoenix didn't seem to mind, and to their credit, the shop owner only smiled. "We'll take two ices, please, and I do thank you kindly."

The shop owner handed Phoenix the sweet treats one at a time, and Phoenix passed the first one to Sev. It was red and smelled of berries. Sev took the provided spoon and scooped some into her mouth.

"Mm," she hummed appreciatively. The fruit-flavored delicacy was tasty and refreshing. Phoenix smiled and, with no extra hand to hold a spoon, took a bite of his right off the top. "On a hot day, there is none like it," he declared around a mouthful of ice.

Sev nodded. "Thanks, Phoenix. Work doesn't seem like work with you." She took another spoonful, flavor bursting on her tongue. "I mean, it goes by fast."

Phoenix did not reply. He nibbled off the top of his own treat, then drank the juice from the cup where it had melted. He slurped loudly, and Sev laughed.

"What now?" He blinked at Sev in faux offense. His hair had dried with sweat and the little white patch stood up in spikes away from his forehead. "Are you calling me out on my manners, girl?"

Sev laughed even louder, finishing her treat and throwing the paper cup in a nearby trash receptacle. She wrapped her hand around Phoenix's forearm, the muscles there firm and warm. She gave it a gentle squeeze.

"Let's have anything but fish tonight," she said, her face wrinkling in disgust. Phoenix grunted, finishing and tossing his own treat. "Anything you wish, little mouse."

After they had each showered and changed, Phoenix pulled the bin of cold cuts from the fridge, and they made sandwiches and munched on vegetable sticks until their eyes were heavy and their stomachs full. Sev got ready for bed, slipping beneath the covers and stretching her legs. Phoenix sat down on the bed next to her.

"No work tomorrow," he said. He braced his arm on the bed where he could look down on her. His hair had gotten long, and it had dried in soft curls from the shower. "How will we ever spend our time?"

Sev turned to him. "Let's go to the beach," she said, and Phoenix just smiled. "Now, how did I know you were going to say that?"

"You've got good instincts," Sev answered around a yawn. "Just like the *Nautica* girl."

Phoenix's eyebrows raised. "Ah, that's quite the esteemed company, then, to be likened to the famed *Nautica* girl." He waved his hand. "I'm honored, little mouse."

Sev closed her eyes. "Will you stay with me until I fall asleep?"

Phoenix pretended to consider, ruminating with a finger under his chin. "Well, seeing as you have put in a hard day of work, and your belly's full, I'm thinking that will get me off the hook before too long."

She punched him lightly on the arm and turned on her side. Phoenix sat on the side of the bed, watching the rise and fall of her chest, her relaxed brow. After a few minutes, he patted her shoulder. "Sleep well, mouse," he said, but she was already gone.

The sun filtered through the heavy canopy of trees, spores catching the light. Sev walked to the edge of the Terra Firma marshes, where the spores belched into the air. A thrill of panic shot through her, but she looked down and realized she was in a suit. She checked the filter, and it was good. This was not her suit, but another one. A newer one.

She remembered Phoenix.

Her breath fogged the inside of her helmet, her eyes wide. He was not with her. *Where was he?* She checked the comms, flipping to the nearest open channel. "Phoenix?" her voice wavered across Terra Firma.

The comm sparked to life. "Now where did you get off to, little mouse? The Pit is ripe for the takin' and I need my right hand."

She looked down, and she held the chem in her hands. Curious, she thought, that she would have the chem out here in the marshes. She picked her way back, ducking under fallen trees and traipsing through the underbrush. Somehow, she arrived at the clearing, and Phoenix rose up out of the Pit to meet her.

He had two hands.

"Little mouse, there you are," he exclaimed cheerily. His eyes were alight with excitement. "We've much to do, now. We best get to it."

Sev stared at him in amazement. Phoenix was wearing a suit…not the ancient thing he'd worn when they first met, but a new suit, something truly fit for Terra Firma. She reached out to check his filter and saw that it was good.

She grabbed his right hand, and he squeezed against hers. There was a mechanical whir of servomotors, and the flesh was cool to the touch.

Synth skin, then. Phoenix had a new arm.

She blinked at him, unbelieving. He was tugging her toward the Pit, his grin lopsided beneath his helmet. She stopped at the edge, pulling her hand away. She ran her hand up the length of the prosthetic, squeezing and touching, enthralled. Phoenix seemed a little bemused. "What is it, mouse? You act like you've never seen a one-armed man before."

She had tears in her eyes, and with no way to wipe them away, they tracked freely down her cheek. "You've got two, now," she stammered, still in awe. "Like before we met."

Phoenix smiled. "That's right, little mouse, just like before." He nudged her forward, and he sank to his knees. "Now help me with this bounty; we'll make our fortune yet!"

Sev looked on as Phoenix harvested the calcet with two expert hands, his knife as steady as it had been against the fish's belly. He sought her face. His eyes in the sun turned to molten, honeyed pools. "The chem, Sev," he said to her, "just as soon as you're ready."

She awoke with a start. It was early, not yet light, and she lay there for a few moments, listening to the drone of Phoenix's snoring sync up with the distant sound of waves. He was on his side, his stump out on top of the blanket.

She frowned. They were back on Dobani, and it was just a dream.

She stood and made her way to the bathroom. She smoothed her hair back into its ponytail and washed her face. Then she crossed to Phoenix's bedside.

She sat on the edge, turned into him. Phoenix's face lay slack and tan against the white pillow. His eyes darted beneath closed lids and his hair was in disarray. She placed a hand on his shoulder right above his stump.

"Phoenix," she whispered. The sun wasn't even up, and it was their day off. She should let him sleep.

She shook him again, saying his name, and he blinked awake.

"Mouse," he mumbled, flipping onto his back and squinting at her. "What's the matter, hmm? Bad dream?"

She shook her head. "A very good dream, Phoenix. Come, let's have breakfast. I'll tell you all about it."

Phoenix wiped his hand over his face, and Sev smiled. There was a distinct pillow crease in his cheek gone red/white from pressure. She pulled him to his feet, and he groaned. "Not just yet now, little mouse. Unless you want to watch the sunrise, it's too early for the beach."

"No, Phoenix, I said breakfast, not beach." Sev huffed and led him to the table. She sat him down and went to the kitchen counter. "Cereal?" she asked.

He yawned. "For now, a glass of water will do." He took the proffered glass gratefully and took a sip. Sev settled in the chair across from him, folding her hands in front of her.

"Now Sev, do you mind telling me why we are up presently and not asleep in our beds, it being our day off and all?" He put his hand up in a placating gesture. "Not that I mind…there's nothing I would like more than to greet the morning with you. That being said, it is awfully early to be up and stirrin'."

Sev leaned forward and steepled her fingers under her chin. "We have to go back to Terra Firma."

Phoenix opened his mouth to say something, then promptly shut it. He grew serious, as serious as Sev had ever seen him. "What's this pertaining to?"

"My dream, Phoenix. It means something. Don't you think it means something?"

Phoenix frowned and tapped the table. "Well now, I don't rightly know, seeing as I haven't heard about this dream of yours. Now spill it, girl. What's got you worked up so?"

Sev drew her legs up to hug her knees, her eyes unfocused in remembrance. "We were on Terra Firma, only I was alone at first. And I had a new suit on with a good filter. But I couldn't find you. And when I did–Phoenix, you're gonna love this part–you had a new arm…a prosthetic arm."

Phoenix pursed his lips. "And what was I doing there on Terra Firma? In this dream of yours?"

Sev brightened. "You were in the Pit. We were harvesting calcet."

Phoenix scratched his chin. "And you think this means…what, exactly?"

"That if we go back, we'll be successful. We won't have to worry about credits anymore." She sought him out, her eyes bright. "But first you need a prosthetic."

Phoenix pushed back from the table and stood, his hand on his hip. "Hold your horses now, little mouse. You're gettin' way ahead of yourself. The barge doesn't run to Terra Firma anymore. And the skiff is in no shape."

Sev lowered her legs and leaned back in the chair. The sun was coming up through the window, painting most of the room in ribbons of buttercream. Phoenix paced in the shafts of light, stirring the dust motes there.

"I think it means something," she repeated. "At least think about it, Phoenix. Think about what you could do with two good hands."

He wiped his hand over his mouth, then ruffled through his hair. The white patch was curled away from his forehead, still spiked with sleep. "Sev, I know you mean well. I truly know. But you told me you didn't want to go back to the Black. You said that. And now you're telling me you do?" He sighed. "I think it was just a dream, sweet mouse, and one we shouldn't read too much into."

Sev lowered her head, picking at her fingers where they lay in her lap. "I said that because of how injured you were," she admitted. "But you're better now. Things are better now."

Phoenix stood leaning against the kitchen counter, one ankle crossed over the other. He was standing in the sunlight, the rising sun slipping over the broad shoulders of his rumpled white T-shirt, his checked sleep pants. Phoenix pushed away from the counter and crossed to where Sev still sat at the table. He knelt in front of her.

"I'll promise you I'll think about it," he reasoned, teasing a smile from her. "That good enough?"

She nodded, then lunged forward, wrapping her arms around his neck. Phoenix smelled good, like soap and fresh laundry, and he was sleep-warm and solid beneath her. He exhaled a laugh, softening against her, and hugged her back with his one arm.

"Now what would you like for breakfast, little mouse?" he said pulling away. "Eggs ok?"

Phoenix took a nap after breakfast, and Sev wrote. The journal Phoenix had bought her at the museum was filling rapidly. The sun was high above them by the time they made it to the shore.

Phoenix sat browning in the sun while Sev searched for shells at the water's edge. She would find one, run back to the dunes to show Phoenix, and then line them up beside him on the sand. She was on her fourth trip when Phoenix caught her arm.

He had been pensive all morning and uncharacteristically quiet. He patted the space beside him, and Sev sat down.

"With all this planning you're doing in that head of yours, have you paid any mind to school?" The breeze off the water was whipping his hair to-and-fro. It appeared to be dancing.

Sev frowned but said nothing. She leaned against him, letting her head drop to his shoulder. She closed her eyes.

"I'd be a sorry man indeed if I let you waste your youth on hard labor and get old before your time. Answer me, girl."

"I haven't," she said. She was hoping he never brought it up again.

"And why not?"

She shrugged, evasive and shy. She glanced over the surface of the water. "Maybe I could go after we get back from Terra Firma."

Phoenix sighed. She was still stuck on that, then. He picked up a shell Sev had collected and turned it over in his hand. "This one's a pretty thing, mouse. What are you going to do with them?"

She looked at him, her eyes imploring. "You said you would think about it," she began, ignoring his attempts to steer the conversation away from her dream.

"Who says I'm not?"

She smiled. "Will you go to the medical center then? Just to ask questions?" She laid her head against him and glanced up at him with large, wet eyes. "Please?"

Phoenix lowered his chin. Maybe if he followed through with it, if she finally heard for herself just how expensive it was, it would satisfy her. He was near helpless against her when she looked at him that way. He would move mountains for her if need be. Surely, he could inquire about a prosthetic arm.

He nodded. "Ok, little mouse. We'll go."

The medical center was all shiny steel and glass, with multiple floors that loomed large in the middle of Dobani Proper. They'd got home from the beach in the afternoon, washed off the sand and surf and shared a meal. Sev had wanted to go into Dobani Proper right after.

Phoenix spoke to the attendant at the desk, signed in on a holopad, and led Sev to a waiting area. She had her journal with her, as she did most days, and sat writing beside Phoenix. There was a nutrition station, and a view panel turned to Dobani news. An artificially pretty journalist was talking about Dobani elections, but Phoenix wasn't interested.

He was nervous.

Phoenix had never liked doctors…could count on his one hand the number of times he'd been to one. Out in the Outer Reaches, field kits were all he had. They were all he'd ever known.

Sev put down her journal and smiled at him. She was truly happy they were there, and it soothed him some. He smiled back at her, and she slipped her hand in his, giving it an encouraging squeeze.

"Mr.–"

"Just Phoenix is fine," he finished, meeting the doctor halfway into the room with his hand outstretched. The doctor shook it, decisive and firm. Sev was beside him in moments.

"And this is your…"

"This is Sev," Phoenix supplied, neatly sidestepping who they were to each other. Sev stepped forward, her eyes keen and her journal tucked under one arm, and held out her hand. The doctor took it. "Nice to meet you, young lady." He turned to Phoenix. "If you'll both follow me."

They followed the doctor down a long hall, his white coat billowing behind. The doctor led them to a large, bright room with exam tables lined up in a row. The doctor patted the nearest table and Phoenix took his cue, blowing out a quick breath of nerves and flexing his hand in his lap. Sev reached for it, interlacing their fingers.

"It's ok," she assured him with a gentle squeeze. "We're just here to ask questions."

The doctor smiled. "You're here about a prosthetic, it says here. May I examine you?"

Phoenix nodded hesitantly, his face pinched. "Do your worst," he said, and pushed his sleeve up over his stump.

The doctor whistled as he probed at Phoenix's skin, the deep scars of his hasty amputation puckered and ugly. "A nasty cut. Was this done here?"

Phoenix shook his head tightly.

"Hmm," the doctor hummed. His eyes flicked toward Sev, then back to Phoenix's stump where he palpated it lightly with both hands. "What do you do for a living, Mr. Phoenix?"

"Fishing industry," Phoenix said. "I was a harvester before."

The doctor's eyes widened. "Harvester, eh? Calcet?"

Phoenix nodded. The doctor made a face. "Dangerous work."

Phoenix smiled his most disarming smile. "So they say."

The doctor huffed and removed his gloves. He leaned against the adjacent exam table, his hands folded in front of him. "You're an excellent candidate for a prosthetic, Mr. Phoenix. Despite your scars, you won't need any reconstruction. We can make the mold today, if you like."

Sev squeezed his hand, looking at him excitedly. He shook his head. "Now, now, little mouse. Settle." He regarded the doctor with a critical eye. "Just how much are we talking?"

The doctor appeared confused. "I'm not sure I know what you mean, sir."

Phoenix blew out an exasperated breath. "Credits, doc, and don't be coy. How many credits for the arm? What do they run?"

Realization dawned on him, and the doctor chuckled. "Mr. Phoenix, there won't be any charge for your prosthetic. Dobani takes care of its citizens. The ruling class provides comprehensive health care for all."

Sev made a little sound and quickly stifled it with her hand. She still held Phoenix's hand with the other. She stared at him, disbelieving.

Phoenix grew sad at the hope on the girl's face. He frowned. Nothing was ever free in the Outer Reaches, and if it was, you couldn't trust it. He turned to the doctor. "Maybe not credits, per se, but there will be a cost, I assure you. So, what is mine?"

The doctor just shook his head. "Nothing, Mr. Phoenix. There's no catch. We can fit you for a prosthetic today if that's something you would like." He patted Phoenix on the shoulder, then looked at Sev. She had tears in her eyes. "Maybe I should leave you two alone…let you talk about it."

Phoenix nodded. The doctor left them in the overly bright room, and Phoenix waited until the door closed behind him before he turned to Sev. "Now I know what you're thinking mouse—", he began, but Sev covered his mouth with her hand. He'd never seen her look more determined, not even when she'd tended his rotten wounds with all the skill and practiced ease of an experienced field medic.

"Just say yes, Phoenix," she pleaded with him. "We've got nothing to lose."

He saw her then. There was a light in her eyes that wasn't there before. His resolve withered. He took her hand from his mouth and pressed a kiss to her palm.

"I'll try it for you, little mouse," he promised her before realizing it. "I'll try it for you."

They went back to work the next day. The doctor made the mold, which Phoenix endured with characteristic grace, and asked them a lot of questions. He sent them home with a holopad of information and a promise to notify them as soon as the prosthetic was ready.

Phoenix forgot about it, and Sev was content. He wondered when his life's main objective had shifted…when the tide had turned from survival to accumulating wealth to making Sev happy.

Because obviously it had, and it didn't bother him much.

In the interim, he taught Sev how to cook.

"You put the butter in the pan first. Let it get all bubbly. Then you place your protein." He took a piece of meat from the cutting board and placed it carefully in the pan. "See?"

Sev had her own pan, and she stood by Phoenix at the stove. She adjusted the heat on the burner in front of her, listened for the crackle of the butter, and then laid the meat down with a sizzle. "Like this?"

"Drek knows," Phoenix assured. "Now wait for it to brown, just a touch, and then we'll flip it."

Sev nodded, face scrunched in concentration. After a few minutes, Phoenix handed her a spatula. "Give it a go, little mouse. Real gentle like."

She regarded him with large eyes. "How do we know it's done on that side? I can't see it."

Phoenix smiled. "Instinct." He sniffed the air. "And scent. Cooked meat smells a certain way…the real trick is knowing when to flip it before it's burned."

Sev slipped her spatula beneath the meat in the pan and edged it over. It was a toasty golden brown. She grinned at him. "I did it!"

He patted her on the back. "That you did, little mouse. That you did indeed."

The holopad flashed on an off day. Phoenix was still asleep, and Sev was eating her cereal by the window when she saw the alert. She read the screen, growing more excited by the minute. She clutched the pad to her chest, her eyes welling with tears. It was really happening. She couldn't believe it.

She let Phoenix sleep. When he awoke around mid-morning, she handed him the holopad.

"It's ready," she exclaimed without explanation. Phoenix blinked at the message, reading it several times before it registered. He glanced at Sev, and she had a bright smile on her face. "Your new arm."

Her enthusiasm was contagious, and Phoenix soon realized he was smiling, too.

They took the chute into Dobani Proper. Sev led Phoenix down the long hall, where the doctor and several other technicians stood waiting. They sat Phoenix down and had him remove his shirt.

Sev's eyes immediately went to the red-brown puckered flesh of his abdomen, the gunshot and stab wounds he'd incurred on Terra Firma. Seeing it reminded her how close he'd come to dying, how close she had come to losing him forever, to being totally and utterly alone.

The technicians brought out a box, took off the lid and there inside was Phoenix's arm. They lifted it out and set it on the table.

Phoenix inspected it dubiously. It appeared large, a foreign thing, but in fact it was the same size and shade as his left one. He chanced a glance at Sev, who was watching the proceedings with wide eyes full of wonder. "Can I touch it?" she asked, and Phoenix realized he would like to touch it, too.

"Let's get it on him first," the doctor instructed. There were straps that went over his shoulder, like a little holster, then the technicians snugged his stump inside the soft interior of the prosthetic.

It was a perfect fit.

Phoenix marveled at it, unused to seeing an appendage there at all. "How does it work?" he asked.

The doctor just smiled. "The sensors inside the arm read your nerve endings. Try to open and close your hand, Mr. Phoenix. Easy now. It'll take some getting used to."

Phoenix did, and the hand opened with a soft whir, then closed, the fingers contracting. Phoenix laughed in disbelief. "By Drek's own hand," he murmured.

Sev gasped, her hand over her mouth. "Oh Phoenix," she stammered. "It really works."

He looked up at her, eyes shining. "I can put both arms around you now, little mouse. Stars alive."

The doctor put Phoenix through several tests, explaining that his grip strength and accuracy would improve with practice. He also brought out attachments, telling Phoenix that if he had need of a claw or hook in his line of work, he could change them out with a hinge on the arm's elbow. Phoenix wasn't listening. He sat there, opening and closing his new hand and looking at it for a long time.

They left the medical center with the little bag of supplies. Phoenix held it in his left hand, and he held Sev's with his new right. "How does it feel?" she asked for maybe the fifth time. His Sev was full of questions.

"Strange," he mused. "I can feel you touching me, but from far away. All pins and needles like."

She nodded, interlocking their fingers. The cool synth skin was smooth against her palm. "What about now?" she asked with narrowed eyes. She pinched his arm, feeling the give of flesh. "And now?"

Phoenix chuckled. "I can feel you, little mouse."

It satisfied her. "Is it heavy, Phoenix? Does it hurt?"

"No little mouse. No to both. Now let's go home, shall we? We both need rest if we're to work tomorrow."

She fell asleep on the chute, and this time, he could hold her against him.

CHAPTER 9

The cold had come to Dobani. Phoenix wouldn't have believed it possible, given his only experience with Dobani before they arrived had been in the blistering warmth of the tourist months, but he and Sev had stayed on Dobani long enough for the off season to come around again.

The streets were mostly empty. The tourists had all gone home. Even some stores were closed half days, adjusting to the slower business. The beach was a desolate waste, one Sev was incurably enamored of. The icy wind glancing off the waves left the dunes and soft grasses and predator birds and little else.

He saw Sev where she sat beneath the window. He could tell she was cold, the way she hugged her knees, the journal balanced atop them. She had closed the window against the weather, but sat in her favorite chair as if she could still hear the waves.

Phoenix crossed to his bed and removed the blanket there. He folded it haphazardly over his prosthetic arm and went to where Sev sat writing by the window. Without a word, he draped the blanket over her and tucked it in. Sev met his eyes and smiled. "Thanks Phoenix."

Phoenix leaned against the kitchen counter, crossing his left hand over the prosthetic he was still getting used to. Sev was pensive, almost solemn. "What's on your mind, little mouse?"

Sev frowned, closing her journal and covering it with her hand. "What did you say this was called? The off season?"

Phoenix nodded. "It is indeed. This is the slowing-down time on Dobani." He flexed the fingers on his prosthetic hand, still marveling at the unfamiliar sensation there. "Does it bother you, little mouse?"

She looked down at her lap. "I miss swimming," she said, "and listening to the waves. It's too cold outside now to leave the window open."

Phoenix smiled. "I'll have to take you to the hot springs," he declared, still looking at her beneath the window.

She brightened. "They have those here?"

"Well, I'm sure they do, being as it's a big world and it has gone mostly unexplored by us." He patted his arm. "They must. We'll ask around."

Sev laid her head on her knees and exhaled. "I'd like to go," she mused.

Phoenix scratched his chin with his new hand, servos whirring with the delicate motion. "We'll need some new clothes if we're to weather the off season on Dobani," he said.

Sev furrowed her brow, her mouth a tight line. "We don't need to spend the credits."

Phoenix huffed. "Now what choice do we have, mouse? If we're to stay on Dobani, we must be well-equipped, clothing included. I hazard that we'll need outfittin' head to toe."

Sev burrowed further under the blanket. It smelled like Phoenix and was warm besides. She relaxed in the chair, letting the warmth lull her. "If you say so, Phoenix."

Phoenix only smiled, lopsided and fond. "We should go before the sun sets, else it will be colder."

Sev only hummed.

Phoenix took Sev to the shopping district, and he wished he could've captured the look on her face when she saw the glittering buildings and gilded shopfronts with brightly painted trim the color of the Dobani sea. Phoenix let Sev choose where they would go first, and they shouldered their way into a store with a fancy-lettered sign. Sev clung to his side before finally succumbing to curiosity, walking dumbstruck among the racks of clothes.

"May I help you?"

Phoenix looked up to find a slight woman with bright red lips and blue hair walking toward them. Phoenix extended his hand (the left one out of habit), and she took it primly.

"If you are the purveyor of this fine establishment, then I bet you might," Phoenix crooned with all his usual charm. "This here is Sev and I'm Phoenix, and we find ourselves ill-prepared for this latest change in weather. So to say, we need something suited for colder climes."

The woman laughed fondly. "Why, I just love the way you speak, Phoenix. It's like poetry."

Sev observed, astounded, as Phoenix's face took on a hint of rouge. "It's a trifle different, I'll give you that," he said.

"My name's Pearla," she began, "and I agree with you about the weather. It's dreadfully cold and only getting colder." She pursed her lips in a little downturn of her mouth. "But we have a new line in that will have you warmed up in no time."

She led them to a set of racks near the back of the store. The myriad of colors and fabrics instantly dazzled Sev. Phoenix knelt in front of her, his hands on her shoulders.

"Pick out whatever you like, Sev. These are clothes for living, not working, so let that guide your choices."

Sev nodded, her face more serious than it should be, and followed Pearla to a rack of clothes that were all in her size.

Pearla helped Sev pick out warm sweaters and slacks, some jeans and boots. Sev's eyes lingered over a black skirt with little pink bows on it, and Pearla perked up.

"Do you like that, honey? There's a pink cardigan to match it, and leggings for the cold. It would look so good on you!"

Sev regarded Phoenix, and he nodded his encouragement. "Go on. Try it on, mouse. And then you can come out here and take a spin."

Sev smiled, clutching the clothes to her chest as she made her way back to the dressing room.

Halfway through the process, Sev was enjoying herself. She'd never had so many choices concerning her wardrobe…in fact, she couldn't even say she had a style. She'd always dressed for the Black, for comfort and utility. That these clothes came in different colors, patterns, and textures astounded her. Deep down, it also pleased her.

Sev came out of the dressing room wearing the skirt and leggings and the little pink cardigan. She walked out to stand in front of the set of mirrors there, her hands clasped in front of her. She was somewhat embarrassed and avoided her reflection.

Phoenix smiled broadly and made a pleased sort of sound. "Don't you look as pretty as a peach, little mouse."

Sev huffed, her cheeks pinking, and pressed her hands against the skirt. "It's not very practical," she murmured. Phoenix tutted.

"Not practical how? Seeing as you are a young girl and you might on occasion have the need to be dressed up, I think it's very practical."

Sev glanced at Phoenix, her eyes hopeful. "Like when we go out to eat?"

Phoenix gestured with his new right hand, stabbing his finger in the air. "That's exactly when," he affirmed with a smile. He turned to Pearla enthusiastically. "We'll take it. And the rest of her things, too. Did you choose a hat, Sev?" He walked off toward the racks of accessories, considering. "Little mouse will need a scarf too," he muttered to himself. "That's it, and a scarf to match."

Pearla stood behind Sev, watching her reflection in the mirror. She gave her shoulders a little squeeze. "Your father loves you very much," she told her with a smile.

Sev swallowed. "He's not–"

"You're very lucky."

In the mirror, Pearla was still smiling at her. The cardigan was soft, and the palest pink she'd ever seen, like the inside of a shell. The little bows on the skirt stood out in stark relief, and she ran her fingers over them. She's never had anything so fine in her life, she thought. She'd never had anything so *pretty*.

"I am very lucky," she agreed, her eyes wet with tears.

After Phoenix got Sev outfitted properly, he shopped for himself. Sev justly pointed out that most of his shirts had the right arm cut out of them, and now that he had his new arm, he needed "proper clothes." She helped him shop, choosing bolder colors than he would've chosen for himself, but he let her have her way. She had good taste, his Sev, and by the time she was done, he had enough sweaters and shirts to cover both arms.

Both donned their new coats and headed outside, packages split between them. Sev grabbed Phoenix's free hand, the artificial one, and squeezed it. "Thank you for the clothes, Phoenix."

Phoenix appraised her. She had the coat buttoned up to her chin, closed securely over the cardigan and skirt that had so caught her eye. He smiled to himself. "You're welcome, little mouse."

"The off season is not so bad anymore," Sev mused. "Although I feel a little silly."

The cold had left patches of color on her cheeks. "Why is that?" Phoenix asked her.

"I'm all dressed up for no reason."

Phoenix patted her shoulder. "Ah, but not for no reason, sweet mouse. If it makes you feel good, then it's certainly for a good reason. Besides, we're off to lunch."

Sev sought him out, her eyes imploring. "The diner?"

Phoenix shook his head. "Somewhere far more special," he assured her. "Somewhere that's befitting your fine clothes." Phoenix made a very self-important face, and Sev giggled.

"Ok," she assented.

Phoenix took Sev to a restaurant in Dobani Proper. It was small from the outside, but upon entering, the space opened to a skylight filled with flowers. The attendant led them to a small round table and took their packages and coats.

Sev was beaming.

"This is so nice," she breathed, looking around in wonderment. The attendant seated them in the sun, and strands of ivy and dappled leafy vines hung down around them.

They ordered, and Sev rested her chin in her hand. "Do you remember my dream, Phoenix? The one where we were on Terra Firma?"

Phoenix shook out his napkin, placing it in his lap. "I do indeed. What of it?"

Sev took a sip of water. "We should go back. You're getting better with your arm, now. I think it's time."

Phoenix thought for a moment, and the attendant brought them their salads. Sev sat across from him, twirling greens onto her fork. "If we're to go back to Terra Firma, we'll need new suits," he began. "And packs. And the skiff is not fit for traveling; we barely made it through Dobani atmosphere without being cooked alive."

Sev's eyes took on an excited gleam. "We'll fix up the skiff first. Save our credits. Buy what we can and earn as we go. We can figure out what we need and have parts ordered as soon as tomorrow."

Phoenix chuckled to himself. Sev's enthusiasm was catching, as usual. "What if it's not there, little mouse? What if Drek has smited us for our greed and given the Pit to some other harvester? What then?"

Sev thought, her eyes narrowed, for a long few moments. "Then we can always say we tried." She stuck her hand out across the table and Phoenix took it. "Even split?"

He smiled, squeezing her hand. "Wouldn't have it any other way."

They made their way back to the apartment. Sev carried her packages to the clothesline they'd strung across the corner of the living room, a makeshift closet, and began hanging her new clothes. Phoenix looked on, something growing soft in his belly. If they found the Pit untainted, he thought, and the harvest was good, perhaps they could have a little house by the shore and Sev would have her own room.

She smiled as if she could read his thoughts. He watched as she pulled the little footlocker out from under her bed and unpacked her everyday clothes, heading off to the bathroom to change.

Phoenix sat on his bed and ran a hand through his hair. His fingers tugged at the little white patch, a nervous habit, until he'd teased it straight up. There was much to do before they could return to Terra Firma, the skiff first among them. It needed repair, and they didn't have the credits to hire it done. So, they'd do it themselves. As Sev had said, they would work for the parts and fix what they could along the way. It would take time, but as Drek allowed, they were in no rush. The Pit would wait, and with the route shutdown, it was unlikely anyone had been to Terra Firma since them, seeing as how it was a perilous journey and fraught with difficulty.

Then, the moral implications of bringing a child to Terra Firma settled in his gut. He remembered how horrified he had been when he first saw Sev on that fateful day with Del. Her very presence in such a Drek-forsaken place had affronted him greatly. He couldn't believe anyone would bring a child there, and here he was contemplating the same thing. He shook his head.

Sev exited the bathroom with her new cardigan and skirt hung neatly on a rack. She crossed to what passed as their closet in the small room and hung it near the back. She ran her hand over it once, pressing out the wrinkles, a faraway look in her eyes.

"Come here, Sev," Phoenix began. "Come sit a spell. I want to talk with you."

Sev took one of the kitchen chairs and pulled it over to sit in front of him. She settled there, her hands folded in her lap.

"Little mouse, why do you want to go back to Terra Firma? It's not a place for children."

She blinked, her large seafoam eyes searching his face. "Because all that calcet is just sitting there. It could change our lives, Phoenix. And you need me!" She folded her arms. "I've been before. Besides, things are different now."

Phoenix savored it, wondering exactly what she meant. He placed his hand on her arm, the one that was fully his, and traced her skin with his thumb. "I worry for you, mouse. I don't want to put you in any position that would cause you to come to harm, is all." He met her eyes, his face going soft. "You understand?"

Sev nodded, then fell into his arms. She lay her head on his shoulder, breathing in his warmth.

Phoenix hugged her back, both arms going up to hold her against him. "You're not like my father," the words souring in her mouth. "I know that's why you're worried about going back. But no one is making me this time." She tightened her hold on him. "I'm old enough to know what I want."

Phoenix rubbed little circles on her back. She was a slight thing, his Sev, but headstrong and capable. "That I know for sure," he said. "You're your own person, little mouse. Have been for a while. If you truly want to make a run for the Pit, then you'll find me a willing partner."

She withdrew, a bright smile on her face. "Yeah?"

Phoenix nodded, feeling better. Feeling, for the first time in a long time, a rush of anticipation…the thrill of the hunt. He tensed his right hand, touching each finger to his thumb in a rhythmic exercise. The sensation was there. He could harvest. He could teach Sev. This could work.

He grabbed her hand. "Come on, little mouse. Get your journal. We've got much to do."

They detoured by the beach on the way to the hangar, because of course they did. Sev was helpless to its pull, and Phoenix was helpless to Sev's whims. They walked barefoot in the cold sand, holding their shoes, and gasped and laughed as the frigid water lapped at their toes.

Sev turned to Phoenix, the dusty rose of the setting sun highlighting her hair. "We should fish sometimes," Sev said, walking along the shore holding Phoenix's hand. "We could cast off the pier or stand knee deep in the water here and see what we catch."

Phoenix laughed. They were wearing their new coats, so the wind didn't bite as bad as it could have. He squeezed her hand. "When warmth returns to Dobani, then perhaps. Perhaps we'll fish, although I thought you would've had enough of fish by now."

Sev smiled. "That's work. This would be something to do for fun. And for food. Have you ever fished before?"

Phoenix nodded. "Not for recreation, no, but I would be open to try." Truth be told, he thought he would be open to trying most anything if Sev suggested it.

She leaned into him with a sigh. "Will you tell me about it?"

He wrapped his arm around her as they walked. She shook slightly even in her coat; Phoenix wondered how she'd made it all those years in the cold expanse of the Black.

He would have had her raised in someplace warm, not in the cold reaches of space.

"It was a long time ago, little mouse. There were twelve of us; we oversaw the nets and baskets. We set the bait, and we would reel them in by turning a big crank. It was hard work, but I never minded being on the water."

Sev went quiet. "I've never been on a boat," she mused. "What's it like?"

Phoenix leaned into her, knocking her off balance and then pulling her back before allowing her to right herself. Sev giggled. "A lot like that. The sea is all topsy-turvy. It takes some getting used to."

Sev dropped her head onto his shoulder. "Take me?" she asked.

Phoenix kissed the top of her head, resting his cheek against it. The sun was nearly gone, taking its meager warmth with it. "One day, little mouse. One day."

The skiff sat where they left it. They had paid the man well to watch it, back when their credits had been plentiful, and they were so new to Dobani. And sure enough, it sat undisturbed.

It looked even worse than he remembered.

The skiff's exterior was pock-marked and scorched, scarred from their shaky re-entry. They'd need new thrusters, new flaps, just to get it off the ground.

Sev walked all around it, taking stock of the needed repairs. Sev had lived her whole life around ships and drop pods; she knew as much as Phoenix at least, and she was taking notes in her journal about the parts they'd need.

"Come on, mouse," Phoenix called to her. "Let's take a look inside."

They opened the hatch to a puff of stale air. The interior was bleak and bare, with no insulation. Phoenix took a mental note to order that too; he wouldn't have Sev cold in the Black if he could help it.

There on the floor of the skiff were a few bloody rags.

Sev crossed to them quickly, gathering them up and tossing them in the corner, out of sight. She glanced at Phoenix, her eyes filled with some unnamed emotion.

"I never thanked you, mouse. For saving my life." His voice wavered a bit, and he cleared his throat. "I don't remember much, but I know enough to know you shouldn't have had to do it." He swallowed, his eyes on the bloody rags instead of Sev's face, but he knew she was looking at him.

"Hey," she said, and he glanced up at her. "You don't have to thank me." She smiled, and something inside him broke. "What are partners for, anyway?"

Phoenix felt a twinge of some unnamed emotion. How could he tell her he no longer considered her just a partner, but that she was somehow *other*? Something more?

He only nodded. "Indeed," he said, his voice thick with emotion. He gestured to her. "Let's get our list together so we can get back home."

They sat on the floor between their beds, the list between them. It was late, and Phoenix had his ledger and was calculating exactly how much they could spend on parts and still have enough left over. He wrote a figure and passed it to Sev.

Her eyes widened. "We have that much?"

Phoenix hummed. "A little more, if we live lean for a while. We can talk to the man at the hangar, order the parts tomorrow."

She smiled, her eyes gleaming in the single lamplight. "It's really happening," she breathed. "We're really going."

Phoenix took the ledger back, a lopsided grin on his face. "We're as good as there, mouse," he replied. "With some time and work, we're as good as there."

Sev stood and extended her hand. "We better get to bed," she instructed, sounding much older than she was. "We've got work tomorrow."

Phoenix let her pull him up by his left hand. He favored it, after so long without the right, and given his general mistrust of such things. The arm would be useful, though, when they were back on Terra Firma.

Sev disappeared into the bathroom and then reappeared, slipping beneath the covers with her journal and a small penlight. She turned it on and held it in her mouth, reading. He would get her some books, he decided, maybe build a little shelf for her next to her bed where she could store them.

"Not too long now, little mouse," he said. "It's late already."

Sev hummed, unable to speak around the penlight, and turned another page in her journal.

Phoenix drifted off to sleep, listening to the rhythmic sound of Sev's breathing and the intermittent rustle of paper.

CHAPTER 10

Phoenix lay under the skiff, the engine assembly in pieces all around him. Sev crouched off to the side, cleaning the intake valves, dunking them in soapy water and scrubbing them free of grease. They'd transmit fuel better that way, Phoenix had said. In between tasks, she watched him work, staying close in case he needed her to pass him a tool or a part.

It'd been thirty days since they'd decided on a plan…twenty since they had enough credits to order parts, and thirteen since they'd started repairing the skiff.

And it was the day on which Del always celebrated her birth.

Sev didn't *feel* any older, except she did. She felt decrepit sometimes, old in her bones, but only when she was alone with her thoughts. Phoenix never made her feel that way, not like Del had. Even now, when she was helping Phoenix work, she knew she had an equal stake in the results…they were fixing up the skiff for *them* and not for him. Not like when she had helped Del.

But Del had always remembered her birthday. Sometimes they were on a job, and sometimes they were in the Black. Just when she thought he had forgotten, when the day was nearing its end and she grew weary with her tasks, he would come out with a hastily wrapped present and the rare kind word.

"Pass me the phase adjuster, little mouse, if you're nearby and so inclined."

Sev blinked, drawn from her revelry by Phoenix's gabbiness. He was half under the skiff, knees up. They still wore their work clothes; they had, like most days, come to the hangar straight from the docks.

She rifled through the toolbox, finding the phase adjuster and crouching down beside the skiff. Phoenix slid out from under it, reaching blindly with his left hand before working his head out.

He was grease-smudged, his tan face dusted with streaks of dirt and grime. The white patch in his hair was gray with soot and stuck out in all directions.

He smiled up at Sev and took the tool from her. She went back to washing the intake valves, fingers tender from scrubbing. Phoenix hummed the wordless tune he sometimes hummed when they were on their way home from work, and the sun was warm, and they had showers and supper to look forward to.

"What's that you're humming, Phoenix?" Sev dipped another valve into the water, brushing it and bringing it up clean. She had a pile of them drying on the floor of the hangar and another pile waiting.

A clatter of engine parts rang out in the hangar, followed by a string of curses in a language she didn't understand. Phoenix blew out a breath, picked up the phase adjuster and started again. He was nothing if not persistent.

"*Caro do,*" he replied, his voice sounding far away beneath the skiff. "It's an old, old song, little mouse. As old as Dobani, I suspect." He slid out from under the skiff and sat up with a groan, wiping his hands on a rag. He peered at her intently, and she stopped washing the valves. "The words escape me, but the tune...ah, the tune is etched on my heart." He smiled somewhat sadly. "My mother used to sing it."

Sev swallowed, not expecting that. She had never considered Phoenix's beginnings, but now her mind was fertile soil for those kinds of thoughts. She wanted to know more, but she did not say.

Phoenix caught her wrists with his left hand (he still favored it, although he was getting better with the right) and pulled them out of the water, suds dripping. "Your hands, little mouse. They've gone red." Something inscrutable passed over his face, and his eyes softened. He pursed his lips. "I've worked you too hard."

She flexed her fingers, and indeed they were raw and aching. Perhaps she should've kept her gloves on, after all.

Phoenix's large hand enclosed both of hers, and he thumbed over her knuckles. His hand was rough and grease-stained, but she didn't mind.

"I've got some salve. When we get back to the room, I'll tend them." He smiled, and she nodded before plunging them back beneath the water again.

She thought of Del. If he were here, he'd accuse her of being lost in her head. But she was, she realized…caught up in memories of birthdays past.

Del always remembered, and Phoenix didn't know.

Her cheeks flamed. She shouldn't feel cross with him for something he was ignorant of. Phoenix was good. He was kind. He was tender with her. She shouldn't hold him accountable for forgetting something he never knew.

It was a silly ire, but an ire all the same. Del wasn't here to be angry with. There was only Phoenix.

He laid his hand on her shoulder, the cool synth skin contracting around the ball and socket joint just a little too roughly. Phoenix was still learning its finite motor control. It brought her back to the present, the gentle pressure, and she saw Phoenix crouched before her.

"That's enough for now," he said. "We've got a long walk, and it's dark already."

She nodded numbly, her mind still very far away. She helped Phoenix clean the work area, putting away the tools and ordering the clean intake valves away from the still-dirty ones. Looking at the two piles, she realized she had accomplished more than she thought.

Sev walked a little behind Phoenix as they made their way out of the hangar. The stars were bright around a pregnant moon. Gossamer strands of clouds obscured much of them, enrobing the ambient light in a pleasant glow.

She folded her arms over her chest. They'd bought insulated overalls, but the night was chill. Phoenix said it would be warm again soon, but it didn't seem that way. It seemed like the cold would go on forever, stretching on into the infinite Black.

Phoenix slowed his pace, thinking she would pull alongside him. She did not. She kept one or two steps behind, observing the stoop of Phoenix's wide shoulders, his overalls filmed in dust from the hangar floor. He must be tired, she thought, though Phoenix never showed it.

They mounted the steps to their apartment, and Sev kept her head down against the wind. Her face was chapped, and her fingers ached from scrubbing. She stuffed them in her pockets and ducked inside.

It was warm within, and she was grateful. Phoenix dropped their tools by the door, dusting his hands, and said something she didn't catch.

"Hmm?"

Phoenix smiled, easy and fond. "I was asking if you would be too put upon if I grabbed the first shower, little mouse," he asked. Her silence worried him, she could tell. The way his brow furrowed, the tight line of his mouth. But there was nothing to be done. Her mood was low, and there was no shaking it.

Sev hummed her assent and collapsed on top of her coverlet. She was tired, and she felt very old. She reached under the bed and withdrew her headphones, placing them tightly against her ears and turning the volume high.

Sev lay there for a good while, lost in her music. She thought of Del, how he only minded the headphones when he was ordering her to do something. She realized, in all her time with Phoenix, she had forgotten her music. It had been an escape before, and she had never needed to withdraw from Phoenix. Not until now.

Sev never heard the shower shut off. She cracked her eyes open long enough to see Phoenix's broad back, skin still damp and hair dripping. There were water spots on his white T-shirt, and he didn't wear his arm.

"Let me see those hands, little mouse. I'm no medic, but this salve will sort you out. Come on now."

But Sev never budged. She lay on her bed, knee up and one leg crossed over the other. The music was so loud he could hear it where he stood, and she had her eyes closed.

Phoenix frowned. Sev had seemed distant since the hangar, and since they'd returned home, she seemed to slip further and further away. He approached her carefully, not wanting to startle her, and placed his hand on her arm.

She opened her eyes, eyebrows up in question. Phoenix withdrew the tube of salve and gave it a little shake. He knew if he spoke, she wouldn't be able to hear him, anyway.

Sev slipped the headphones down, letting them rest around her neck. The music seemed louder without Sev's ears to take the brunt of the noise, and she kept her hand on them as if she could slip them back on at any moment.

"Your hands, mouse," Phoenix coaxed, trying to be as amicable as possible. His girl was distant, and it troubled him. "Let's treat them lest they get worse."

Her lips turned down, and she sat up. "Let me wash up first," she mumbled, heading to the bathroom and slamming the door before Phoenix had a moment to process what she'd said.

She left him standing there holding the tube of salve and feeling quite lost.

He walked to the kitchen, eager to find something to do. Perhaps Sev was just hungry and tired from work, and that had her all out of sorts. He rubbed his chin, taking stock of what they had in the pantry.

Flatcakes, he settled on with a smile. They were Sev's favorite and sure to boost her mood. He got to work mixing the honey and grain, so used to doing things one-handed, he didn't miss his other arm.

He had taken the last one off the griddle when he heard the bathroom door open. Sev came out dressed for bed, followed by a puff of steam. She still seemed quite dour.

She took a cursory glance at the table, at the stack of flat cakes that was set at her place. It was slightly taller than Phoenix's and glistened with a honey glaze.

Phoenix stood in the kitchen, a hopeful smile on his face. He'd tied an apron around his waist somehow, and he still held the spatula.

She turned away from him, toward her bed. She lay down and put her headphones back on, this time facing the wall.

Phoenix's eyes stung. Sev had never refused food before, and it hurt him to see her so despondent. She obviously wanted time to herself, so he let her be.

Not knowing what else to do, he left the flatcakes on the table and went to bed.

Sev turned the headphones down low. She listened to the creak of Phoenix's mattress. She heard him grunt as he turned on his left side. Lying on his stump made it sore sometimes, so he favored his left.

He had made her flatcakes.

The tears came unbidden, leaking down the side of her face and spilling onto her pillow. She wiped them away quickly, careful to be quiet. The guilt of ignoring his efforts was almost paralyzing.

She warred with herself for a long moment, the music still pulsing in the background of her thoughts, and removed the headphones to sit on the edge of her bed.

Phoenix had turned out the light. He was on his side, like she figured, with the covers tucked under his stump. She stared at his soft outline in the dark for a long time before, without thinking, she walked across the floor to stand over him.

Phoenix rolled over and turned on the lamp. The light cast his face in soft relief, warm and open against the shadows on his side of the room. He blinked up at her. "Mouse?" he inquired roughly. She realized he must've been almost asleep.

She sniffled, and another tear escaped her lashes. Sev thought of the flatcakes, gone cold now, of the salve she had refused out of a childish desire to punish him.

"I'm sorry," she said, her voice thick with tears. "I'm so sorry, Phoenix."

She had crossed her arms in front of her despite the warmth of the apartment. She lowered her head, unable to look at him.

"Ah now...none of that, sweet mouse." He slid over closer to the wall and rolled onto his right side. He patted the space in front of him. "C'mere."

Sev went wordlessly, slipping under the covers into the place that was still warm from his body heat. She lay there rigidly until the solid weight of his hand landed on her shoulder. He gave it a gentle squeeze.

"What's been bothering you, mouse?" he coaxed. "Out with it now."

Sev pressed her cheek into the pillow. It was still damp from his hair and cool against her fevered skin. "I've been thinking about Del," she confessed, and she could feel his intake of breath.

They never talked about him. It lay an ugly thing between them, how Del died, and while Sev no longer blamed Phoenix (if she had ever blamed him), they did not discuss it.

Phoenix lay uneasily until Sev relaxed against him. She let her shoulder hit his chest, a warm and solid thing, and her muscles unspooled. "Do you want to talk about it?" he asked, his breath feathering her hair.

Reluctantly, she nodded.

He settled against her, thumb tracing little circles on her forearm. They said nothing for a long time, him waiting her out. Phoenix was a patient man…he would've waited all night if that's what it took.

Sev sighed, closing her eyes. "It's my birthday," she said. "Or at least Del said it was. I can't be sure."

The light sweep of his thumb stilled, leaving gooseflesh in its wake. Phoenix was uncharacteristically quiet, but Sev knew he was just letting her have space for her thoughts, for the memories that seemed bigger than the room, now.

"Drek, you've worked the whole time," Phoenix said. "Had I known sooner, little mouse, I'd–"

"He…wasn't a good father," Sev struggled to get out. "I know that now. But sometimes he tried. And he always remembered my birthday."

Phoenix let his arm go over her middle in a loose embrace. Sev blinked against a fresh onslaught of tears, and she moved to wipe them away. Phoenix stilled her hand halfway to her face and did it himself, his callused thumb sweeping over the apple of her cheek. "How would he remember?" he asked, voice low, almost reverent.

"Nothing special. Sometimes he gave me a present, an odd thing wrapped in an old scrap of cloth. He wouldn't make a fuss. Del never did. But he always remembered."

Sev worried her lip with her teeth, realizing how childish she'd been. "Somehow I thought—"

A sob strangled her throat, and she turned into him. She buried her face in his chest, pressing her nose to his shirt. He smelled of soap, of something that was uniquely Phoenix. It made a familiar warmth buzz through her. He held her against him, ghosting his hand down her back.

"It's ok, little mouse. I know. I know."

Sev shook her head, tears now soaking the front of his T-shirt. "You don't," she asserted, her voice muffled. "I was mad at you for not knowing. It's stupid. It sounds so stupid now."

Phoenix tutted, rocking her gently. He held her through her sobs, smoothing over her quivering shoulders, reaching up to trail a hand through her flaxen hair. She quieted, turning her cheek to rest against his chest. Her fingers twined in his shirt, and she could feel the steady thud of Phoenix's heart. She closed her eyes, imagining that beat marching in time with her own.

When her breathing had evened out, he rested his chin on her head.

"My mother died when I was just a young thing," Phoenix began, running his fingers through her hair. Sev grew still, afraid if she moved, he would stop, and she didn't want him to stop. She wanted to know more…all that he would tell her.

Phoenix huffed a bitter laugh. "And my father took off long before that."

Sev flattened her hands against him, breathing in the warm-laundry scent. "When you were a baby?" she asked.

"Lil' older," Phoenix added, and Sev suddenly imagined Phoenix as a child, as a young man. She had never thought of Phoenix like that before…he was always just there, a fully formed adult. But he hadn't appeared on Terra Firma, she knew; he'd come from somewhere.

"What did you look like?" she asked.

Phoenix chuckled. "Scarcely any different. Lean and angry." He tightened his arm around her. "You wouldn't have liked me, mouse. I was a hard man even in my youth."

Sev looked up, and Phoenix's eyes looked far away. She gestured to his hair. "What about that?" It was something she'd wanted to know for so long, how that little white patch had come about, but never knew how to ask.

He quirked his mouth. "Born that way. 'Drek's Kiss,' my mother called it. Said it made me special." He sighed. "Of that, I am not so sure."

They said nothing for a long time. Sev rested against him until she thought he was asleep, lulled by the rise and fall of his chest. "Is it still today?" she asked sleepily.

Phoenix checked his chrono. "Indeed, it is, little mouse. We've time left to celebrate."

He left her then, climbing out of the bed and reaching under it. He withdrew a brown paper package and presented it to her.

She observed him, stunned, and realized he was blushing. "I've been saving this for, well, I'm not particularly sure. But I was certain the right time would present itself." He thrust the box in her direction, and she took it with tender hands, placing it in her lap. "And so it has."

Phoenix settled on the bed next to her, and she weighed the package in her hands. It was heavy but neatly wrapped. Phoenix waited expectantly. "Drek waits, girl," he chided. "Open it before I'm an old man."

Sev licked her lips, her mouth suddenly dry. She slid her fingers beneath the brown paper, fighting the impulse to preserve its integrity, to save it. She untied the twine and let it fall away.

There in her hands was a set of books.

"That's all of them," Phoenix said, "or that was all when I made my purchase. It's been so long, there may be another by now. Bought this with my first credits earned, I did." He waited, brown eyes searching her face. "What have you to say?"

She turned them over in her hands. It was *Nautica*, the entire set, the beloved copy she'd memorized and some titles she had never heard of. She blinked away tears, her throat tight. "Phoenix. Oh, Phoenix."

He smiled as if he'd just made her flatcakes and not given her the entirety of her world wrapped in brown paper. She dropped the books, precious as they were, and threw her arms around his neck.

He laughed and hugged her back. "I take it you like them, then? And I made a fair choice?"

Sev smiled, burying her face in the juncture of his neck and shoulder. "Very fair," she assured him.

He patted her arm. Then he stifled a yawn. "We never took care of your hands, little mouse."

She pulled him down with her, settling in the crook of what was left of his right arm. "Tomorrow," she murmured. "First thing."

Phoenix pulled the covers up over them. "First thing, then."

Sev settled against him, warm and easy. She thought of the books that lay beside her on the floor. All she had ever wanted, but not all. "Will you sing to me, Phoenix?"

Phoenix huffed. "I know only one song, little mouse, and not the words to that besides."

Sev snuggled in close. "Hum it then. I want to hear it. I want to hear *Caro Do.*"

So, Phoenix hummed. When he'd finished, he reached for the lamp and plunged them into darkness. Phoenix wrapped his arm around her middle, leaving it loose. He bent his head to her ear. "I'm not your father, Sev," he said, "but I am here. I'll always be here."

Sev blinked away tears. Then, a wild thought...a small and desperate thought occurred to her, one she could not keep to herself. "Could you be?" she asked, her voice small. Her heart pounded, and she was suddenly glad she faced away from him under the cover of darkness. "Could we get...papers?"

Phoenix caught his breath, weighing the magnitude of what she was asking against his own heart. They came up in equal measure.

"Of course," Phoenix answered against the lump in his throat. "Whatever you wish, mouse. Whatever you wish."

He smiled to himself. Papers were hardly necessary, given the way he cared for her, but if Sev chose him and wanted all Dobani to know it, by Drek, he would not deny her.

"We'll go to Dobani Proper," Phoenix said, "and then we'll go to the hot springs to celebrate. The hot springs, little mouse, just like we talked about."

Sev sighed. "But we don't know where they are," she protested.

He kissed the top of her head. "We'll find them, sweet mouse, if they're there to find. Don't you worry about a thing."

And she didn't, and they drifted off into a dreamless sleep.

CHAPTER 11

S ev lay in her bed, the early morning sun slanting through the windows. She had the curtains open, and the shaft of light that had slowly crept its way along the floor since sunrise was almost at the foot of her bed now. Sev looked over the top of her book, then back down again to the glyphs on the page.

"She was happiest when she was alone, where she could get lost in her thoughts and not leave anyone out."

Sev read the line three more times, rolling it over in her mind. She set the book face-down on her coverlet and scribbled the line in her journal. She would remember to tell Phoenix that way. Sev was curious to know what he thought.

They had been working nonstop on the skiff. The weather had warmed, but it was not yet balmy; the bite of the off-season still lingered in the air. Across the room, Phoenix lay in his bed. He had one leg out from under the blanket, his left arm thrown over his face. She smiled; he had never been an early riser.

Sev placed her book back on the little shelf Phoenix had built her, right above her bed, and grabbed her work clothes. She ducked into the bathroom and dressed hastily, eager to see the skiff and run through its final checks…eager to show Phoenix the interior, the tasks she'd worked so hard on these past weeks.

When she emerged from the bathroom, Phoenix was still asleep, sprawled on his back over the small bed and limbs akimbo. She walked over to him, stripping off the blanket. She tugged at his toes. He grunted in his sleep, flexing his foot against her hand, but did not wake.

Sev bent over him, positioning her mouth at his ear. "Phoenix?" she whispered, and he startled awake, hand going up to pinch the bridge of his nose. "Morning, little mouse," he mumbled, his voice rough with sleep. "What has you stirring this early?"

She sat beside him on the bed, crowding him in the small space. "The skiff," she said. "It's almost finished."

Phoenix smiled lazily, his eyes still closed. "That it is, mouse. Our toils will not have been in vain, given she passes our inspection."

Sev patted his shoulder. "She'll pass," she said. Her stomach rumbled. "Can we make breakfast? I'll help."

Phoenix cracked his eyes open. "Now who could pass up such an offer...generous and capable hands are a truly rare thing." He sat up, rubbing the sleep from his eyes. "Come along now, little mouse, and let's see what fruits the kitchen will bear."

They stood together, Phoenix prodding protein sticks in a skillet with the point of a knife and Sev spreading jam on bread. The heady, salt-rich smell of frying meat was thick in the air, and the morning sun filled the small space, lighting the dust motes in a butter-warm glow. Sev hummed something tuneless and happy, and it made Phoenix smile.

After breakfast, Phoenix changed, indulging Sev's desire to get back to the skiff as early as possible, as if it had moved somehow overnight. They walked along the near-empty streets, the off-season and early hour doing much to clear them. Phoenix grabbed Sev's hand, endeared by the girl's enthusiasm and by her eagerness to see her vision come to fruition.

Sev moved her hand just so to ensure their fingers interlaced. "I can't wait until you see what I've done, Phoenix. You won't believe it. You truly won't."

Phoenix gave her hand a little squeeze. "Of that I am entirely sure, little mouse. You never fail to surprise me."

It pleased her. She'd been working on the interior of the skiff for the last several days while Phoenix labored beneath. It was soothing, doing her work on the inside while hearing him knock and bang his tools against the innards of the ship. During those moments, she felt closer to him, somehow. Connected.

They arrived at the hangar and Phoenix spotted the ship immediately, the deep blue of its hull glinting in the morning light. Sev had painted it blue because it reminded her of Dobani, of the sea and the sky. "That way we can always have a bit of Dobani with us even when we're in the Black," she'd said.

They stood looking at the skiff. Phoenix put his arm around her and pulled her to him. "You did good, little mouse," he said, and Sev preened. "A finer ship I've never seen."

She grinned. "Wait until you see inside," she teased, then took off, running ahead of Phoenix and blocking the hatch with wide open arms. "You have to close your eyes, Phoenix, or it's not a surprise."

He did so dutifully, allowing her to lead him through the hatch. The air was no longer stale…it smelled of metal and recent paint, of something like fresh beginnings.

She led him by the hand and halted him just inside the hatch. "Now," she announced.

Phoenix opened his eyes. The interior of the skiff was practically unrecognizable. Granted, he had only grainy memories of it before, when he'd been bleeding out on the floor of the ship, but he could recognize the amount of care and effort that had gone into its restoration.

Sev had scrubbed the instrument panel clean, every switch and knob shining. She had reupholstered the two chairs. The view panel gleamed. There wasn't a speck of dirt anywhere.

Sev led him excitedly through the curtain into their sleeping quarters. They had proper beds, now, although small. All the filth and rubbish left behind by the previous owners was cleared away, wiped clean by Sev's own hand.

Phoenix whistled. "My, my, little mouse. We'll never leave the Black, with such a ship as this. Shiny as a piece of calcet."

Sev smiled proudly. She walked him back through the cockpit, toward the hatch, and pressed her hands over his eyes. Phoenix sighed, long-suffering and patient. "One more time, Phoenix. For me?"

He followed her lead.

"Hold out your hand. The left one." Phoenix did so, palm up, and she quickly turned it over. She grabbed his hand and pulled it down to press into a shallow tray of paint.

Phoenix gasped at the cool, sticky wetness. "What in Drek's name, girl? What's that my hand is in?"

Sev giggled, pulling him by the prosthetic arm to a space beside the hatch. She flattened Phoenix's painted palm against the wall of the ship, withdrawing it to reveal a perfectly whorled print.

Phoenix opened his eyes and eyed the print fondly. He flexed tacky fingers against the drying paint. "But you're entirely too clean, little mouse, seeing as how we are equal partners and all." He glanced at her then, all mischief and devilry, and swiped his wet fingers across her cheek.

Sev shrieked, shying away, her laughter ringing out in the cockpit.

He grew serious, his eyes shining. "Now you, little mouse."

Sev nodded. She touched her hand to the paint and pressed it to the wall beside Phoenix's print. When she withdrew it, her smaller one was right beside Phoenix's larger. They belonged together, side by side. Phoenix's throat grew tight.

"It's truly ours now," Sev mused. "It's official."

Phoenix nodded, a soft smile on his face. "That it is indeed."

They washed the paint off back at the apartment. Sev came out of the bathroom wearing one of her new sweaters and a coordinating pair of pants. She crossed to where Phoenix was standing over the sink and slipped her arms around his waist.

He turned in her grasp, drying wet hands before hugging her back. He pulled away to get a better look at her. "You're dressed so smartly. What are you up to, Sev?"

She smiled and inclined her head. She walked to their closet area and withdrew one of Phoenix's new shirts. "I thought we might go to Dobani

Proper today," she began, "since we're not working, and we finished the skiff." She held the shirt out shyly. "You could wear this."

Phoenix took the shirt from her and laid it on his bed. He held both of her hands. "And what are we doing in Dobani Proper, little mouse?"

Sev regarded him shyly. "Going to the records office," she said. "I mean, if you want to."

He released one of her hands, his going up to cradle her face. He thumbed over her cheek. "Of course I do, little mouse. Of course."

Sev sighed, closing her eyes. Phoenix quirked his mouth. "You best bring your swim clothes and some besides, if I'm going to make good on my promise."

The ride into Dobani Proper was quiet; Sev read *Nautica* while Phoenix sat beside her, his head back on the seat, eyes closed. He thought of the magnitude of what was about to transpire; all his life he'd been a loner, one person against the universe. Suddenly (but no, not suddenly) he would become two. Sev would be his to take care of, to keep safe, to make happy. Sev would be his daughter.

He stole a glance at her. She read her book, absorbed in her imagined worlds, her profile blurred against the fast-moving scenery. The book was the one she had memorized…she hadn't started on the others yet. He slipped his prosthetic arm around her slight shoulders, and he felt her relax.

He suddenly realized that he had been a father for a long time.

They would get papers. It wouldn't change anything. Phoenix knew since he had orphaned her on Terra Firma that Sev was his responsibility. Even when he had carried her unconscious through the wilds of Terra Firma, laid her on the cot in the miner's tent and fed her a ration bar, he understood she was a girl that was newly aggrieved. That she needed someone. Maybe he did too.

She took him completely by surprise with her strength and fortitude, the way she had stitched him up and tended his wounds. As unfortunate as those circumstances were, he was so unbelievably happy with the result. This girl had changed him…this slight but strong slip of a girl who was wise beyond her years had stoked life back into the ashes of his heart, had sheltered the embers and coaxed them into a flame that threatened to consume him whole.

Phoenix realized he was staring at her, and she caught him out of the corner of her eye. She smiled, and he couldn't help but smile back. *How did I get so lucky?* He wondered. *How in all Drek's kingdom did I become so rich?*

Sev nudged his shoulder. "I can hear you thinking," she murmured, head still in her book. Phoenix looked past her, through the window. The scenery zoomed by in flashes of color and light. "Nothing to worry about, mouse," he settled on, because how could he tell her? What could he say? He squeezed her shoulder, and she turned into him, putting her feet up on the seat and bracing her book with her knees.

After a lengthy ride, they stepped out of the chute and into the middle of Dobani Proper, the records building looming on the horizon, all steel and glass. Phoenix had changed into the shirt Sev had picked out for him, and he wore his good slacks. He had gelled his hair in a careful style…the little white patch lay flat instead of standing straight up. Sev wasn't sure she liked it, but she appreciated the effort all the same.

They walked together into the records building. It was a stark place with a few fake plants and a severe-looking woman behind a computer terminal. She asked them several questions and took their thumbprints. Phoenix signed his name and Sev signed hers. The woman handed Sev the document and gave Sev a small smile. Sev clutched it close to her chest as they walked out into the blinding light of Dobani Proper.

Sev held it out, tracing the glyphs on the thick paper; it was midday, and Dobani teemed with life. Still, to Sev, they were the only two in the world.

She cleared her throat before she read.

"The Records Office of Dobani affirms that a human male (Phoenix) has formally taken a human female (Sev) to be his daughter and assumes all responsibilities for her well-being." She glanced at Phoenix as they walked along the sidewalk. *"To be his daughter,"* she recited. "That's my favorite part."

Phoenix's heart swelled with the words. He saw her run her fingers over their thumbprints; they reminded him of the handprints they'd left on the wall of the skiff. They were one and the same.

Sev grabbed Phoenix's hand, lacing their fingers together. "I don't feel any different," she said, her voice taking on a bemused, almost disappointed air. "I thought I might."

Phoenix squeezed her hand. "But do you feel good?" he asked her, his brows raised in question.

Sev smiled. "Of course, Phoenix."

He nodded, moving his hand to the small of her back. "That's all that matters then, little mouse."

He led her to a bench by the stop and they sat down. Sev took her bag off her shoulder and sat it beside her. "Where to, now?"

Phoenix squinted and ran a hand through his hair, disturbing the careful styling. He inclined his head. "Far from here, little mouse, if we're to make the hot springs by dark."

Sev's eyes grew wide. "You know where they are?" She frowned. "You knew, and you didn't tell me?" She shoved at him playfully, spurred on by his impish smile.

"Some things are not for knowing," he offered with a shrug. "Besides, we can only take the chute so far. Then a transport will have to do."

"I've never been on transport before...not a land transport, anyway. What's it like?"

"You'll soon know for yourself," Phoenix replied as the chute pulled up to their stop. They boarded and settled into their seats.

Once the chute left Dobani Proper, the land opened to rolling hills and green as far as she could see. She'd never seen so much green outside Terra Firma...never in her life. As time wore on, the hills rolled into valleys, and the open space on either side of them became close with trees, the sort of which she'd only read about in books. When the chute ended its route, they boarded a transport and bumped along a dirt path under a canopy of leaves.

"How much longer?" Sev asked, and not for the first time. Phoenix drew her head to his shoulder, pressing a kiss to her hair. "It's not far, now, little mouse," he reassured her, knowing that it wouldn't be long before she asked again.

The transport eventually arrived at a village of multi-colored buildings arranged in a circle. Phoenix disappeared into one of them, leaving Sev to wait outside. She stayed there long enough to befriend a sar-cat, delighting in the way the little animal rubbed against her legs and mewed for scratches.

She raised her head, and Phoenix was walking toward her. He held out his hand. "We're walking from here. Let's get to it, little mouse."

They walked until the close canopy of trees led to a clearing. A little stone cabin with a thatched roof sat on a hill, a fire in the hearth already churning out smoke. A single light was on. It was the only house they'd seen since the village.

"I wonder who lives there," Sev mused. "It's so pretty."

Phoenix only smiled. He lay his hand on the back of her neck, squeezing slightly. "Us, for a time. We're having ourselves a holiday, Sev."

She sought his face, her eyes filled with wonder. "You mean it?" she asked, throwing her arms around his neck and all but jumping into his arms. "It's all ours?"

Phoenix laughed, lowering her back down again. "For a time, mouse. For a time. You best run ahead now and get changed; the hot springs are just beyond the meadow there."

He followed Sev as she skipped along the stone path to the cabin and opened the door. It was clean and well apportioned, like the man in the village said it would be. Phoenix was pleased.

Sev disappeared into the bedroom and came out in her swim clothes. She regarded him. "You're not getting in?"

Phoenix shook his head. "I think I'll just watch you for now," he replied. "Does that suffice?"

She nodded. They made their way down the footpath that led to the hot springs. It was rough and laid with stubby grasses. Sev could see the hot springs in the distance, the cattails that lined it, and the soft green expanse of the meadow.

Phoenix settled in the tall grass to watch Sev. She stepped into the water and her face lit with surprise. "It's warm!" she exclaimed, and still she went further. Steam rose from the water, clinging to the glassy surface like early morning mist. She submerged herself up to her chin and began swimming.

He was a *father* now. He let the word settle in his mind as he kept a watchful eye on her. Phoenix thought of the document that Sev had lovingly tucked into her bag, of her placing her thumbprint beside his. Such a small thing...such a monumental thing.

The water was clear and bathwater-warm, and she could see straight through to the sandy bottom. There were creatures living here too, long slithery things that tickled her legs but otherwise did not bother her.

She swam until her arms were shaky and her legs ached.

It was growing dark when she stepped out of the water and joined Phoenix on the bank. She lay beside him, the cool air drying her skin. They watched the stars appear, one by one, against the dusky sky. Sev grabbed Phoenix's hand where it lay over his chest and pressed her palm to his.

"You're truly mine now," she mused, looking at their fused hands. "It's official."

Phoenix turned on his side facing her, the tall grasses making his face appear soft and out of focus. The sun set behind him, bleeding through his hair now tousled by the gentle breeze. "I've always been yours, Sev. Ever since you hooked me to your filter on Terra Firma. By the by, we've been tethered ever since."

Sev smiled and then stood, holding out her hand. Phoenix took it and let her pull him up. Her clothes were basically dry, and the first of the night creatures filled the woods with music. Phoenix dusted himself off, slipping an arm around Sev's shoulders as they began walking back to the cabin.

It occurred to him then, as the sun set and the little light in the cabin grew larger, floating there in the dark like a ship out to sea, that he had never been happier.

CHAPTER 12

They were in the Black. Sev had forgotten how it felt, the weight of the gravity condensers, the cold of space seeping into her bones. The engines whirred softly on their trajectory; the instrument panel made music of its own. This ship differed from being in a drop pod. Drop pods were quiet. Ships were alive with sights and sounds. This ship, too, was far more personal. This ship had history, acquired and written. It might've started out as someone else's, but it was theirs now, a product of their own hands. She glanced at the long-dried handprints by the hatch, his and hers, and warmth stirred beneath her ribs.

Sev took an inventory of the items before her. They had plenty of packs, Phoenix had seen to that, and Sev had insisted on a new field kit...top of the line. Too much could go wrong on Terra Firma to go off into the Black unprepared. She grazed her hand over it, reassured by its solid presence.

These were tasks she'd done with Del...charging the air guns, checking the packs. But Phoenix wasn't Del, and everything she did now was because it was her choice to do so.

They were a solar day deep on the way to Terra Firma. Phoenix had split his time between piloting the ship and hovering over Sev; he was worried she was working too hard...she was worried he wasn't getting enough nutrition. They were a matched set that way.

Sev settled beside him in her navigator's seat, the two of them staring out into the Black. The ship hummed around them. She saw her own face reflected in the triangular view pane, a faded gray impression on the blank canvas of space.

"What do you think is out there?" she mused, her voice as soft as the reverberation of the engines.

Beside her, Phoenix appeared contemplative. "Drek only knows, little mouse. Maybe the beginning of all things…maybe the end." He put his hands behind his head and leaned back in his chair. "As for knowing or not knowing, I care not."

Sev thought on that for a moment, letting Phoenix's words settle. She had learned that Phoenix was accepting and skeptical at the same time…skeptical of people and their motivations, certainly. But on matters like simple faith in the unknown, he appeared satisfied. It was, in a way, like the ease with which they'd blended their lives. Seamless. Without question.

She checked her chrono. "It's nighttime on Dobani," she said. "We better turn in."

Sev stood, taking a last look at Phoenix before she disappeared behind the curtain to prepare. Phoenix sat for a moment, looking out into the vast nothingness of space and listening to Sev as she milled about in the sleeping quarters.

He was unsettled. A creeping anxiety clawed at his chest, something he'd never experienced in all his time on Terra Firma. He knew without a doubt what the difference was…why he was worried now when he had never been worried before.

Sev.

She was his to look after, now. His to protect. In his previous trips to Terra Firma, he'd only had himself to consider; not even former partners or the loose assemblage of a crew had inspired any concern in him. Now, however, everything had changed.

If something happened to Sev, he could never forgive himself. Life without her was anathema, unthinkable.

He leaned forward, resting his head in his hands. A helplessness closed around his heart, and he reached out past the Black and into the hazy realm of a long-forgotten faith.

"It's been a tick," he said, his voice quiet, "but please see fit to spare my little girl in this forsaken place and forgive me for putting her in harm's way."

Sev heard him murmuring something, and she pulled back the curtain to peer around it. Phoenix sat bent over his knees, his shoulders slumped. The very sight of him like that, so burdened by the immensity of his thoughts, was enough to bring tears to her eyes. She blinked them away.

"Phoenix? You ok?"

He straightened, schooling his features in a peace he didn't feel. "Right as rain, little mouse." He turned to her, a reassuring smile on his face. It never reached his eyes.

Sev frowned and made her way over to him. Whatever was bothering him had his shoulders tense, his brow creased. She placed a hand on his upper arm, the muscles firm beneath her hand. "Let's get some rest," she encouraged.

He smiled and, for a moment, seemed to relax. Phoenix stood and leaned over the control panel, putting the skiff on autopilot and turning out the console light. It plunged the cockpit into a cotton-wrapped darkness…soft, but impenetrable.

Sev slipped a hand into his, and she led him behind the curtain. The light there was on, illuminating the little space in stark relief.

Sev had pushed their bunks together.

She blinked up at him, a shy smile on her face. This was her first night in the skiff since they had broken through Dobani's atmosphere all those months ago, a ball of fire in the sky. This was her first night in the Black since they'd both come close to dying. The memories of those days, fraught with tension and fear, were never far from her mind. Sometimes, back on Dobani, she still dreamed of arriving planet-side and Phoenix dead already…of Phoenix incapacitated in the Black and her piloting the ship to the nearest populated world. She dreamed of walking lonely streets, standing before the boards rife with gutter jobs, of sleeping in alleyways as cold as the Black. On nights like that she'd wake up gasping, and Phoenix would push their beds together then, or simply turn back the covers on his own and welcome her in.

So, when Phoenix only nodded, she knew he understood.

They climbed beneath the covers, Phoenix sliding his prosthetic arm beneath her head and pulling her close. Sev was warm and soft against him…she tucked her face into his chest and stretched her arm across. They lay in quiet for long moments, Phoenix listening to Sev's even breathing while she grazed her fingers over his T-shirt. She fisted the fabric, watching it bunch and wrinkle in her hand.

"What were you saying back there, Phoenix? To Drek?" Her voice was quiet, almost hesitant. She had never heard Phoenix pray. It unsettled her.

Phoenix reached with his left arm to hold her against him, his face going soft. "I asked for protection, mouse. For you. For me." He went quiet, perhaps considering. "Doesn't hurt to ask."

Sev closed her eyes. Phoenix's hands against her were soothing; he was a warm and solid thing, an immovable anchor in the near-dark. "Are you worried, Phoenix? Do you have a bad feeling?"

Phoenix smoothed over her hair, gathering it away from her collar and then letting his hand rest at the base of her neck. He trailed his fingers over her back, feather light, and she settled her face against his shoulder. She inhaled. Phoenix always smelled good, even in the Black. He kissed her head. "No, little mouse, nothing like that. I've just got a lot on my mind, is all."

She rolled onto her back, staring up at the ceiling of their sleeping quarters. "Is it me?"

Phoenix traced her profile with his eyes, committing it to memory. "You're always on my mind, little mouse. Even more so now. I want to make sure nothing ever happens to you." He grew quiet, contemplative, and Sev counted the breaths until he spoke again. "Terra Firma is not a place to be taken lightly."

She rolled onto her side and snuggled in closer against him. "Nothing will happen," she affirmed. "We have good suits, and your hand is true. Both hands." She turned her face into him, stifling a yawn. "But most of all, we have each other."

Phoenix smiled. The rhythmic motion of his hand against her back had Sev nearly asleep. If there had been one positive from acquiring the prosthetic, it was that he could hold Sev properly, like she deserved.

She let the quiet stretch between them, allowing the buzz of the engines to drown out her thoughts. "I never slept much in the Black," she confessed. "Del took phials. They knocked him out straight away. I had to watch the controls. Besides, the Black always made me feel like I was asleep already."

Phoenix made a disapproving noise, his mouth turned down. Sev lying against him felt like a completed circuit, as vital to him as his remaining arm. *How could he?* Phoenix thought to himself. *How could Del just throw her away?* Sev had such a warm and giving nature. Del never even gave her the chance to show it.

He brushed her hair away from her face. "You're here now, with me," he soothed. "You can take your rest. I'll keep watch." He pressed his lips to her hair, and after a few more moments, she exhaled, and her weight settled properly against him. Phoenix stretched, careful not to disturb her, and turned out the light. He did not sleep.

The proximity alarm went off, alerting them of their approach vector. Aside from the klaxon, a light blinked on the instrument panel, casting their faces in blood-red shadow. He had keyed in the coordinates for the Pit, hopefully taking them straight to their destination. There would be no wandering through the wilds of Terra Firma this time. Phoenix didn't want them to be on the deadly planet any longer than was necessary.

Phoenix settled behind the controls. He cast a glance at Sev; she was concentrating on the navigation screen, and they were calling out numbers back and forth between them.

"Vector 2774 approach at 30 degrees," Phoenix announced, and Sev keyed in the command.

"30 degrees confirmed," she replied, flipping switches and turning dials.

"Arc at 45, thrusters at 20 percent." Phoenix's hand moved over the controls with all the confidence of someone who had been in the Black most of his life.

"45," Sev repeated. "Confirming now."

She focused on the view pane. With the new commands, the ship canted, and the planet swung into view. Her eyes widened as the green orb expanded, rushing towards them until the entire view pane filled with a viridescent hue.

Phoenix eyed Sev, his smile tight and illuminated by the halo of spores over the planet. "Buckle up, sweet mouse. We're going to Terra Firma."

Sev took a shaky breath and strapped herself in. The shape of Terra Firma came into view, and she reached for Phoenix's hand. They shared a look before turning toward the view pane and watching as the upper atmosphere blazed past. Flames licked the hull, but Phoenix's insulation held true. The skiff shook, vibrating them in their restraints. The thrusters engaged and threw Sev's head back against the seat. There was a loud roar as the skiff broke through the atmosphere. Sev blinked at the view pane as a ribbon of blue sky appeared, dotted below by a canopy of green. Sev could see the haze of spores over Terra Firma, making a green corona around the planet. The skiff slowed, trees rushing past as the clearing opened below.

Sev held her breath as the ship righted itself, stuttered on firing thrusters and settled, scorching the ground beneath.

The skiff settled roughly on Terra Firma. Phoenix cut the engines with a few decisive flips of a switch, and they sat for a moment getting their bearings. Phoenix regarded Sev, his eyes roving over her face. "You ok love?" he asked her. He was shaky with adrenaline.

Sev nodded, a little breathless. She began working on her straps. Phoenix unbuckled and climbed out of the seat, getting his legs under him once more. Sev was already at work, gathering nutrition packs and prepping the suits. Phoenix placed his hands on her shoulders. "Slow down now, little mouse. It's not going anywhere."

Sev looked up at him, seeking calm in the lines of his face. "I know," she said. "I just want everything to go right."

Phoenix pulled her in, and she tucked her face against him. "Breathe, sweetheart, just breathe," he reminded her. "We're gonna be fine."

Sev took a shaky inhale, then blew it out slowly, just like he'd shown her. She wrapped her arms around his waist, and he simply held her. They were here. They were back on Terra Firma.

Phoenix withdrew, cupping her face in his hands. He smiled. "Let's get you suited up, hmm?" He took Sev's suit and unzipped it, holding it out for her to step into. She remembered the last time she had dressed for Terra Firma. She had been on the transport barge with Del. He hadn't offered to help.

Phoenix took his time, making sure she tucked into the suit properly. He began on the zippers and buckles, methodically fastening each one. It settled her. He tapped her filter. "Brand new for Terra Firma. No problems out of that, I don't suspect." He reached for her helmet, but she stayed his hand.

"Now you," she said, gesturing to where his suit lay folded on the console. Sev held it out for him, just as he had done for her. She thought of the last time she'd seen him in a suit, of that ancient thing, hardly viable and with a worthless filter to boot.

Sev took the same care and attention with him as he had with her, checking every seal and valve as she went. Phoenix squeezed her arms fondly, then bent to kiss her forehead. "Thank you, sweet mouse," he said, his lips lingering over her skin. "Don't you worry about a thing. Ok?"

Sev nodded and let him seal the helmet in place. "Ok," she agreed through the helmet, though he couldn't hear it.

Phoenix pulled his helmet on, sealing it and checking the comms. The channel clicked on, and Sev was relieved. "Ready to go?" Phoenix asked her, and Sev nodded. "Ready," she asserted, although her nerves were apparent.

Phoenix opened the hatch and helped Sev down from the skiff. They stepped out onto Terra Firma. Sev observed her surroundings, her breath echoing in her ears. The horrors of that night came flooding back...the battle with the harvester, Phoenix's injury. She struggled to regulate her breathing, and the comm sparked to life. "We get the gems, and we get out," Phoenix said. He sounded as tense as she felt. "No need to press our luck."

Sev nodded, following Phoenix into the clearing.

The wilds of Terra Firma had encroached upon the clearing; it was no longer the flat expanse of dry ground the harvesters had used as their campsite. The soil was supple and moist...sumptuous ferns and mosses grew where once there was only dirt. Plants with broad, dewy leaves now stood taller than Sev, making the clearing almost unrecognizable.

Off in the distance was the Pit.

Phoenix must've seen it too, because he was walking in that direction. Sev followed Phoenix through the spore-thick air, both picking their way through the underbrush. Phoenix had an air gun on his hip.

It was the one she'd charged back on the ship...like the one her father had shot him with on this very planet.

The Pit lay before them, seemingly undisturbed. Overgrowth corroded it, too, but nature had marred it and not man. Phoenix gestured to it, his eyes bright. "As I live and breathe," he murmured, his voice awed. They stood at the edge, and Sev set down her harvesting kit. Phoenix was already on his knees, preparing for a dig. He pulled up a membrane, and Sev knelt beside him, holding the scalpel. Phoenix pulled it taut, and Sev made the cut. Fluid poured out onto the ground. Phoenix held the sac in his hand, the gem hidden within.

Phoenix had taught Sev how to harvest. Back on the docks, when they were gutting fish, Phoenix showed her how to feel for the blister, how to cut around it. He taught her how deep to cut and when to pour the chem. Sev harvested fish innards like they were calcet, cutting around organs like the entire thing would spoil if she made a wrong move. These steps ticked through her mind as she assisted Phoenix with the first gem. At his signal, she poured the chem, letting it flood the membrane. She stared, wide-eyed, as Phoenix made the last cut. The membrane fell away, leaving a whole and pretty gem.

Sev released a breath she didn't realize she'd been holding. Phoenix retrieved the gem with his left hand, all wet and gleaming. He handed it to Sev, a soft smile on his face.

"We split the labor. You take that side, and I'll continue here."

Sev considered, her mouth turned down. "Me harvest by myself?"

He chuckled. "If I didn't think you were ready, I would say as much. Now get to it, girl."

She smiled and started digging in the soft ground. She withdrew a membrane, fat with calcet, and made the first cut.

They harvested well into the night. It started to rain, soaking their suits and running off their helmets. The harvested calcet lay in a bin between them, dull and milky pink in the lights from the skiff. There was so much of it...more than Sev had ever imagined. They were both waterlogged and sore, and the night grew chill.

Sev made a cut, and the scalpel slipped.

She looked down at her left hand, blood staining her glove. It ran in rivulets, mixing with the rain. She sat back on her heels, staring in disbelief.

"Phoenix?"

There was something in her voice, a tremulous note that let him know something was wrong. He whipped around, dropping his tools. Sev was sitting in the mud, cradling her hand.

"Sev?" he exclaimed, breath giving out at the end. His heart was in his throat. His head pounded in time with the rain. Lightning cracked the sky, illuminating Sev in strobing flashes before blinking out against the black expanse of night.

He was beside her in seconds.

"Lemme see, baby," he stammered, taking her hand. His were shaking. "Lemme see."

He probed the little cut with his fingers; it was a deceptively small thing, no wider than a fingernail. Blood ran true, soaking her glove. *Small but deep.*

"Get to the ship," he gritted out. "Now, Sev."

She nodded and took off at a sprint. Halfway to the skiff, she looked back. "Get the gems!" she yelled over the comm as the rain thundered down. "This can't have been for nothing."

Phoenix wavered, momentarily paralyzed with fear. Sev ran back, her left hand tucked under her arm. She activated the gravsled on the calcet bin and it slogged slowly out of the Pit.

Sev turned and ran toward the ship, slipping in the mud. She fell with a cry, but Phoenix was on her heels. He hefted her in his arms, holding her against him as he carried her the rest of the way to the skiff.

Phoenix set Sev down long enough to open the hatch. He pushed her inside, then loaded the calcet bin that was just catching up to them. The gravsled whined up the ladder, and Phoenix pulled it inside, falling to the floor with a grunt.

He closed the hatch, sealing them in. He stripped off his helmet and let it clatter to the floor. Sev was panting on the floor of the skiff, her helmet still on.

Phoenix began working on the buckles of her suit, hands slippery and shaking. Sev caught him by the wrist with her good hand, and he locked eyes with her.

"Dad," she said, barely audible through the helmet. "It's ok. I'm ok."

He unlatched her helmet, and there were tears in his eyes. "Oh mouse," he said, "Mouse, I'm so sorry."

Sev shrugged out of her suit, leaving it a sodden mess on the floor. She stretched her hand out, and Phoenix was already waiting with the field kit.

He flushed the cut, and Sev hissed with pain. The edges of it were clean, but it was still unclear if any spores had gotten in.

Phoenix paused as if suddenly remembering. "The rain...it didn't take," he assured her. "The spores didn't take. The rain rid it all."

Sev nodded, trying to convince him—trying to convince herself. Phoenix pulled the needle and thread from the field kit and, with trembling hands, pulled it through the severed flesh.

She bit her lip, determined not to make a noise. Phoenix tied off the catgut and pulled her into his lap. He stroked her hair, damp with sweat and humid from the helmet.

"It's all ok, sweet mouse. It's all ok, now. It was the rain, see. The rain washed it all away."

Sev squeezed her eyes shut, and a few tears escaped her lashes. Phoenix rocked her gently, holding her injured hand to his chest.

She pulled away to look him in the eyes. "If it goes black, then you know what to do."

Phoenix shook his head, an adamant refusal. Maim his little girl? Leave her lacking like him? "No, no. No." Threads of panic tinged his voice. He framed her face with his hands. She was already feverish, he could tell. Spore-sick. His blood went cold. "Nothing's going black sweetheart. It's just a scratch. See?"

He spread her hand, thumbing the stitches over the meat of her palm. "It's sealed up good." He kissed her cheek, pressing his lips to her tears. "Let me get you some tablets."

She stiffened. "Want to stay awake," she rasped, but she was hurting, he could tell. He gave her the fever tablets, then something for the pain. She curled into his lap, tucking her face into his neck. The world went fuzzy. The rain beat down on the skiff and lightning lit the landscape in flashes of white and gray.

Phoenix checked her hand again for what seemed like the hundredth time, taking it up from where it lay against the covers and turning it over in the light. There was no sign of pinking, no rot. He watched her as she slept, her face peaceful and unbothered. He touched the back of his hand to her forehead; it was cool and dry. The tablets had done their work. *By Drek, we caught a bit of luck after all*, he thought. He left her then, disappearing beyond the curtain.

Sometime later, Sev blinked awake. The hum of the ship was a steady drone, almost soothing. Her hand throbbed. She was in bed, the covers pulled up. Phoenix was gone.

She staggered to her feet, pulling back the curtain where Phoenix sat at the controls. Her head swam, and she pressed her hand against the skiff, feeling it rumble beneath her.

They were in the Black. Sev gazed past Phoenix into the infinite vastness of space. He saw her reflection in the view pane and turned around.

"Mouse," he said with a smile. "You're awake."

Sev flexed the fingers of her left hand. They were tingly from the phial. She examined the stitched-up wound. It was pale and dry.

Phoenix held out his hand to her, and she walked slowly forward.

"You're going to be fine, little mouse. Just a little spore-sick is all. No black rot to be seen."

Sev blinked, unbelieving. She had been prepared to lose her hand, or worse. She'd seen it in Phoenix's worried eyes, the possibility. Relief flooded over her like a cool balm.

Phoenix handed her a hydration pack, and she took it gratefully. She settled in the navigator's chair and put her head back against the seat, still lethargic from the tablets. "How long?" Sev asked a little breathlessly. "How long 'till Dobani?"

Phoenix couldn't stop looking at her. "Two days, little mouse," he informed her, his smile soft. "Two days and we'll be home."

CHAPTER 13

T he sun was warm, the off-season making way for balmy weather again not long after they got back to Dobani, and Sev was glad. They sat in the sand just before sunset, the pink and orange of the sky reflecting on the water. Gulls bobbed and weaved near them, fighting for the bits of bread Phoenix threw into the air. One squawked and dove just over their heads, catching the morsel in its mouth. Phoenix laughed.

He leaned back on his arms, his ankles crossed in front of him. His shirt was unbuttoned and blown back by the breeze, his tanned chest taking the brunt of the evening sun. They'd been on the beach since midday; they were both golden brown and glistening with a fine sheen of sweat.

Sev was building something in the sand.

She had a little spade she used to smooth the edges, and a pail of water nearby. She concentrated on her task…tongue pressed thoughtfully against her upper lip. Her hair blew willy-nilly in the breeze off the water, whipping her face and momentarily blinding her. She huffed, her nose scrunched up, and rubbed her cheek against her shoulder to clear her vision. It had gotten long, and her hands were gritty with sand.

Phoenix saw her struggle and slowly stood, leaving his bag of bread for the birds to fight over. He eased onto the sand behind Sev and pulled her hair back, threading it delicately through his fingers, letting his fingertips smooth over her scalp until her hair was in three sections.

Sev smiled, looking at him over her shoulder and then leaning back over her task. Phoenix braided her hair, weaving the sections into each other while stealing brief glances at her project. "What's that you're building, sweet mouse?"

Sev patted the side of her structure, smoothing it with her hand. "You'll see," she teased. She scooped up more sand with the spade, heaping it upon the structure and smoothing it out. It was square, Phoenix could tell, with a pitched roof.

He finished her braid, pleased with his work and thankful again for his new right arm that allowed him to do such things for her. Phoenix fished a hair tie out of his pocket and tied off the ends, keeping the strands together. He pressed his lips to her newly trussed hair, closing his eyes. "All done."

She stood, dusting her hands, and bent to kiss his cheek. "Thanks, Daddy."

It never failed to make his heart swell, this new development. She didn't say it often, nor did she use it to get her way (which was, if he was honest, hardly necessary), but when it happened, usually out of nowhere, it made him immeasurably grateful.

"You're welcome, little mouse," he replied after her, but she was halfway to the shore by then, and his words were lost on the wind. He watched her pick at the water's edge, skirting the foam that lay upon the beach. She was gathering the items that had washed up there, twigs of driftwood and seaweed and little shells, collecting them in the well of her T-shirt.

He loved her.

This was no revelation…he had known for some time that the depth of feeling he had for Sev must be love—the pure, selfless and abiding love that only a parent can have for their child. He had not yet told her. He didn't know why.

Perhaps, he thought, she already knew.

Sev returned, her shirt filled with ocean jumble. She dumped her treasures near the structure and settled behind it. She cupped her hands into the pail of water, drew them up, and emptied them into the sand in front of her. Sev shaped and formed the wet sand until satisfied, placing it nearby the structure she'd built.

Sev picked up the seaweed she'd gathered and started decorating the roof of the structure. It was some sort of dwelling, Phoenix surmised. He leaned in, arm propped on his knee. "May I be of assistance, gentle lady?"

Sev quirked her mouth and handed him some seaweed. "Put it along the edges of the roof, and I'll place the shells," she instructed. He followed her lead, decorating the little house while she laid a path leading up to it. She took two twigs of driftwood, standing them upright beside the path. She considered Phoenix, who was still decorating the eaves. "It's us," she said, her eyes bright. "You and me."

Phoenix looked at the two sticks by the path that led to the door of the sand structure. One was taller than the other. They were both weathered and smoothed by the ocean.

"Why, it is indeed," he said. "In fact, if you squint just so," he said, pointing with his mechanical finger to the taller stick, "you can even make out the bit of white in my hair."

Sev giggled, pleased by Phoenix playing along. She had pulled her braid to one shoulder, and the setting sun painted her profile rose gold.

"Have you made us a house, little mouse?" Phoenix could see it now…the sloping roof, the carved sand door, the little windows inlaid with shell. And out beside it, a larger mound.

Sev nodded. "Just for the two of us. And look here…the skiff."

Phoenix smiled. "Sat right by the house. How convenient. No more long walks to the hangar, then."

Sev leaned against him, resting her head on his shoulder. It was getting dark, now, and Phoenix knew they would need to make their way back to the apartment. He swept her braid back over her shoulder.

Sev sighed, her face crestfallen. "Will it be here tomorrow?" Her green eyes searched his face, large and doleful. Phoenix put his arm around her.

"I'd do anything to say it would, little mouse, but the tide will have its way, I'm afraid."

She stood, and Phoenix followed. "Maybe if we look at it long enough, we'll remember it."

118

Phoenix inclined his head, a soft smile on his face. "I'm not likely to forget."

She grabbed his hand. She appeared younger and older both, with her hair pulled back and the last flames of the sunset licking over her face. Sev smiled at him. "We'll look anyway, just to be sure."

So, they looked, and then they made their way back to the apartment.

They had not yet talked about the calcet. The bin sat where they had hustled it in, under cover of darkness, in a corner of the apartment. Phoenix had thrown a blanket over it just so he could enjoy the warmer weather with Sev, temporarily avoiding the treasure's burden.

But the time had come (indeed, it was past time, after so many weeks), that it needed to be dealt with.

Having so many gems on hand, and such fine specimens at that, was dangerous. He'd seen men kill for just one of those shiny stones, let alone the mounds of wealth that sat there, unassuming, in their little room on Dobani. Aside from his air gun, it was not secure. They needed rid of it. They needed to put the credits to good use.

When they returned to the apartment, Sev coerced him into making flatcakes with little effort; he was always happy to cook and even happier when she insisted on helping, like she did now. She flipped the last of the flatcakes and added it to the tall stack. It was a little wobbly and jiggled precariously as Sev walked it to the table. She drizzled the honey and flourished her hands, magician-like, in front of the meal she'd helped prepare.

Phoenix smiled, something warm loosening in his chest. The braid was still in her hair, although pulled loose from the wind. Little wisps framed her face. Her cheeks and nose were sun-kissed; she'd forgotten her hat. He sat down opposite her and took a few of the flatcakes off the stack. The first bite was warm and sticky sweet.

"I've been doing a bit of thinking," he began, pausing around a mouthful and swallowing it down. "I think it's time we found a suitable buyer for our cache of gems."

Sev grunted, eating heartily like they hadn't had sandwiches by the seaside for lunch. "I've been saying that ever since we got back," Sev mumbled around a forkful of flatcakes, her voice muffled and cheeks stuffed.

Phoenix huffed a laugh. "Slow down, now, little mouse. Taste your food a bit. The mouth can't talk and eat both."

Sev visibly slowed, taking a few steadying breaths and a sip of water. She set her fork down. "Let's sell them privately," she offered. "Pawn them off a few at a time. We'll make more credits that way."

Phoenix shook his head, his lips pursed. "That'll take time. I was thinking wholesale. Find one buyer. Be done with it in one go."

Sev frowned, twirling her fork in a bit of honey. "We won't make as much," she supplied, watching for any reaction from Phoenix. His face remained impassive.

Del would have never sold wholesale, she thought. He also would've never left gems on Terra Firma, but as soon as Sev had cut herself, Phoenix had forgotten the harvest.

She shrugged, taking another bite of her meal and chewing slower this time. "Whatever I can do to help," she finally agreed. They'd built their early partnership on trust, on compromise. Even now, as they were clearly more to each other than partners, it was no different.

She pushed her plate back, empty and sticky with honey. "What are we going to do with the credits?"

Phoenix leaned back, a thoughtful look on his face. "I thought we might get us a house to start."

Sev's eyes narrowed. "And leave the room?"

Phoenix nodded. "I reckon we would. How would you feel about that?"

Sev appeared thoughtful, mulling over her answer. She collected their spent plates and placed them in the sink. She turned, leaning against the counter with her arms folded. "Would we buy, or would we build?"

Phoenix inclined his head. "We could do either, little mouse. If we don't find one we like, we'll build our own."

Sev smiled then and began walking toward him. She placed her hands on his shoulders where he still sat at the table. "Can I have my own room?"

Phoenix chuckled, breathy and fond. "Of course, little mouse. And bathroom, besides."

Sev looked surprised. "My own bathroom? Drek, I can't imagine."

Phoenix wrapped an arm around her waist where she stood next to him. She leaned into his warmth, listening to the prosthetic whir and flex as he tightened his grip. "Can it be by the ocean?" she asked.

Phoenix nodded. "On the beach itself, if that's what you wish," he replied, eyes warm.

Sev nodded excitedly. "I want to hear the waves from my bedroom window," she said.

He swept the stray strands away from her face, letting his hand hover there to cup her cheek. "I'll make sure of it."

Phoenix lay awake for a long time, thinking of a suitable buyer for the calcet. Someone maybe in the jewelry industry, he thought. He could talk to some people. Find a supplier. See if they were interested. The market was hotter than ever, with calcet next to impossible to find now that the rush had passed.

He listened to where Sev lay in her bed, breathing slow and even in the still dark. Phoenix had her to consider, too. He had not yet told her his plans. She would be resistant, he suspected. It didn't matter. It was necessary.

He turned on his left side, stump tucked under the blanket, and eased into a dreamless sleep.

The next morning Phoenix and Sev sat polishing calcet on the floor between their beds. They'd picked the largest, clearest stones to show to their potential buyer. Sev held one up to the light, marveling at it.

"It's so pretty," she said. "Maybe we could keep one?"

Phoenix made a little noise. "That one's worth 15, maybe 20. Too risky to have it just lying around. I'm sorry, sweetheart."

Sev seemed downcast, but made no reply. She polished the gem and laid it with the others. They had chosen six, all large and gleaming, enough to tease the palate of any prospective buyer.

She finished her task and stretched, then headed to the bathroom to change. When she was out of sight, he tucked the piece of calcet she'd been admiring into his pocket and replaced it with another.

When they left the apartment, Sev carried the calcet in her bag...again, Phoenix thought it was best to be unassuming. A locked case would bring too much attention, and attention was not something Phoenix wanted. They were making a life here on Dobani. He wasn't looking for trouble.

They rode the chute into Dobani Proper's business district. Phoenix had a few contacts from his trading days, and he was hoping their first stop would be their last.

They walked into the little shop, and Sev's eyes filled with wonder. She'd never seen a jewelry store before. Everything glittered and shone. Glass cases of polished calcet glowed warmly under the lights. The stones were smaller than theirs by far, but they were still beautiful. Beside her, Phoenix extended his prosthetic arm and shook hands with a smartly dressed man who had a chrono clipped to his vest. Sev took her bag off her shoulder.

He appraised them both. "Let's step into the back, shall we?"

They settled in what could only be the man's office. Two chairs stood waiting in front of a shiny desk. Someone offered them tea, which Sev accepted, sipping the hot, bitter liquid to give her something to distract her from her burgeoning nerves.

Phoenix motioned to her, and she withdrew the bag and took out the gems one by one.

The man whistled, his eyes wide. "May I?"

"Go ahead," Phoenix encouraged. The man tenderly took a gem, holding it up to the light. He used a device to scan it, the tool emitting a sharp trill.

"It's pure alright," he announced, placing the gem back on the desk and shaking his head. "And how many more of these do you have, approximately?"

Sev glanced at Phoenix. He was tapping his chin with one mechanical finger. "Can't be sure," he said. "We haven't counted."

The man nodded, a bit dumbfounded and more than a little excited. "And what are your intentions, Phoenix?"

Phoenix straightened, placing his hand on the desk. "We want to sell them all, for a fair price, of course. If you could take the whole lot off our hands, then you would be doing us a service."

The man leaned back, wiping his brow. He was balding, and there were little wisps of white hair curled over his ear. "I'm interested…make no mistake. I just don't have the funds right now to make such a purchase. But my supplier might. He and I could go in on it, as partners."

Phoenix thought it through. "Is this man trustworthy? Someone you regularly do business with?" he asked.

The man nodded. "As trustworthy as they come. What do you think?"

Phoenix turned to Sev. "What do you say, little mouse. Are you acquiescent to another buyer, here after we had agreed on just the one?"

Sev looked at Phoenix. She knew the man was watching her, probably realizing only now that she had the power to bring the entire proceedings to a halt if she so chose. It gave her an odd sense of satisfaction.

"If you think it's good, then so do I," she said. "If the man is as trustworthy as you say."

The man nodded eagerly. "I'll contact him today. If the rest of the gems look like this, and there are as many as you say, then 500 credits, at least, would be my estimate. Enough for you and your girl to settle down." He smiled, and Sev shifted uncomfortably under his scrutiny. "You'll never have to work again, Phoenix." He gestured crudely to his prosthetic. "I'm assuming Terra Firma took your arm. You'll never lose the other."

Phoenix grunted, not bothering to correct him. Sev realized he was as unmoored as she was. 500 credits was a greater amount than she had ever heard of anyone having. It was far more than she had ever imagined they would get, though she admitted she hadn't given it much thought. He gestured to the gems, and she began packing them up. When she was done, she tugged at

Phoenix's sleeve. "Can we go now?" she said. She suddenly wanted to be far away from this store and its shiny baubles and its owner with the oily smile.

Phoenix patted her shoulder. "Wait outside, little mouse. Don't wander off. I'll only be a moment." Phoenix smiled at her, and it settled her some. Sev rushed outside into the bright sunlight of Dobani and let the door of the shop close behind her.

Phoenix waited until Sev was gone. Then he withdrew the gem he'd hidden in his pocket.

"You're a jeweler by trade. Is that a fact?"

The man nodded solemnly. "For more years now than I remember."

Phoenix hummed. "See to it then, that you make something for my daughter." Phoenix handed him a piece of paper and the gem. "Use this stone as payment."

The man reached for the piece of calcet, turning it over in his hand. He unfolded the piece of paper, reading it intently. When he finished, he placed it into his pocket. "Certainly, Phoenix. Shall I have it delivered?"

Phoenix nodded. "I'll be in touch with the address." He stood to leave, then turned back to the man. "Make sure it's as special as she is," he added.

The man smiled. "You'll be pleased!" he called out after him. "You'll be pleased with everything; I'll see to that."

Phoenix shouldered his way through the door to find Sev waiting for him, her hair bright in the midday sun.

She slipped a hand in his. "Is everything ok?"

He pulled her to him, pressing a kiss to her forehead. "Everything's perfect, sweet mouse."

Within a few days, they'd sold the calcet. The supplier picked up the gems and transferred the credits to Phoenix's card within the hour.

But this did not satisfy him, not yet.

It was past the midnight hour. Sev lay against him, skin humid and sweat-warm. She'd had another nightmare about Terra Firma. This time, in the dark realm of her dreams, they hadn't made it back.

Phoenix shushed her, whispering nonsense words into her hair. She trembled against him, and he pressed his palm against her back as if he could infuse peace into her bones.

"We have somewhere very important to go today, mouse. And after that, we can look for a house."

She sniffed, still shaken from her dream. "I'm going to miss the room," she murmured into his chest.

Phoenix smiled. "So will I, little mouse. The very walls have memories." He pressed his cheek to her head. "But we'll make more."

She quieted, and the trembling eventually stopped. She had her fingers twined in his T-shirt, the fabric bunched in her fist.

"Tell me what our house will look like," Phoenix soothed, trying to distract her, his hand moving in a constant circuit over her back and down her arm. "How will we know it's ours?"

He could feel her smile against him. "Lots of windows," she mused. "But not too big. Big houses aren't cozy."

His left hand went up to cover hers where it lay against his chest. "And my sweet mouse likes to be cozy."

She nodded. Phoenix smiled to himself. Sev was a child of the Black. She felt safest in small spaces…tucked in against the outside. So, a small house, then.

"Will you build it?" she asked, her voice sounding tired and far away.

"If it needs building," Phoenix assured her. "We may find one that is whole already. How would you like that?"

Sev pressed her face against him rather than answering. "Will my room be near yours?"

Phoenix held her close. "Of course," he replied. "After sharing a space for as many months, I couldn't bear being too far away from you, girl."

He stroked her hair, still sweaty from her sleepless night. She was almost asleep, struggling against her body's desire for rest and the conscious fear of her dreams, yet unknown. "Will you cook in the new house?" she mumbled. "I like it when you cook."

Phoenix smiled, tucking her face into the crook of his shoulder. "Things will be exactly the same, only better," he assured. It pleased her. She said nothing for a long time, her feathery breath against his neck evening out. He realized she had drifted off to sleep.

Phoenix thought of the day ahead, eager to take care of this bit of business. They could relax, then. They could finally start living. With that thought, he nodded off himself, Sev snuggled against him.

Later that morning, when they had showered off the restless night and readied for the day, Phoenix took Sev to the finance office.

Sev wondered why they were there, but she did not say as much. She trusted Phoenix had his reasons, despite having expressed distaste for the finance office in the past. She followed him to a room that read "accounts" in Central glyph. A woman stood to meet them.

"I'm Phoenix," he said with his usual charm, "and this here is my daughter Sev." Sev preened as she did whenever Phoenix introduced her as his daughter, which was often. She stuck out her hand, and the woman took it gingerly.

"Nice to meet you, Phoenix…Sev. What can I do for you?"

They settled at a long table, the woman on one side of it and Sev and Phoenix on the other. Phoenix took a breath, then leaned forward. "I need some credits moved. Quite a few, to be true. I need them put into a trust in my daughter's name."

The woman jotted a few notes, nodding and listening all the while. She stopped writing. "How many credits exactly Mr. –"

He waved his hand. "Phoenix will do. And 250. I need it for Sev, for when she comes of age."

Sev's eyes grew large. 250 credits? It was exactly half of their calcet sale. *Even split.*

Phoenix rambled on, but she wasn't listening. All she could digest was 250 credits, all in her name. She had never had credits of her own before. Her eyes misted. Phoenix had kept his part of the bargain they'd struck deep on Terra Firma so long ago.

126

"I'll be the executer of the trust, for now. In the unfortunate event of my demise, I would like an impartial third party of your choosing to make sure Sev is cared for."

"No," Sev interjected. "Don't say that." She grabbed his upper arm, both hands fitting around his bicep. "I don't want the credits," she refuted weakly. She glanced up at him, eyes brimming with tears. "I just want you."

Phoenix patted her hands, then cupped his hand around the apple of her cheek. "It's just a fact of life, now, dear heart. It doesn't mean anything is going to happen. But we best be prepared all the while."

A tear escaped her lashes, and Phoenix wiped it away with the pad of his thumb. The woman cleared her throat.

"Sev, your father just wants you to be seen about. Just in case." She smiled. "It's just a precaution."

Sev blinked at her. She had lovely dark skin and red hair. Her eyes were kind.

Phoenix nodded, giving Sev's hands a little squeeze. Once they'd come to an unspoken understanding, he turned his attention to the woman across the table.

"Split the credits. Get Sev put to rights, and we'll make our departure."

The woman made a few keystrokes on her holopad, making one last entry with a decisive click. She looked up from the viewscreen. "It's done. You can rest easy, Phoenix. You and your daughter are taken care of."

Phoenix could feel the pressure in his chest abate. He shook the woman's hand again, a wide smile on his face. "I thank you kindly," he supplied a little breathlessly. "I do thank you kindly."

They walked out into the warmth of Dobani. Phoenix grabbed Sev's hand, entwining their fingers. He was lighter now that it was done. Sev never had to want for anything, and that's all that mattered.

Sev swung her arms a little, also moving his, and it made him smile. She considered him. "Can we get ices?"

Phoenix moved his hand to the small of her back, leading her around the foot traffic on the sidewalk. "Of course we can, little mouse. I know just the place."

The quaint little diner sat on a less-busy corner of Dobani Proper, quite close to the finance office. They sat at the counter with their ices, Phoenix sipping loudly from his straw just to make Sev laugh. Hers was berry, and her lips and tongue were stained red.

She scooped some of the sweet treat into the spoon, pausing halfway to her mouth. She set it back in the cup. "Why did you give me all those credits, Phoenix? It's not like it was back on Terra Firma. Things are different now."

Phoenix put his treat aside and met her eyes. "We may be family, and I thank Drek for it, but we're still partners, you and I, and I take partnership something serious."

She blinked up at him, eyes searching. Phoenix laid a hand on her shoulder.

"I want you to hear something mouse, and hear me good. Half that calcet was yours. You harvested it. You bled for it. You should enjoy the spoils of a job well done. A future. Understand?"

Sev nodded. Then she smiled. "Will we get a house now?"

He squeezed her arm, letting his thumb brush the skin there. "We'll look straight away, sweet mouse. Today, if you're amenable."

She lowered her eyes. The gravity of what had transpired settled with her. Phoenix had made sure she got her share. If they were careful, they'd never have to worry about credits again. She felt full…complete. It was some feeling that she didn't have a name for, but it seemed right all the same.

She slid off the bar stool and held out her hand. He took it. "Ready when you are."

They walked out of the diner together. Sev squinted against the sun as they made their way back to the chute. "Can we go to the beach first? I want to check on our little house. Maybe the tide didn't take it, after all."

Phoenix laughed. "Of course, mouse. But don't fret if it's not there. We can build another."

CHAPTER 14

The diner buzzed with people and beings from all over, some dressed for the day and some, students from the neighboring university, Phoenix suspected, appeared as though they'd just tumbled out of bed, their clothes rumpled and hair in disarray. Some of them sat with plates of food, others with the morning paper, and still others hunched over steaming cups.

Phoenix and Sev sat across from each other in a red vinyl booth, elbows propped on the scarred tabletop. The morning sun was bright, slanting warm through the window blinds. The neon sign outside the window cast them both in a muted orange glow. Sev was contemplative, staring down at her half-eaten breakfast scramble and sweet cream fruit with her chin propped on her fist. Her hair was in another braid, a product of Phoenix's own hands.

"What's on your mind, little mouse?" Phoenix's smile was serene, the light from the window catching the white patch in his hair and setting it on fire. On the table between them were several spec sheets for different houses for sale on Dobani. There were holographs attached to each sheet. Sev had been studying them intently.

"I don't like any of these," she asserted. Any other child would've sounded petulant, but not his Sev. He knew how important this decision was to her. She wanted things to be right. To be good for them.

Phoenix just wanted Sev to be happy.

He slipped his prosthetic hand past his own empty plate and tapped the edge of one spec sheet with a mechanical finger. The holograph there was of a large yellow house they had toured the day before. "What about this one?"

Sev scrunched up her nose. "It's too big." She glanced at him, her eyes sad. "The bedrooms were too far apart...a whole floor!"

Phoenix chuckled. "We could talk to each other on comm," he said playfully. "Or, if we were so inclined, we could simply yell back and forth...make a game of it."

She frowned. "That's not funny," she replied, turning the spec sheet face down on the table. *So*, Phoenix thought, *that one is out for good.*

They went through the other selections like that, Sev discounting each definitively in a similar fashion. "Too many trees," she would say, or "not enough windows."

Phoenix began to think she was simply reluctant to leave the little room they'd grown so accustomed to.

He leaned back in his booth, flagging a server to order one of the steaming mugs that most tables featured. He tapped the table with his fingers. "We've one more, mouse. One more to look at before we start exploring our other options."

Sev brightened. "One we haven't seen? Where is it?" she asked. "Can we go?"

Phoenix smiled. "We'll go presently, just as soon as we're done here."

Sev folded her hands in front of her. "What do you know about it?"

Phoenix took a careful sip from his mug and set it back down on the table. It was hot, the slightly bitter liquid spreading warmth throughout his body. "Don't know much," he said. "The agency just said it had been there for a while. It's a little out of town. We'll have to take a transport."

Sev nodded. She sipped her juice, looking out of the window at their bustling neighborhood just waking up to the day. Phoenix watched her in profile, her braid over her left shoulder. She'd requested a ribbon, today, tied at the end. That was something new.

Phoenix finished his mug and gathered the spec sheets. "You ready, little mouse?"

Sev averted her eyes from the window and gave him a small smile. "Let's go."

The ride on the transport was mostly silent. Apartment complexes and the shopping district gave way to squat homes, then sparse trees and grasses. The highway ran parallel to the ocean, the silver thread of it shining in the distance as she sat against Phoenix in the backseat. He wrapped his arm around her, pulling her close. He observed her. She appeared content, watching the scenery from the back of the transport. "Don't be upset, mouse, if we have to build. It'll take time, but by the by, we'll get it done."

She nodded, then laid her head against him. The transport slowed, pulling off onto a sandy road lined with trees. The clearing opened and all she could see was the beach, the ocean beyond. They took a sharp left around a grove of palms, and there stood a house.

It was a small, whitewashed clapboard cottage with peeling blue trim. Two bay windows faced the ocean, their glass dirty, one on either side of the faded door. A little boardwalk marked the way to the beach, stubby grasses pushing up through the boards. The porch was small, barely enough room for two chairs, but there they sat, as if waiting for someone to fill them. In the sandy front yard, a fire pit sat cozy and black with ash from the last inhabitants. From the looks of it, there hadn't been a fire there in a long time.

Sev ran past Phoenix, up the stone path leading to the front door. She twisted the doorknob and shouldered her way inside, stirring the dust motes within.

"Sev!" Phoenix called after her. "Slow down, doll, you might hurt yourself."

But she was already gone.

Phoenix sighed, hurrying to catch up with her. He found her in what was probably the living room, all hardwood floors and sheet-covered furniture. There was a sizeable skylight in the roof, quite opaque now…he'd have to check if the seal was good.

He found the light switch and flicked it on. Warm light filled the room.

There was a fireplace on the right side of the living room, a natural rock hearth jutting out around it. A driftwood mantel hung above it, knotted and smoothed by the ocean. Sev was standing in the middle of the room, directly under the skylight, her face aglow in its murky light.

"It's beautiful Phoenix. Don't you think?" Her eyes were alight with joy, with curiosity.

He walked over to stand behind her, a hand on her shoulder. "It is beautiful, little mouse," he agreed in a hushed voice. "Do you want to see the rooms?"

She nodded enthusiastically. He took her to the first room on the left; there were two bedrooms, he surmised, separated by a short hall that led into the living room.

Sev walked into the first room, and her breath caught. Even without the light on, the room was warm and bright, the natural light from the bay window spilling across the floor. There was a single bed, the head of it against the adjacent wall, its white bedframe scratched and chipped. A lamp stood on a nightstand, and Sev turned it on. She walked over to the bay window and pressed her hand against the glass. When she withdrew, she had that same sparkle in her eyes as before.

Sev returned to Phoenix's side. Phoenix observed his surroundings, considering. There were dust and cobwebs everywhere. If Sev was sold on this one, they would need new furniture. It was badly in need of a paint job, and maybe a few boards on the exterior would need replacing. He brushed his hand over Sev's hair, hand settling at her neck. But the house had good bones.

Sev turned, burying her face in his chest. "Oh, can we buy it?" she asked, her voice muffled.

Phoenix chuckled, rubbing his hand down her back. "Let's see the other rooms first, little mouse, then we can think on it."

Sev hummed, pulling Phoenix by the arm and leading him to the other bedroom. It was much like the one Sev had become so enamored of, without the bay window, but two plain windows let in plenty of natural light. There was a larger bed against the interior wall, a chair, a closet, and a bathroom. Phoenix tested the plumbing in the bathroom by turning on the facet. A claw-foot tub stood under a showerhead. The fixture protested with a loud shrill sound, sputtering brown. After a few moments, cool, clean water started flowing into the basin there.

Phoenix nodded, satisfied. He turned and Sev was gone.

He found her back in the living room, the central room of the small house. She was making her way to the open-plan kitchen, running her finger along a dust-covered counter as she went.

Phoenix caught up to her and looked around. The kitchen was pale yellow, with white cabinets that were grimy and had lost their luster. Many of the appliances were old, and he was unsure if they would work at all, but when he turned the knob on the ancient gas range, the flame caught easily. The refrigerator hummed, and when he opened the door, it was predictably empty, but cold inside. Sev was sitting at the bench-style kitchen table in front of the bay window there, her legs swinging carefree beneath her.

"This is it," she declared, her eyes all starry. "This is the one, Phoenix. I can feel it."

Phoenix placed a hand on his hip, considering. "You won't have your own bathroom," he cautioned her.

She shook her head. "There are two. There's one off the living room. That one can be mine." She sought his face, large green eyes pleading. "Please Daddy? I think we could be happy here."

It melted him, as it usually did, whenever she called him that. He was at her side in moments, kneeling in front of where she sat at the kitchen table. Phoenix could see it now, the two of them sitting in the morning sun eating flatcakes, or at night with sandwiches or whatever else Sev wanted. He could see it so clearly. Even more, he wanted it.

He drew her head down and kissed her forehead, letting his lips linger there. "Oh, little mouse, I'd be happy anywhere as long as I'm with you."

He pulled away, and she was smiling. "We'll fix it up," she said. "It'll be like brand new. Better than new. We'll do it together."

Phoenix nodded, awed by her even more than usual. He tucked a piece of hair behind her ear; it had shaken loose from her braid. "Do you want to go down and check out the beach?"

She gazed at him, mouth turned in a soft smile. "Let's go Daddy. Let's go see our beach." She threaded her fingers through his mechanical hand and tugged him through the living room towards the front door. They walked the little boardwalk, too narrow to walk side-by-side, but Sev still never let go of his hand. The pathway took them by the palm grove, opening into the bright sun and grassy dunes of the beach. It stopped just shy of the shore, and Sev released him, taking off running until she was knee deep in the cool spray. Phoenix watched from the sand, his eyes gritty with tears.

They'd made it, he thought to himself. They were finally home.

Phoenix and Sev worked on the house during the day, taking the transport home at night to sleep in their own beds. Phoenix entertained the thought of buying a transport, a small one for him and Sev, and saving on fares. It would be a practical purchase now that they lived out of town. He tucked it into the back of his mind, something to dwell on later when they had finished the house and settled.

Phoenix was nailing boards, standing on a ladder. The roof was good; he'd checked it himself, but some of the siding needed replacing. Sev stood below him, handing him nails.

"You haven't peeked, have you?"

Sev giggled. She knew what he was referring to. Phoenix made her promise not to look in her bedroom until he had finished preparations. Unbeknownst to her, he had a few surprises planned.

"I haven't peeked, Drek knows," she swore solemnly.

He nodded his head. "Ok then, little mouse. I'll just have to believe you."

Sev passed him another nail. "When do you think we'll be done?"

Phoenix pursed his lips, striking the clapboard he was replacing with a hammer…once, twice, and a third time. He sighed. "Exterior is almost done.

135

I'll let you clean up the fire pit, if you're so inclined, and pressure wash the deck out back. I'll work some more on the interior tomorrow."

Sev perked up. "I want to help in the kitchen," she added, and Phoenix nodded. "I would be much obliged if you did," he said. "Make a list of what we need to purchase, and we'll have it delivered."

Sev held the ladder for him to climb down. They were wearing their work overalls. She had not asked, but she was wondering when they would go back to the docks.

When they had deep cleaned the entire house and decided what furniture they would keep (the sturdy kitchen table, for one, and the little nightstands) and what they would replace, they started moving in some of their belongings.

At first it was small things…blankets, toiletries, pots and pans. All their clothing was in the apartment, still, along with the few personal items they owned. Sev's books still lay on the shelf above her bed, and she was loath to remove them just yet.

They were arranging the furniture in the living room. The new couch and loveseat had arrived, and Sev was making sure of their proper place. There were lamps on the end tables and a new plush rug on the floor beside the fireplace. It was getting late, and if they were going to call a transport back to the apartment, they'd better do it now. But Sev remained lost in her work.

"Sweetheart, we better head back," Phoenix said.

Sev stopped where she was fluffing a throw pillow and straightened to meet her father's gaze. She turned suddenly shy. "I thought we could stay here," she said. "Just for tonight."

Phoenix quirked his mouth. "Sweet mouse, we've no beds yet. Just a day more and they'll be here. Remember?"

Sev acknowledged him, but only in passing. She withdrew the blankets from the hall closet and laid them on the floor in front of the fireplace. "We could sleep here," she persisted. "We could build a fire."

Phoenix saw that she'd made a little pallet on the floor. She'd thrown down a few pillows from the couch with a nest of blankets in the middle. His bones ached from all the physical exertion of the last few days. He didn't have the heart to tell her he was getting too old for sleepovers on the floor. He didn't think he could stand the disappointment in her eyes.

Instead, he sighed. "Tonight, it is. Did you pack a bag?"

She reached beside the couch and held it up. "Enough for both of us."

So, she had prepared, then. He ran a hand through his hair and settled in the nest of pillows and blankets. He didn't bother to hide the grunt at his cracking joints. "Did you bring any snacks? The kitchen is not yet fit for cooking, as you well know, and we've not a speck of food anywhere."

Sev grinned and withdrew a couple of sandwiches, placing them on the blanket in front of him. His Sev really had thought of everything, he mused.

Sev disappeared into what she had declared as her bathroom, the one off from the living room, and came out dressed for bed. Phoenix settled back on the pillows, staring up at the skylight and the canvas of stars beyond. Out here, away from the city, he could count each one.

While she was gone, he had made a fire, and it crackled merrily in the hearth. The flames licked the dry wood, casting shadows over the rug. Phoenix closed his eyes. He was just falling asleep when Sev settled at his back.

She slung an arm over him, grabbing his left hand. She had tucked herself in behind him, sharing one of the throw pillows. "I brought something for the house," she murmured. "A present."

Phoenix hummed. "A present, you say? That will be its first one." Phoenix sat up, leaning back on his arms, the blanket falling to his waist. Sev had brought him sleep pants but no shirt, and the light from the fire danced over the smooth bare skin of his chest.

Sev laughed, getting up to get her bag. She removed something large and rectangular and climbed up on the natural rock hearth, reaching up above the mantelpiece. Before he'd had time to caution her to be careful, she had situated it just so and stepped back to appraise it.

Phoenix turned, looking above the fire at what Sev had hung in such a prominent place in their home.

It was the papers…the ones that affirmed they were father and daughter now. Phoenix blinked, his eyes stinging with tears. Their thumbprints shone even in the shadow cast by the low firelight, clearly visible behind the glass.

Sev hugged him close, resting her face against his bare chest. She sighed. He smoothed a hand down her side, giving her a little squeeze. "Mouse, when did you have time to do this?"

Sev did not answer. She lay back, and Phoenix followed. She burrowed into his back, his skin smooth and warm, and pulled the blanket up over them.

Phoenix lay there, feeling Sev's light breath on his shoulder. Lying on his right side, he could see the papers plainly, preserved there in a simple black frame. His face was wet before he realized he was crying, and he was asleep before he could wipe the tears.

Moving day arrived like any other day. All the furniture was in its place. They had scrubbed and checked the kitchen, opting to leave the old appliances. There was a certain charm in them, and if they worked, it was only wasteful to replace them.

When it was time to leave the room for good, they had very little to take with them.

Sev stuffed her books in her bag and made her bed for the last time. Phoenix had a rucksack slung over one shoulder. They'd moved most of their clothes already.

They stood together at the threshold of the room, memorizing every shape and angle. Sev squeezed his hand, tugging him toward the door. She seemed melancholy, but not as sad as he had feared. They shut the door with a definitive snick, locking it behind them.

Surprisingly, he had a lump in his throat.

The ride in the transport seemed different this time. It would be the last trip they would take with no intention of coming back. Phoenix was sure they would need to return to the city…for supplies, for other reasons, but they would never return to the little room with its too-small beds and stockpile of memories. It was no longer home to them, and he was strangely affected.

That little room had been where they had woven the threads of their lives together…tenuously at first, then strong and true. Sev was looking out the window, a tear tracking down her cheek.

He pressed his lips to her temple, and she leaned against him. "It's ok to be sad, sweet mouse. Truth be told, I'm a mite sad myself."

She worried her lip. "I'm sad and happy both," she murmured. Her brows knit in confusion. "How is that possible?"

He grazed his hand down her arm. "We are complex creatures, little mouse. Full of different emotions. It's quite alright to feel two or more things at once. It's how we know we're alive."

Sev nodded, wiping her eyes, and Phoenix tutted. Her bag was in her lap, those precious books she treasured so, and Phoenix would hazard a guess that her headphones and journal were in there, too.

The transport turned off onto their sandy drive and bumped along until they reached the grove of palms. The clearing opened, and there set their house, gleaming in the sun with a fresh coat of white paint and trim as blue as the Dobani sea.

Phoenix paid the driver, and he left them standing there in front of their home.

Phoenix appraised the yard. Sev had done a fine job on it. She had trimmed the little scrubby hedges low and scooped the ash out of the fire pit. The yard was sandy save for a few nubby grasses. The little rock path leading up to the door had been pressure washed to shining. Phoenix held out his hand. "Shall we?"

Sev slipped her hand in his, and they walked together to the front door. Phoenix twisted the knob and pushed inside.

It smelled clean…new. Like leather and fabric and no trace of its previous staleness. The skylight shone clearly into the living room; he'd scrubbed off the film of sea spray with his own hand. Phoenix put his bag on the couch, and Sev headed directly to her room.

She stood at the threshold, her hand on the knob. She was vibrating with anticipation. "Now Daddy? I want to see it."

He caught up to her, his hand on her shoulder. "Go on, girl. I've made you wait long enough."

Sev opened the door and walked into the shaft of light pouring through the bay window. She had a dresser, she realized. It was a fine wood dresser, the knobs carved into little flowers. She pulled open a drawer and Phoenix had folded all her shirts and pants and put them away. She realized, then, that she was standing on a rug.

It was a woven rug in various muted colors, lush and soft. Her bed stood atop it. It was twice the size she was used to, and Phoenix had meticulously made it up with a pale blue comforter and pillows besides. On the other wall, near her closet, was a bookshelf. It was mostly empty, but there were a few titles she had never seen before. She ran her fingers over each one reverently, as if she could leech the words into her skin.

He had painted the walls the same peachy hue as a calcet gem. It was a calming color. Her gaze fell upon the window, then, and she caught her breath. Phoenix had built a little shelf into it with a padded cushion. It was someplace where she could sit and read, or dream, or listen to the ocean with the windows open. A sob strangled her throat, catching her completely off guard.

Phoenix knelt before her and gathered her to him. "Do you like it, baby? Don't cry, now," he soothed. He swiped at her tears with the pad of his thumb. "We'll fix whatever's wrong."

Sev shook her head, sniffling. "Nothing's wrong," she managed between sobs. She met his gaze, her eyes red-rimmed. "It's perfect. It's more than I ever dreamed."

Phoenix kissed her fevered cheek, wicking away her salty tears. He bent her head to his shoulder and held her. "Why don't you put your books away on the shelf I built you, hmm? Let's give them a home, too."

Sev nodded, unzipping her bag and placing it carefully on her bed. There was a stuffed sar-cat there, white with black stripes and blue eyes. She held it to her, giving it a little squeeze.

It was the first time she ever remembered doing that…hugging a stuffed animal. In fact, she didn't remember having one at all. She must've, as a very young child, but she couldn't recall it.

"You'll have to give him a name, dear heart," Phoenix's deep voice intoned behind her. "You have any in mind?"

Phoenix, she immediately thought. It was the only name she cared for, aside from her own. It was the only name that mattered.

She laid the sar-cat back down against the pillows and put her books away. She'd stopped crying, but her face was still puffy and red. "Can we see the other rooms?"

Phoenix held out his hand. "This is our home now, Sev. You can go wherever you like."

They headed across the hall to Phoenix's room next. Sev opened the door. Phoenix had a sizeable bed, just like hers, but the walls were dark blue. Everything was blue/brown/tan. It seemed very Phoenix to Sev.

They walked back into the living room. Sev noticed with pride that their papers still hung over the mantel, where they should be. Sev led him outside to the deck. There was a round metal table with an umbrella looking out over a stand of trees. She had washed the deck and scrubbed it spotless. Sev looked up at him proudly.

"Beautiful job, little mouse. A nicer one I have never seen. We'll spend many a happy time here, I know for sure."

Sev beamed under the praise. They stepped back into the cool of the house and walked into the kitchen next. Phoenix had left the yellow paint, only freshened it up a bit. He had repainted the cabinets too, and they were pure white. Sev opened the refrigerator, and he had stocked it with food. She laughed. They'd been moving little by little for cycles, but to see the old fridge stocked now was still a bit of a novelty.

Phoenix grabbed her hand. "One more surprise, little mouse. Let's go down to the beach."

Sev followed him to the end of the roughhewn boardwalk, where they shucked their shoes. In the distance, Sev could see a small wooden structure with a saw grass roof.

They traipsed through the sand, the warmth sinking between their toes. Sev arrived at the structure first; it was cool inside, away from the sun, and there was a little bench there.

Phoenix smoothed the hair away from her face where it blew in the wind. "For when you get tired of the sun, little mouse. You can take your rest in the shade here."

She smiled up at him. "There's room for two," Sev noticed, pleased.

Phoenix nodded, his hand at her back. The wind blew his hair away from his forehead, and the sand swirled around their feet. "Indeed, there is. Should we sit?"

Sev nodded, walking under the structure and sitting on the bench. Phoenix sat too, and Sev moved closer to him. The little hut smelled of sea oats and sawdust. It made her smile.

"You worked so hard," Sev mused, looking out over the glittering sea. "You made everything so *right*."

Phoenix looked too. The birds over the ocean swooped down to fish from the sea, an intricate ballet. He could hear their calls even from where they sat. "Don't thank me, mouse. You're worth it. Don't ever let anyone tell you you're not."

She found his hand where it rested against his thigh and entwined their fingers. Her throat grew tight. "I won't," she said, but she didn't think he heard her.

The hour grew late. Sev and Phoenix sat on the couch, reading from one of her books. Her eyes grew heavy, and Phoenix knew she was fading fast.

"Mouse," he whispered. "It's time for bed. Go wash up and I'll meet you there."

She nodded, finding her way to the bathroom. When she returned, Phoenix was sitting on the side of her bed.

He stood, holding back the covers for her to climb in. When she had settled, he held out the stuffed sar-cat, and she took it gratefully.

It was a new thing, having something soft to hold against her. It was not unwelcome.

Phoenix raised the window enough so she could hear the ocean, and then reached to turn out the light. Sev stayed his hand. "Could you leave it on for a little while?"

Phoenix dropped his hand to her head, caressing her hair. "Of course, mouse."

He bent to kiss her forehead. He was halfway out the door when she turned to look at him, one arm looped around the stuffed sar-cat. "Phoenix?"

He stopped in his tracks, turning with a soft smile on his face. "Yes, hon?"

Her mouth turned down a little, but it wasn't exactly a frown. "I'll miss you."

He chuckled fondly. "Oh mouse, I'm just across the hall. Would you like me to leave my door open?"

She nodded, hugging the stuffed sar-cat closer. Phoenix patted the doorframe. "Goodnight, love. Sleep well."

She closed her eyes. When she opened them, he was gone.

Her stomach flipped. *Not gone. In his room. In his bed*, she reminded herself. She closed her eyes and listened to the waves, letting her breathing match the soft rushing in and out of the water. After a while, she drifted off to sleep.

Sev showed up in Phoenix's doorway past midnight. She was dangling the sar-cat by the tail, her shadow framed by the light in the hall.

Phoenix rolled over, turning on his lamp so he could see her clearly. She seemed skittish, unsettled. "What's wrong, sweet mouse? Did you have a bad dream?"

She shook her head. "Were you asleep?" she asked.

Phoenix sighed. "Yes mouse, but it's ok. C'mere."

He motioned to her with his left arm, his right arm put away for the night. She drew near to his bed and climbed up next to him.

"I see you brought your friend," Phoenix mused, pointing to the sar-cat. Sev shrugged. "He didn't want to sleep alone, either," she reasoned.

Phoenix smiled. "Oh, is that right? Well, Mr. sar-cat," Phoenix began, affecting a humorous tone, "maybe you can just sleep between us then. That way, you won't be alone."

Sev laughed. She stretched her legs…she wasn't used to having so much space beside Phoenix. Their beds had always been so small.

"I love my room. I don't want you to think—"

Phoenix rolled onto his side to face her. He cupped her cheek. "Oh no, little mouse. I would think nothing of it. It's your first night in a new place. It's ok to not want to be alone."

Sev nodded, leaning into his touch, her eyes closed. "It really is the perfect room," she mused, "but yours is nice too."

Phoenix's mouth quirked. "It is. Even nicer now that Mr. sar-cat is here."

Sev punched his arm, and Phoenix feigned injury. They both lay there, laughing until their giggles had faded away. Phoenix kissed the top of her head. "You'll get used to your new room, dear heart. But I'll always be here, regardless."

Sev rolled over, clutching the stuffed animal. She was small there in the enormous bed, huddled under the dark comforter. He could almost hear her thinking.

"Why?" she asked him, and Phoenix wasn't sure what she was asking.

He was at a loss. "Because you're mine," he finally managed. "Because I love you."

The word lay between them, irrevocable. Undeniable. As if Phoenix would've done either, given the chance.

He heard her sniff, then saw her wipe her eyes. "I love you too, Daddy," she replied. "I love you so much it hurts sometimes. It scares me. There's so much of it, I don't know what to do with it all. And then I think, what if something happens to you? I'll be all alone. I don't wanna–"

Phoenix pulled her to him, shushing her, his lips pressed to her hair. "It's alright babydoll," he soothed. "Nothing's going to happen. We've got the rest of our lives in front of us, and Drek willing, that's a while yet."

She quieted and curled her body so that she lay in his arms. He closed his eyes, listening to her breathing. "It's ok to be scared, little mouse. Love is a powerful thing. It's bigger than us, and sometimes that's scary."

"Yeah," she breathed. It was the last thing she said before sleep claimed them both.

CHAPTER 15

They were growing things. Sev was growing things, Phoenix mentally amended, although he had contributed to her little hobby by building the raised beds that now lined their back deck. They were on their knees, a soft rubber mat beneath them. Sev was digging in the rich soil with the little spade she often used at the beach, lovingly aerating around her plants.

The morning sun was bright, but dew still shone on the leaves of the herbs, vegetables, and fruit they had planted. Sev's hair was in a ponytail, and her hands were black with dirt. She sat back on her knees and wiped an arm across her brow.

"Drek, it's hot already," Sev said with a sigh. "Wanna swim later?"

Phoenix hummed. "I think that's a fine remedy to the oppressive heat we currently find ourselves subject to," he agreed. "When we're finished here, perhaps a cool drink in the shade?" Despite the breeze, he had a fine sheen of sweat on his forehead.

Sev nodded. She continued pruning her plants, fussing over each leaf and muttering something about pests.

Phoenix wiped his forehead. "Now, little mouse, there's bound to be a solution. Something we can contrive around here, I suspect."

She stood, stretching her back. The morning sun had slipped over the roof of their house, casting her face in a warm glow. She wiped her hands on her work overalls, leaving dirty streaks on the sides. She scrunched up her nose as if suddenly remembering. "When are we going back to work, anyway?"

Phoenix pursed his lips, looking up at her where he still knelt by their little garden. He stood, grunting at the stiffness in his joints. He wrapped a hand around her arm, clutching it gently. "Will you sit with me, mouse?"

Sev blinked up at him, concern slipping over her face. She let him lead her to the patio table, settling in the chair across from him. There was a pitcher of ice water there, frosty with condensation, citrus slices floating within. Phoenix took it up and poured her a glass, handing it to her.

She could tell something troubled him…that he was having difficulty parsing out his words. It was very uncharacteristic of him. Phoenix always had a volume of words at the ready.

He slipped his hands across the table to cover hers. He met her gaze, eyes soft. "About that," he started hesitantly. He cleared his throat, obviously nervous. "We're settled now," he began, "and I think it's time we start thinking about school."

Sev swallowed, but didn't withdraw her hands. "I know I said I would go after we got back from Terra Firma," she hedged. "But this is—" she averted her gaze briefly, tears springing to her eyes. "This is the first real home I can remember. I don't want to leave it just yet."

Phoenix shook his head, squeezing her hands. "I know," he said, his voice impossibly tender. "I know. I'm not asking you to leave, baby. I just—"

Sev gasped, taking her hands away and hiding them in her lap. "Are you trying to get rid of me?" she asked him. "Is that what this is about?"

Phoenix's eyes widened, alarmed, and he put both hands up defensively. "Drek knows, little mouse," he began, his voice shaking. "Drek knows how much you mean to me." He swallowed, looking away. He took a breath and ran a hand through his hair. "I just—I just want you to have everything you deserve. To have the things I can't give you."

Sev's lip trembled. "Dad, I don't need anything else. Just you."

Phoenix swiped hurriedly at his face. To her dismay, he was crying. He met her eyes, an unreadable expression on his face. "I talked to a school, Sev. In town. It's not far from here. You could—"

The look of betrayal on her face was almost unbearable. He saw her eyes well, witnessed in anguish as the first tear tracked down her cheek, knowing he put it there. "You did this without talking to me first?" He could hear the anger there, the slight tremor in her voice.

He swallowed, his face flushing. *Drek*, he thought. He'd screwed up. He'd screwed up big time.

Sev was on her feet and through the back door before he could say anything. He followed her inside, making it through the living room just in time to see her bedroom door slam in his face. The sound it made was deafening.

He placed his hand against the door, his brow furrowed. "Little mouse, please come out. Just talk to me."

He heard sniffling behind the door, but nothing more. He could imagine her lying on her bed in her dirty overalls, maybe hugging a pillow or even her sar-cat. She was distraught, all because of him.

"It's an art school, little mouse," he pressed on. "I thought about your writing…you're so talented, Drek knows. That needs cultivating. Developing. Things I can't do for you."

Phoenix pressed his ear to the door, his heart breaking every moment. "You can draw too, Sev. I know you draw a little in your journal. You'll create beautiful things there, sweetheart. I know it."

The doorknob turned and her puffy face appeared in the crack. "You should've asked me," she said, her voice low and still laced with ire. He hadn't seen that steel in her gaze since he'd first noticed her on Terra Firma.

He tapped his head against the doorframe twice, for good measure. "I should've," he said. Sev still stood with just her face visible. She had her mouth turned down in a severe frown, but she wasn't crying. "Mouse, please come out. I'm sorry." He shook his head, his eyes closed. "I'm so sorry."

He stepped back from the door when it swung open, giving her space. She'd changed out of her overalls and wore one of her soft T-shirts and a pair of jeans. She walked out slowly with her arms crossed in front of her and sat down on the couch.

Phoenix approached her, tentatively at first, hating the distance still palpable between them. He sat down on the far end of the couch, body angled toward hers.

"Hardest and best thing in the wide world," he began after several long moments of stony silence. "Being a parent. Doing what you feel is right. When you care for someone, when you're responsible for them, you just try to make the best decisions." He met her gaze, his eyes sheepish. "But I was wrong. I am wholly aware of my transgressions. I should've talked to you, mouse, before I did anything." He blinked away tears, flexing his hand at his side. "I never meant to hurt you...would never embark on such an action as to cause harm, intentionally or not, but that appears to be exactly what I've done. I–"

"Phoenix?" she asked, her mouth quirked, her eyes softer than before. "Shut up."

Phoenix huffed a laugh, relief flooding through him. Sev slid over to him, covering his hand with hers where it lay pressed against the couch. "Can I at least see it? Before...before I have to go?"

Phoenix smiled a little crooked, the light returning to his eyes. "Yes baby. Of course. And if it doesn't meet your expectations, then we'll call it all off. You have my sincere word."

She raised her eyebrows. "You mean it? If I don't like it, then I don't have to go?" She blinked at him, her eyes as green as the sea.

It wounded him. "No Sev. Of course not. I would never, ever force you into anything you didn't expressly want, even if I thought it was good for you. You should know that."

Her frown lessened, and she closed the distance between them. She leaned into his chest, and he wrapped his arms around her. She was warm against him, her hair floral and familiar. "Oh, sweet mouse," he whispered into her hair. He dropped a kiss to the top of her head, and she sighed. "Can you ever forgive me?"

She relaxed into him, her face turned into the juncture of his neck and shoulder. "I already have," she murmured, her voice muffled by his skin.

He gave her a gentle squeeze, his eyes wet, and silently thanked Drek or whoever was listening for Sev's tender mercies.

Their transport was waiting outside, parked under a palm tree. Phoenix had purchased it secondhand, but it was in good condition and had more than paid for itself as he and Sev had explored their new neighborhood. Phoenix liked it for the price; Sev liked it for the berry red color, showy and bright under the Dobani sun.

They bumped down their sandy drive, Sev in the passenger seat and Phoenix driving. Sev was quiet as they turned off onto the main road. After a while it opened into a town with little shops, their new stop for dessert, and a diner Phoenix favored. The scenery sped by with little reaction from Sev; her thoughts fixed on the school. A little tremor of nerves rattled through her, and she stole a glance at Phoenix. His eyes were on the road, hands loose on the wheel of the transport. He felt her gaze and turned, a lazy smile on his face. "It's not far now, little mouse," he assured her. He meant to put her at ease, but she was still slightly off center.

Around a curve, the school came into view. It was a large, sprawling campus with tall, colorful glyphs in the school's name standing on the carefully manicured lawn. The building was gray, with an asymmetrical roof and tall windows out front. The gray contrasted well with colorful glyphs, she thought. Off to the side, students sat on a hill, blankets spread and eating their lunch. Some were throwing a flying disc; others were drawing in sketchbooks.

Phoenix parked out front. He nudged her shoulder, and she glanced at him a little apprehensively. "You get the final say, Sev," Phoenix reminded her. His smile was soft. "Wanna have a look around?"

Sev worried her lip, nodding once. They slipped out of the transport and made their way up the sidewalk to the glass double doors. Sev reached for Phoenix's hand, and he could feel the slight tremor there. He pressed his palm to hers with a gentle squeeze.

Inside there was a long, carpeted hall. Large plants hung from the high ceiling, leaves broad and green. A sizeable skylight lay above, much larger than theirs at home. A mural of Dobani covered most of the far wall. It made her smile.

Phoenix led them into the office. The administrator was there, and he greeted Phoenix warmly.

"You must be Sev," he said. He stuck out his hand for her to shake. "I've heard so much about you, young lady. Your father is a proud man."

Sev couldn't stop the small smile from spreading, nor could she stop from leaning shyly into Phoenix's side, her cheeks red.

The administrator straightened, addressing them both. "I'm Mr. Davenport. I would love to show you around. Would you like that, Sev? Meet some of our students, perhaps?"

Sev regarded Phoenix, her jade eyes questioning. He gave her an encouraging pat, his arm wrapped around her.

"Thank you," Sev said, turning to the administrator. "I'd like that."

Mr. Davenport led them down the long hall. Sev craned her neck, looking up at the long chains that suspended the plants above them. "How do you water them?" she wondered aloud. "A ladder?"

The administrator chuckled. "Let me show you," he offered, leading them into what appeared to be a supply closet. He pressed a button on the wall and one of the large plants descended.

Sev watched, amazed, as the plant went slowly up and down, seemingly on its own. "It's an electric pulley system," the administrator informed her. "One of our engineering students designed it."

Phoenix ran a hand over her hair, pulling it away from her collar and letting his hand rest at her neck. "My Sev is quite the gardener. She loves anything that grows."

Mr. Davenport smiled. "We have a wonderful horticulture program here, Sev. You'll have to tour the gardens."

Her eyes brightened. "You have gardens? How big?"

They came to two wooden doors, an archway of books painted above them. "Sizeable," the man enthused. "We grow many vegetables and flowers here, all tended by the students."

He turned the handle, and the door opened to a large room with shiny wooden tables, lamps, and plenty of natural light let in from the tall windows she'd seen from the outside. And there were books. Shelves upon shelves of them. More books than Sev had ever seen in her life.

She walked ahead, looking around in awe. There were couches and chairs too, and some students sat writing, some sat lounging in the sun streaming through the windows, headphones on and a book in hand with several stacked beside them. Mr. Davenport motioned to her. He was standing with Phoenix at a desk chatting with a pleasant-looking woman there.

"Sev, this is Ms. Allen. She's the director of our library. Do you have any questions for her?"

Sev swallowed shakily, still a bit dumbfounded by the sheer immensity of the library. Phoenix gave her a little smile. "Go on, mouse. You know how much you like to read, now. Surely you must have something on your mind."

She wet her lips. "Do you have *Nautica*?"

Ms. Allen laughed, lilting and sweet. "Oh, several copies. It's a favorite here among the students. In fact, it's the subject of our book club this month. Have you read any of the author's other works?"

Sev bit her lip, shaking her head. "I…I didn't know they had any."

Ms. Allen grew visibly excited, gesturing with her hands. "Oh, quite a few. All are wonderful. You'll have to check them out!"

Sev frowned. "I'm sorry, but I'm not a student here."

Ms. Allen gave her a small smile. "If that changes, dear, then come back and see me."

With that, Mr. Davenport steered them back into the hall. Sev's head was abuzz with thoughts. "Ms. Allen was nice," she blurted out. She turned to Phoenix, her eyes warm. "She knew about *Nautica*."

Phoenix placed his hand at her back, guiding her. "And some we never heard of, to boot," he added. "Very nice indeed."

Mr. Davenport nodded. "I want you to see our art studio, Sev. I told the instructor we might be stopping by. The students will be busy, but you can observe a little of what goes on here."

They knocked on a large door in the hall and then pushed inside.

There were shapes and colors and forms everywhere. Aprons hung on pegs by the door. The large sink on the counter gleamed chrome, and bottles of paint and cups of brushes stood on a table pressed up against the wall. There were cabinets and drawers, some half-opened, revealing pastels and charcoal pencils.

Sev had to press her hands to her side to keep from reaching out to touch them. She'd only ever used a pen.

There was a circle of students, some sitting and some standing, easels in front of them and palettes besides. They were all painting a still life, a conglomeration of odd shapes and textures in the middle of the circle. Sev observed the two, comparing canvases. They were alike, but also very different.

"Is this Sev?"

Sev raised her head, following the voice. There was a young woman wearing an apron spattered with paint. She had a bright smile and kind eyes. "I heard you might be stopping by. So, you're thinking of joining us?"

Sev's mouth turned down. "I haven't decided," she admitted.

The woman only smiled. "That's ok. Come see what's going on in the ceramics room. It's at the back of the studio here."

Sev walked past the students painting, then past more students sketching on drafting tables, their tools spread out neatly beside them. Sev saw the drawings, some very technical, others more organic, all flowing shapes and lines. A feeling very akin to hunger settled beneath her ribs.

She looked back, and Phoenix and Mr. Davenport were still standing in the doorway. She stopped, her eyes wide. Phoenix had told her he wouldn't leave her here. She still believed him. He saw her looking back and gave her a little wave.

It settled her. She gave him a shaky smile and followed the woman in the apron back to where a large space opened. The room smelled damp and earthy, like her garden after a rain. Students sat hunched over their sculptures, hands wet with slurry. Others worked at the wheel, crafting bowls and mugs and forms Sev couldn't yet discern.

The woman knelt in front of Sev, her eyes catching hers. "Mr. Davenport tells me you're quite the writer. And that you draw?"

Sev nodded quickly. She could feel Phoenix's absence like a cold shadow, but she tried not to let it distract her. "Just doodles. Nothing exciting."

"Oh, I think that's very exciting," the woman interjected. "People have made entire careers just by doodling."

Sev blinked at her. "Really?"

The woman pressed her lips together. "Really Sev. Art is a beautiful way to express yourself. Writing is art, too." She placed her hand on Sev's shoulder, gentle and fond. "So, you're already an artist."

Sev's eyes were wet, and she squeezed them shut. When she opened them, the woman was at the sink. She returned with an apron in hand and a ball of clay. "Would you like to try?"

Sev stared at the clay, her mouth agape. "I–I wouldn't know what to do."

She led her over to an empty stool and sat her beside a student. "We're making coil pots today. They're easy. Just roll this clay into little snakes and coil them around each other."

The instructor pinched off a bit of Sev's clay and rolled it on the table. It made a long piece. She wrapped it around itself until it was two levels high. "Now you try."

Sev pulled her lip between her teeth. She smiled shyly at the student next to her, and they caught her gaze before she could turn away. "Hi," they greeted. They were building a grand pot with many clay snakes. "Are you new?"

Sev's face burned. "No," she replied. "Not yet." She turned back to her clay, then. She pinched off a piece and set to work.

Sev found her father and Mr. Davenport sitting in the man's office. She held the pot she'd made, misshapen and a bit wobbly. Phoenix saw her enter and stood, his hand outstretched.

"Careful Dad. It's still wet."

Phoenix whistled appreciatively. "Little mouse, what have you made?"

Sev held it up to him. "It's a pot. I made it for you."

Phoenix pulled her to his side, careful of the pot she was still holding. "Thank you, sweetheart. I shall cherish it always."

Mr. Davenport stood from his desk and regarded her. "Did you enjoy spending time in the art studio, Sev?"

She nodded, a sincere smile on her face. The man put his hands in his pockets. "I have one more place I'd like to show you if you still want to go."

Sev smiled, handing off the pot to Phoenix who took it in his large left hand, the tacky clay cool beneath his fingers. "I'd like to see it," she said.

The three of them made their way down the hall, then down one more. The first door on the right had a little plaque that read "Writing Room" spelled out in Central Glyph. Sev's heart skipped a beat.

Mr. Davenport opened the door and Sev walked in first. There were computer terminals everywhere, and soft armchairs, and somewhere music was playing. At a back table, two students sat with notebooks in front of them. One was reading to the other, and they were laughing.

Phoenix nudged her forward. "Go introduce yourself, sweet mouse. Go on, now."

She made her way back to where the two students were sitting, and they looked up at her. "Hi," one of them offered. "I'm Jesse."

"Sev," she replied. "What are you reading?"

Jesse waved her hand dismissively. "Just this funny story my friend Rhya wrote. Do you want to read it with us?"

Rhya nodded excitedly. "Why don't you sit down? I'll read it to both of you."

Sev smiled, tremulous but sincere, and sat down to listen. Within moments, she was laughing, too.

Phoenix looked on, his eyes filled with tears, as his daughter made her first friends.

They were late starting dinner. They had the windows open in the kitchen, the cool breeze off the water dispelling the heat from stove. The tide was coming in, and Sev could hear the waves crashing relentlessly against the beach.

She stood at the counter, chopping vegetables. She was humming happily, a towel thrown over her shoulder. Phoenix was stirring the stock. They were making soup tonight. "It's fit weather for it, when the moon is high like this," Phoenix had said.

Sev's knife work got slower and slower as she became absorbed in thought. When she finished, she carried the cutting board over to Phoenix and raked the vegetables into the bubbling stock. He brushed her cheek appreciatively, teasing the hair away from her face. "One day we'll be eating from the garden," he told her. Sev closed her eyes, leaning into his touch.

"Dad?"

Phoenix stirred the pot once more, then replaced the lid, setting it to simmer. "Yes, baby?"

"I'm sorry for getting mad about school. I know you only want the best for me. I know that, and I still got mad."

He wrapped her in his arms. Sev pressed her face to the front of his apron; he smelled like red sauce and spices and something that was uniquely Phoenix. "You have nothing to apologize for, little mouse. It was me who was out of line." The ocean roared its agreement, crashing heavily onto shore. "Is that to say—and correct me if I'm just totally off the mark, little mouse—but are you saying you liked it, and that you could see yourself going to school there?"

Sev withdrew, her eyes wet. "I do like it, Daddy. I tried not to. I was still cross with you. But I *do* like it." She burrowed into him again, drying her eyes on his shirt. "Will you take me every day?"

"And be there waiting every afternoon to pick you up," Phoenix assured her, threading his hands through her hair. "Have you thought of a place for my pot?"

Sev huffed a laugh. "Over the fireplace?"

Phoenix's eyes lit, and he gestured with a mechanical finger. "Now there's an idea I have been waiting to hear. And I chance a better one I've never come across. Should we place it together?"

Sev nodded.

Phoenix took her by the hand and led her into the living room. "Let's do that, and you get ready for bed. The soup should be ready by then." They stood in the living room, Phoenix's arm draped over her shoulder, both staring at the spot on the mantelpiece that Sev had reserved for Phoenix's pot.

"I'm proud of you, sweetheart. So incredibly proud."

She met his eyes. "You mean it?" she asked him. "Because I'm kind of scared, Dad."

He knelt in front of her, holding both of her hands. "Oh honey. You'll do fine. More than fine. I guarantee."

Sev's lip quivered, and she tucked it between her teeth. "What if they don't like me? I'm not like them. I won't fit in."

Phoenix cupped her face, letting his thumb gentle her cheek. "You're not like them at all," he agreed. "You're not like anyone. You're my wild bird, Sev. And wild birds are born to fly."

He caught the tear that rolled down her cheek, wiping it away with his thumb. She hugged him close, letting her head rest on his shoulder. They stayed that way for a long time.

Phoenix was up before dawn. He sat on his bed, the room still dark, holding the little red box in his hand. It had come the day before, by courier, but he'd upset Sev with his misguided secrecy and the time had not been right.

He would give it to her today, her first day of school.

Phoenix swore to himself. He was already feeling the pangs of her loss, even if it was just for a few hours. They had not separated, not one moment since Terra Firma where Sev had literally tethered them to each other. It was selfish, and he hated himself for it.

This was good for her. This was right. It's what he'd been thinking when he'd talked to the administrator before he'd talked to Sev. But he'd been too eager. It's what a lesser man would do. *It's what Del would've done*, he thought wretchedly. Plan her future without her.

He gripped the little box in his left hand; he had not yet put on his prosthetic. Sev didn't belong on the docks, ground down under the boot heel of manual labor. Her gentle hands would grow gnarled, after a time, and her back stooped. He'd seen it happen too many times. Sev deserved better.

"Daddy?"

He slipped the box under his pillow and saw where Sev stood in his doorway. Her hair was in disarray, and she was still in her pajamas.

"Good morning, love. I was just thinking about you." He held out his hand, gesturing to her. "C'mere."

Sev smiled, inclining her head as she walked toward her father. She settled on the bed next to him, leaning in close.

"I was just about to wake you," he said with a smile. "You'll have to get ready for school soon."

She sighed, her slight form heavy and relaxed against him. "What is that under your pillow?"

Phoenix chuckled. "Nothing gets past you, does it, little mouse?" He pressed his cheek against her hair, unable to wrap his missing right arm around her but wanting to all the same. He exhaled. "It's a surprise."

She brightened, looking up at him. "For me?"

Phoenix smiled. "Of course, for you. None other."

Her small hand dug into his left side as she wrapped her arm around him, fingers splayed over his warm, bare skin. "When can I get it, Daddy?"

"After breakfast," Phoenix said. "Directly."

Sev pulled away to look at him. "You're cooking? I thought I would eat at school."

Phoenix huffed. "Far be it from me to send my girl off to school on an empty stomach. You may eat there, and I say you should, but you'll eat with me first. I'll make sure of that."

She leaned into him and closed her eyes. "Ok," she agreed, satisfied.

Sev pushed her plate back, eggs and toast mostly finished. Phoenix had served her fruit, too, and her favorite juice, and some jam they'd found at a produce stand in town. She was wearing a brand-new shirt, and Phoenix had twisted the sides of her hair in a careful braid, securing the rest with a hair tie.

Phoenix cleared the table, excusing Sev from helping. She sat at the table near the window, her chin in her hand. "What will you do, Phoenix?"

He dumped the dishes in the sink, turning on the hot water. Suds built, spilling over the pots and pans. He shut off the tap.

"Oh, I'll abide," he said. "There's plenty to be done, little mouse. You just enjoy yourself. Don't give it a thought."

She angled toward him, her eyes soft. "Will you water my plants?"

Phoenix nodded gravely. "As soon as I get back."

Sev smiled, a mischievous glint in her eyes. "Will you talk to them?"

Phoenix made a face. He put a finger to his lips, pretending to give it a great deal of thought. "Now I don't believe mine is the voice they'd prefer to hear." He walked toward her, grabbing her hand and coaxing her to her feet. "You'll just have to resume your conversation with the plants when you return," he said, patting her hand as he walked her into the living room.

He sat her down on the couch. "You just wait right here, girl. I'll be right back."

Phoenix walked to his bedroom, slipping inside and withdrawing the little box from under his pillow. He put it in his pocket and walked out, returning to where Sev sat waiting in the living room.

He sat on the low table in front of her and withdrew the little box.

Sev's eyes lit up, her mouth falling open. "What is it, Daddy?"

Phoenix smiled. "Open it and find out."

She took it in her hands, holding it tenderly. She turned it over, finding the seam, and lifted the top.

There, against the black velvet, was a little calcet pendant in the shape of a bird.

The carved bird was intricate; she could see the etched wings, the little beak, the delicate tail feathers, the careful eye. It shone beautifully. The peachy center of the calcet was near-translucent and catching the light.

"Oh, Phoenix," she breathed, lifting it from the box by its silver chain. "It's so pretty." She blinked away tears and regarded her father where he sat watching her, a sense of wonder on his face. "Put it on for me?"

"Of course, little mouse. Turn around."

Sev did so, sweeping her hair over her shoulder so Phoenix could easily fasten it around her neck. When it was done, she closed her fingers over it. The gem was cool and smooth against her skin.

The pendant had a little weight to it, but it wasn't uncomfortable. It was grounding. Solid. She turned toward him. "How does it look?"

Phoenix leaned forward, his hand cradling the back of her head. He pressed his lips to her forehead in a chaste kiss. "Why on you, sweet mouse, it's the most beautiful thing I've ever seen."

She fell into him then, arms snagging his waist. "I love you, Daddy. Not just for the necklace. But for everything."

Phoenix wrapped his arms around her, feeling the immensity of her love in the ferocity of her embrace. "I know, baby. And I love you."

After watching Sev walk up the sidewalk to the school, Phoenix drove back home alone. He walked through the front door, the silence of their little house suddenly oppressive. He opened the windows, letting in the breeze. Phoenix watered Sev's plants, observing the little blooms. There would be a harvest soon. It made him smile.

It made him think of Sev.

A twinge of loneliness twisted his gut, settling there cold and unmistakable despite it being unfamiliar. Phoenix had never been a lonely man; many times, he'd been alone…in his work…in his personal life. And certainly, in the Black. But he had never been lonely. It was a piercing sort of pain.

He wandered into the living room, settling on the couch. Phoenix read some, trying to distract himself. When his eyes grew heavy, he napped, sprawled there with one arm hanging off the edge. He awoke with a start. He'd dreamed of Sev.

After a while, he checked his chrono. Only a few hours had passed. He wondered briefly what Sev was doing. It was midday, so she was probably eating lunch. His lips twitched into a fond smile. He hoped she was well.

He found himself in the kitchen, finishing the morning's dishes. Phoenix put everything away, wiping his hands on a dish towel and leaving the counters spotless. The spot by the bay window was devastatingly empty; Sev had sat there just this morning.

He sighed. Not much time had passed since last he checked the chrono. He didn't even look. Phoenix went outside and settled into one of the rocking chairs on their small porch. He gazed at the ocean, a green-blue ribbon on the horizon. That reminded him of Sev most of all.

Phoenix was at the school early. He sat in the transport, listening to it idle, and eyed the entrance to the school. The thought had occurred to him while he was moping around the house. Sev was at school, away from him. But what if he was there, too?

He turned off the transport and walked into the office. Mr. Davenport was there talking with a student. Phoenix waited, then knocked on the door.

"Phoenix!" Mr. Davenport greeted him. "I wasn't expecting to see you so soon. Checking on Sev?"

Phoenix appeared sheepish. "Something like that," he admitted. He stuffed his hands in his pockets. "I don't suppose you've seen her?"

Mr. Davenport nodded. "Indeed, I have. I helped her find one of her classes only a while ago. Do you need me to call her in?"

Phoenix held up his hands. "No, no, don't disturb her. I'm actually here to see you."

They both sat, and Mr. Davenport beckoned Phoenix to continue. Phoenix swallowed, nerves and embarrassment getting the best of him. "I was wondering…" he wavered, then collected himself. "I was wondering if there wasn't something I could do here. Volunteer, if you like."

Mr. Davenport considered, leaning forward with his hands folded on his desk. "You miss her, don't you?" he asked, and Phoenix flushed red. "It's quite alright, Phoenix. You're a single parent. I can't imagine how difficult it's been for you both, it being just the two of you."

161

You haven't a clue, Phoenix thought.

"We would love to have you volunteer," Mr. Davenport said. "The library always needs help, and we may even need you to substitute from time to time. You think you're up for that?"

Phoenix laughed nervously. He wasn't sure if he would be any good with a child that wasn't Sev, but he could certainly try.

He smiled, his nerves dissipating. "Why, that sounds fine," he asserted. "I'm much obliged." The icy fist of despair that had settled in his gut not long after he dropped off Sev eased some.

"A day or two a week?" Mr. Davenport asked. "We can start you tomorrow, if you like."

Phoenix nodded appreciatively. "If it's alright with Sev, that is."

He shook Mr. Davenport's hand and began walking out of the office. "The students will dismiss momentarily," Mr. Davenport called after him. "You're welcome to wait here if you like."

Phoenix smiled. "I'd like that."

He was standing outside the office when a soft tone sounded, marking the end of the school day. A large group of students made their way down the hall, some of them chatting, all of them headed for the exit. He spotted Sev almost immediately, her blonde hair bright under the skylight, the calcet pendant he'd given her shining like glass.

"Daddy!" she exclaimed as soon as she saw him, running up and throwing her arms around him. She kissed his cheek. "I can't wait to tell you all about it."

He touched the little bird around her neck, then kissed the top of her head, taking her backpack and shouldering it for her. Something clicked into place with her by his side again. He felt whole. Complete. He grabbed her hand, leading her out of the double doors and into the bright Dobani sun. "And I can't wait to hear."

CHAPTER 16

The fire crackled between them, flames licking the dry wood. Little sparks danced into the night sky, swirling upwards in the dark before burning out. Sev and Phoenix sat around the fire pit, comfortable in the low wooden chairs there. They pressed their bare feet into the cool sand of their front yard, Sev's half-buried, burrowed into the sand like a crab. She had a stick in her hand and was languidly poking the fire, her face aglow in its warmth.

"This is my first campfire," she mused, her voice soft. "We never stayed in one place long enough to do anything like this."

Phoenix frowned. He had a lifetime of experiences planetside. He often forgot his Sev had spent most of her time in the Black.

And he knew what she meant by *we*.

He leaned forward with his hands on his knees and caught her gaze over the flames. "You know what we used to do, when I was a boy? We'd camp out under the stars. We'd build a fire, cook our food over it. Sleep with nothing but the songs of the forest creatures to keep us company."

Sev listened, entranced, her eyes filled with longing. "Can we do something like that?"

Phoenix leaned back, crossing a foot over his knee. He was keen on any opportunity to make memories with Sev. There was a painful past there that he hoped to erase, in time, one where she'd had to grow up too fast…one in which she'd been an extension of Del's own greedy hand, a tool rather than the child she was. The child she still is.

"I don't see why not. You don't have school again for several days, yet." His eyes brightened. "Say, that's what we'll do. Get us a boat. Journey until we find a little island. Eat what we catch."

Sev's eyes went wide, the light from the fire catching on her calcet pendant. "Fish for our food? Not pack anything?"

Phoenix chuckled. "Not a thing, little mouse. Live off the land, as they say, or more accurately, the sea. And if the sea is unkind, and we're hungry, we'll simply come back home."

Sev smiled and gave the fire a final poke, a shower of sparks ascending skyward. She tossed the stick into the fire pit, watching it catch. "I've never been camping," she mused, her gaze far away.

Phoenix brightened. "Adventuring, Sev. And you're a skilled enough hand at that. A brief night under the stars will be no large thing."

Sev yawned, checking her chrono. It was well past midnight, but Phoenix always let her stay up when she didn't have school the next day. "Want to turn in?"

Phoenix regarded her fondly. "Sure baby. I'll douse the fire. You go get ready for bed. I'll be in directly."

He saw her leave, his heart twinging at the sight of her. He would charter the boat tomorrow. They could head out beyond the waves, discover what lay waiting for them. It would be good for Sev…the sun and the salt air. She'd been working so hard at school. And he had missed her.

He had not yet mentioned volunteering. He was hesitant to misstep, as he had before…worried he would infringe upon her privacy, her right to have a life away from his own.

Phoenix doused the fire with a pail of sand, plunging the yard into total darkness. He took the stone path to the front door, walking it by memory. He eased into the familiar comfort of their warmly lit little house, so still and quiet. Phoenix could hear Sev in the bathroom, brushing her teeth. She came out in her pajamas, her hair in waves from the braid she'd worn all day. She eased up to him, slipping her hand in his. "Read to me?" she asked, eyes green and questioning.

He smoothed his hand over her head, fingers dancing over the soft waves there. "Of course, mouse. Go wait for me and I'll be right there."

Phoenix stopped by the kitchen, filling Sev's water glass to set by her bed. He carried it into her bedroom, where she lay beneath the covers.

She scooted over, patting the space beside her. Phoenix wanted to laugh; it was something he would do, something he had done many times when she'd been roused by a bad dream, or was cold, or simply needed to be close to him. He dutifully settled beside her, placing the glass of water on her nightstand. "What book are we reading tonight?"

Sev crawled to the edge of the bed and stretched toward her bookcase. She handed him her selection. "The one about the explorers," she said, settling back on the pillow. Her hair spread out like a halo, framing her face.

Phoenix smiled. "My favorite one."

Sev laughed. "You say that about every book, Dad."

He didn't deny it. He opened the book and leaned back, getting comfortable against the pillows propped behind him. Sev made a little noise, letting her head fall against his shoulder, and Phoenix began to read.

Chartering the boat was a straightforward affair; Phoenix, still unused to the freedom that came with a card full of credits, had anticipated problems. They packed lightly…two sleeping bags, their fishing gear, a change of clothes, and some water. Phoenix took snacks just in case their catch was skimpy. He wanted this to be a novel experience for Sev, but he also wanted her to have fun.

They drove the transport down to the pier, where they found a boat there tethered to the pilings. Phoenix had assured the man that they would not need a captain…Phoenix, in his youth, had manned the helm of many boats. They unpacked their gear, and Phoenix hefted it onto the deck. He helped Sev climb aboard, unmoored the boat, and fired the engines.

165

Sev was quiet as they pulled away from the pier. She had her eyes closed against the feel of the wind on her face, the way it whipped her hair as Phoenix picked up speed. The soft bouncing of the boat over the waves was rhythmic, almost soothing. She looked at the whitecaps breaking on the water, then back toward the pier, watching it recede the further out they got.

Soon, it was just the two of them and the Dobani Sea.

Sev stood, making her way up to where Phoenix steered the boat. He seemed at peace, skin already brown from the sun and hair blown back away from his forehead. Sev watched, transfixed, as the little white patch danced in the wind.

He reached with his left arm and pulled her to him, leaving his prosthetic to steady the wheel. "How do you like it, babydoll? Your first ever boat ride."

She put an arm around his shoulder, looking out over the vast expanse of water in front of them. "It's so beautiful, the sea. And so big. I never realized." She pressed her lips together, leaning into him a bit. "Makes me feel small."

Phoenix nodded. "Me as well, little mouse. We are just a speck in the universe out here. It's a humbling feeling."

They continued for a while more until Sev spotted some fish on the horizon, and Phoenix reduced their speed. The fish were silvery with a rainbow sheen; they were jumping out of the water almost in unison. They both watched them for a little while, leaping over the waves. Phoenix tucked a piece of hair behind her ear, securing it away from her face. "Would you like to drive, little mouse?"

Sev appeared incredulous, then hopeful. "Really?" she asked. "You would let me drive the boat?"

Phoenix smiled. "Of course, sweetheart." He stood, motioning to the seat he'd just occupied. "Hands on the wheel. Keep it straight, now."

Sev sat down, and Phoenix checked the maps. He had navigated them to a sandbar a few miles off the coast. Though they were still in open water, he could see a sliver of land in the distance.

Sev gripped the wheel, turning when Phoenix said turn. She pointed to a spot on the horizon. "Is that where we're going?"

Phoenix hummed. "It is indeed. Would you like to fish here, in deeper waters, or take our chance in the shallows?"

Sev thought for a moment. "We better fish here. More likely to catch something, I think."

Phoenix patted her shoulder. "Smart girl." He reached across her and shut off the engines. They cast anchor, and Phoenix baited their hooks. Sev stood there on the swaying boat, holding her fishing rod and a little unsure of what to do next.

Phoenix wrapped his hand around hers, moving them just so. "Hand on the rod here," he instructed. "Other hand on the reel, in case you get a nibble."

Sev met his gaze, her eyes lighter in the sun. "How will I know?"

He huffed. "You'll know, sweetheart. Want me to cast it for you?"

She bit her lip, nodding. Phoenix took her rod, cast it out far. Sev observed the baited hook where it sank below the surface and disappeared. Phoenix handed it back to her. "Reel it in a little," he instructed. "Now we wait."

An hour had passed, the sun hot and too little breeze blowing. Phoenix got her hat from their pack, the straw one she favored with the floppy brim, and placed it on her head. "Patience, little mouse," he'd said. "We're on their turf now."

Not long after, Sev's line pulled. It was a sharp, decisive tug, nearly yanking the rod from her relaxed hands. Phoenix was on his feet, helping her hold it.

"Reel it in Sev and pull up besides. That's it."

Sev reeled, her arm cramping, and pulled against whatever she'd caught. Even with Phoenix helping, it was quite the task. Still, a thrill of excitement went through her.

She'd drawn the line in until it was flush with the boat. Something flopped, large and cumbersome, against the hull. Phoenix scooped it up with a net, and Sev sat back, exhausted from the struggle.

"What a catch, mouse!" Phoenix exclaimed. He dislodged the hook and emptied the fish into the live well. It swam free, happy to be in the water again even if not in the large free real estate of the ocean.

Sev laughed. "I can't believe it," she said a little breathlessly. "I really can't believe I caught him, Daddy. By myself, too."

Phoenix squeezed her shoulder. "That you did, little mouse, all by yourself. And he's big enough for the two of us."

Sev glanced up at Phoenix, a hopeful look on her face. "So, we can stop now?"

Phoenix chuckled. As much as Sev loved the ocean, she seemed to be not too keen on fishing. He closed the lid on the live well and took Sev's rod. "We can stop, hon. We've more than enough for supper."

Sev smiled, settling back in her seat. She kept her hat on. When Phoenix started the engines again and picked up speed, she held it to her head against the wind.

Phoenix ran the boat aground at one end of the sandbar. Sev climbed down, her pack on her back, and touched down on the sandy beach with a look of awe on her face.

Waves lapped at her feet. A cool breeze blew off the water, stirring her hair. Phoenix was already collecting driftwood, firmly in his element. There was nothing around them for miles…just them under the sun on this strip of beach surrounded by the Dobani Sea.

"Let's make camp, sweet mouse," Phoenix called to her, his arms full of driftwood. "Find us the perfect spot."

Sev traversed the sandbar, letting the foam at the water's edge tickle her feet. She walked until she found a sunken bit of ground in the middle of the sandbar under a small grove of trees.

She called him over, her voice carrying easily over the flat expanse. Phoenix brought the driftwood over and the rest of their gear, settling it under a palm.

Phoenix dusted his hands and surveyed the area Sev had chosen. "Good job, mouse. A better spot I've never seen. Wanna help me build the fire?"

Sev nodded, digging out a place in the sand while Phoenix snapped off pieces of driftwood. He took his starter and ignited a spark. The wind caught it, and the fire flamed to life.

The sun was setting, painting the sky in strokes of pink and orange. Sev sat by the fire, watching the first stars light in the sky.

It should feel barren, she thought, sitting on this desolate scrap of land in the middle of the sea with no one around for miles. But it didn't. She felt calm, contemplative.

It was because of Phoenix, she knew. He stood bent over the deck of the boat, cleaning their fish. He worked so hard to make her happy; it still astounded her sometimes. For as long as they'd been together, he'd always treated her with tender hands, measured words. It was jarring at first, the difference from what she was used to. But Phoenix helped her realize that kindness and consideration were a right, and not a privilege.

It had not been easy, learning how to be loved.

Up ahead, Phoenix made his way back to the campsite. She'd seen him gut fish before, had done it beside him for countless hours. He was quick and efficient. He walked toward her in no time, backlit by the setting sun, a large filet in each hand.

Sev had sharpened some sticks and had them at the ready. She'd never cooked over an open fire before, had never really indulged in food beyond ration packs before meeting Phoenix, but Phoenix had taught her the beauty of simple pleasures, had introduced her to the luxury of tasting good food in a beautiful place.

"Are the skewers ready, sweet mouse?"

She nodded, handing them over. He speared each filet and handed one to Sev. "Just a kiss of heat will do," he instructed. "The flesh will tender in little time."

Sev held her meal over the fire, listening to the crackle of the flame, the pop and sizzle of the fish cooking. Phoenix sat across from her, doing the same.

The shadows cast by the fire danced over his face, painting his profile in shifting shades of light and dark. He felt her gaze and met it, smiling.

"After we partake of this delicious meal, we can retire to our sleeping bags," Phoenix said. "The stars are clear, and the breeze is cool. After our bellies are full, we'll want for nothing."

Sev smiled to herself, her eyes falling to where the fish hovered over the fire, close to being done. A swell of pride surged through her. She had provided, for once, instead of Phoenix. She had caught their supper.

"Thank you," she said, feeling oddly emotional. "I really like camping, Daddy."

Phoenix tested his fish by digging into its flaky flesh, then turned the stick over so the flames would lick its other side. "It's my pleasure, little mouse. You've worked hard. You've earned a little time away."

After the fish was done and they had eaten, they settled in for the night. They lay on their backs, the fire between them, staring up at the clear night sky.

"Tell me a story?" Sev asked him. She was close to sleep, warm in her sleeping bag with the fire burning low. The only sound was the crashing of the waves against the shore, the dry rattle of the palm fronds above them.

Phoenix shifted on his left side so he could see her across the fire. "Well, you've heard tell of me on a boat already, but what I never told you was what happened one night, far out into the ocean. Strangest thing I've ever seen, or nearest."

Sev turned to face him, still bundled in her sleeping bag. Her eyes were intent. "What happened?"

"One man I was working with had a son, probably around your age. We had been pulling nets all night long. We were tired...dead on our feet. Well, the boat hit a wave—now this was a massive wave, fifteen foot at least—and a wall of water came down and deposited a fish right there on the deck. When I tell you it was the largest fish I ever saw, you'll not find me guilty of exaggeration. It was two men across and maybe three as long."

Sev leaned in, her head resting on one of her hands. "What did you do?"

"Well, it wasn't what I did, but what the fish did. Remember the man with the son? Well, after the fish arrived, placed there by an act of nature none of us could begin to fathom, the man couldn't find him. We searched everywhere. Meanwhile, the fish is flopping on the deck, struggling to get to the water again. It finally moved enough for us to get a look at it—and it was dark, mind you— but when we did, all we could see was a foot sticking out from under the great fish. The boy's foot. The fish had crushed him beneath."

"For Drek's sake," Sev said, riveted. "Was he dead?"

Phoenix nodded soberly. "And more than. We had to cut the fish off him in pieces. By the time we got a good look at him, it was nearly sunrise."

Phoenix lay back to look at the stars again. "Terrible way to go…flattened by a fish."

Sev flipped onto her back, the breath rushing out of her. The story had exhilarated her; she was strangely giddy. She started laughing and found she couldn't stop. "Phoenix," she asked between fits of laughter. "Did you make that up?"

He chuckled. "By Drek's own hand, I'm telling the truth." He sighed, still listening to Sev's occasional giggle. He grew quiet, a soft smile on his face.

"I love to hear you laugh, little mouse."

Her giggles subsided. The wind died down, and the rustle of the palms faded into the sound of the waves.

"Mouse?" Phoenix asked after a while. He was almost sure she was asleep, having been silent for so long.

"Yes, Dad?"

"Tell me about school."

Sev stretched, scooting down further into her sleeping bag. "I tell you every day, Daddy."

He nodded, though she couldn't see. "Humor your old man, would you?"

Sev smiled. "This week we're learning about famous artists from Dobani. And I started a painting…my first one. It's a value study. I thought we could hang it in the house when I'm done."

"Of course," Phoenix assured her, wholly interested now. "Anywhere you like, little mouse. And when we run out of space for your creations, why, we'll just build another house."

Sev huffed. "Don't want another house," she protested. "Besides, it will take me a long time to cover everything. And some won't be good. Those will just be for practice."

Phoenix pursed his lips. "What about your writing?"

"I'm finishing my old stories. The ones about *Nautica*. But I'm adding some new stuff too. And some illustrations. The art teacher is helping me."

Phoenix made a pleased sort of sound. "That's fine, Sev. I'm so proud."

Sev turned over to face him where he lay, looking up at the stars. "I know you are Daddy. It makes me want to work hard, because I know you're proud."

They fell silent for a few moments. Sev could tell something was on Phoenix's mind, but she didn't push him. She was getting drowsy when she heard him shift in the sleeping bag, turning toward her.

"What if I helped at school? Just a day or two a week. Would that…bother you, little mouse?"

Sev's mouth fell open. Unbidden, images of her father at school flashed before her eyes. She had trouble picturing it. "What would you do?" She asked him.

"Help in the library. Or the gardens. I might even substitute sometimes. It wouldn't be every day, Sev, and I wouldn't hover…I want you to have your own space…your own life. I know I'm being a selfish man, but I miss you, sweet mouse. I'm afraid I find myself quite lost without you."

Sev hadn't replied, and he was sure he had overstepped. He looked up then and saw her standing over him. She nudged his sleeping bag with her foot. "Scooch over, Daddy."

Phoenix smiled, unzipping the sleeping bag and opening the flap. Sev edged in beside him, the spot warm from his body heat. She put an arm over his middle, her face pressed against his shoulder. "You really mean it? You're coming to school?"

"Yes, little mouse," Phoenix breathed. "If it's amenable to you. Just to make myself useful. I've done far too much piddling these past few weeks. Idle hands, and what not."

She pressed into his side, her fingers digging into his T-shirt. "That's the best news I've heard," Sev whispered. "School will be perfect now…you were the only thing missing."

Phoenix's heart flipped. "I won't interfere, dear heart. I know you'll be busy. I just—"

His words were cut off when Sev pressed a hand across his mouth. "We can have lunch together," she said, enthusiasm lilting her voice. "Out on the grass, as the weather permits. And you can meet my friends."

Phoenix pressed his lips against her hand where it still covered his mouth, and she laughed, removing it. "I can't wait to go back to school now, knowing that sometimes you'll be there, too."

Phoenix blinked back tears. "Then it's a done deal." He moved his arm to press her against him, and she settled her face against his neck. "Who knows, I might learn a thing or two myself, if any more knowledge will fit into this thick skull of mine."

Sev laughed, feather-light against Phoenix's skin. She turned her face up to look at the stars, at the pale moon that hung low over the water. "It's so pretty, isn't it?" Sev observed. "I've never slept like this, out in the open. I'm glad we came here."

Phoenix brushed his hand over her arm, giving it a little squeeze. "Me too, little mouse. Me too."

Dawn broke over the horizon in deep shades of red. Phoenix stood frowning at the water's edge, his hair whipping in the wind that had picked up just overnight.

Sev had put away their sleeping bags and sat by the vestiges of last night's fire rummaging through her pack. She withdrew her journal, turned to a clean page, and began sketching.

They would need to leave soon, Phoenix thought. He remembered what his shipmates long ago had told him about a red sky so early in the day. A storm was brewing. From the depth of that slash of color on the horizon, it would be a big one.

He stood studying the waves until the sun came up in earnest and the red receded from view.

Sev came to stand behind him, her journal tucked under one arm. She slipped an arm around his waist. "Where did you go?" she asked.

Phoenix smiled, rubbing his hand over her hair and letting it settle around her shoulders. "Nowhere, little mouse. I'm right here."

They languished for a while on the sandbar, Sev sketching and swimming, and Phoenix watching the weather. It was past midday by the time they packed up and headed out, Phoenix navigating them through the now-rough waters. There was something coming; he could tell from the unseasonably cool stream of air cutting across the water, the way the clouds hung low. The usually placid sea was dark, the surface clouded and restless.

Sev approached him at the bow, coming to a stop at his left shoulder. She'd taken off her hat now that the clouds had rolled in, blocking the sun. "What's going on, Phoenix? The air feels...strange."

He pursed his lips. "Some sort of storm," he answered her. "But don't worry, mouse. We'll be home before it gets too bad."

She settled into the chair next to him, looking out over the increasingly angry sea. The dark clouds hung low; the air was oppressive. A lightning bolt flashed in the distance. It seemed very close to shore.

They fell into a heavy silence. Phoenix steered the boat, tension framing his shoulders, while Sev sat beside him, watchful as electricity lit the sky.

By the time they had made it to the pier, it was growing dark. The rain came soon after, just in time for them to dock and disembark. Fat droplets spattered the view pane of the transport, slowly at first and then rapid-fire, leaving a watery film behind. The onslaught was torrential by the time they made it to the house, thunder and lightning splitting the night sky.

They dashed to the door, Phoenix's jacket over Sev's head, and once inside, they toed off their wet shoes. They both went to their bedrooms to change.

Phoenix came out in sweatpants and a T-shirt, his hair still wet. He settled in the kitchen, making a few sandwiches for them. Sev met him there, moving up behind him and snaking a hand around his waist. She pressed her cheek between his shoulder blades.

"I hate we had to cut our trip short," she said. "It was fun, Daddy."

Phoenix hummed affectionately, patting her hand where it lay against his abdomen. He took their sandwiches and walked into the living room, stopping at the low table there. "It doesn't have to end," Phoenix said as thunder rattled the windows. "Go get the blankets; we can camp right here."

Sev smiled, heading to the hall closet. She had just opened the door when another round of thunder shook the house, and the lights blinked out.

A cold dread spread through her, the sudden darkness almost smothering. It was black as pitch, the moon hidden by the storm. "Dad?" she asked, her voice timid.

There was a stumbling sound, a muttered curse, and then a beam of light flicked on. "I'm coming, mouse," she could hear Phoenix say from the living room. The light swung in her direction, and she released a shaky breath.

Sev was standing there, the blankets clutched to her chest. There was a haunted look on her face. "C'mere babydoll," Phoenix soothed. He was holding a small flashlight in his left hand and offered her his prosthetic. She took it gratefully, shifting the blankets under one arm. He tugged her forward, and she finally uprooted herself from her spot in the hall.

Phoenix could feel her tremble, and it worried him. He squeezed her hand as they passed by her darkened bedroom. "Want me to get your journal, little mouse? You can use the flashlight."

She mumbled something, and he stood her by the door. "You stay right here, sweetheart. I'll be right back."

Phoenix made quick work of getting the journal; he knew where she kept it, there propped on her bookshelf. He slipped out into the hall and gathered her up. She was shaking.

"What's wrong, baby?" He turned the flashlight on her, and she closed her eyes against the onslaught. She had furrowed her brows, and her mouth turned down. "Let's get settled in," he soothed, taking her by the arm. "I made us some sandwiches."

He led her to the dark fireplace, and they settled on the floor in the nook behind the table. Phoenix took the blankets and wrapped Sev up despite the growing warmth of the dark house. She shivered once, and he tucked his arm around her.

"Why'd the power go out, Daddy?" Her voice was small, tremulous. Phoenix tightened his arm around her.

"It's the storm, little mouse. That's all. They'll likely be out all night."

He heard her sniff and clicked on the flashlight, standing it upright on the table for ambient light. Tears shined in silver threads down both her cheeks.

He pressed his face to the top of her head, an ache forming in the pit of his stomach to see her so upset. "Talk to me, Sev."

She shook her head, but did not pull away from him. If anything, she drew closer, seeking his warmth and comfort against the words she could not say.

He didn't push her; he simply held her. Lightning lit the sky outside, illuminating the inside of the house in intermittent flashes. The wind raged, and the rain beat against the roof. She let her head drop against Phoenix's shoulder and closed her eyes.

"It was a long time ago. We were planetside on a job. I don't even remember where. Del had rented a house, but we were out of credits. I didn't know. When I asked him why there was no food, he snapped at me…told me it was not for me to worry about. He told me that if I worked harder, then maybe I wouldn't be hungry. Then, I woke up one day and there were no lights."

Phoenix tightened his grip on her without even realizing it. He took a sharp breath, willing himself to stay calm. Tears stung his eyes. He blinked them away, pressing a kiss to her head. He stroked his thumb against her upper arm, silently encouraging her to continue.

"It was so dark that night," she continued, her voice watery. "It was cold, too. Del left me there alone. When I asked him where he was going, he wouldn't say."

She turned her face up to him, and he could just make it out in the low light. "I was scared, Phoenix. I was little and I didn't understand." Her lip quivered, and he turned to cup her cheek. "It was so dark," she repeated, her face a tumult of emotions. "I didn't know what to do."

176

Phoenix hugged her close. Rage threatened to overcome him. His thoughts turned toward violence, as if he needed one more reason to fly back to Terra Firma, find Del's spore-ridden bones and kill him again. He took a steadying breath, waiting to speak until his teeth had receded, until his claws retracted into the gentle hands he'd only ever shown Sev.

"I'm here now, sweet mouse. I'm here. The lights will come back on again, the storm will pass, but until then, you have me."

Sev pressed her face against him. A strangled sob choked her throat. "I tried so hard," she cried. "I worked. I tried to be good. I made myself into what I thought he wanted, and it was never enough."

He stroked her hair, tears running freely down his face. The wind howled and there was the deafening sound of splitting wood. They must've lost a palm, he thought distantly, but he cared not. All that mattered was Sev.

He pressed his lips to her fevered cheek. "You listen to me, little mouse. You're good. You're better than good. You're so perfect I can't believe you sometimes." He cradled her face in his hands. "You're my daughter and you're enough. Nothing can change that. Ever."

Sev pressed her forehead against his, collecting herself. "I wish I could've known my mom," she murmured. "Del never told me much about her. Only that she was kind." She sniffed and reached up to wipe her eyes. Phoenix beat her to it, swiping away her tears with his thumb. She pulled away, meeting his eyes. "You think she would've loved me? I mean, had she lived?"

It sobered him. "Oh, mouse, she loved you. You must believe. How could she not, as sweet a babe as you most certainly were?"

Sev smiled, and Phoenix reached up to caress her face. "You wanna work in your journal? You can show me what you've been sketching."

Phoenix moved the light closer to where Sev sat and handed her the journal. She took it gratefully, her eyes still red-rimmed from crying. Something tugged at his chest, his previous ire at her long-dead father evaporating under the warmth of her gaze. Sev opened her journal and handed it to Phoenix.

She smiled shyly, seeking his approval. Images of their trip to the sandbar filled the journal. The boat, the fire, the water. And there were multiple sketches of Phoenix.

In one, he was laughing, his blond patch rendered in white charcoal, his brown eyes crinkled in mirth. Phoenix's prosthetic, every intricate line and angle of it in different poses. Phoenix standing by the water, his hands in his pockets.

In one sketch, Sev had drawn herself, her headphones on, sitting in the bay window of her room.

Phoenix traced his fingers over it lovingly, careful not to smudge the pencil. "Can I…can I have this one, little mouse? To put by my bed," he explained.

Sev nodded eagerly, her eyes lighting. "Sure Dad," she agreed. It made her feel warm, that he wanted a picture of her. It was the first time anyone had ever asked her for something she'd created. That it was Phoenix did not come as a surprise.

They sat there under the blanket, thumbing through her journal until the storm passed and the sun came up, peeking out from behind the scattered clouds.

By midday, they had power. As soon as they'd had some breakfast, they walked out into their yard, surveying what the storm had left behind.

They'd lost a tree, as Phoenix figured, missing the house by just a few feet. *Drek's provisions*, he thought to himself, grateful for no one being injured and for their little house being intact. Sev pulled him down to the beach, her face falling when she reached the end of the boardwalk.

The little shade Phoenix had built her was gone, swallowed by the sea.

She ran out to where it usually stood, face crestfallen. The beach itself had transformed, sand whittled away to the dunes by the churning water. Driftwood and shells littered the beach, and gulls picked at the small fish washed up there, stranded by the overnight storm. Phoenix came to stand behind her, his hand on her shoulder.

"The shore will heal," he said. "And your shade can be rebuilt. Like new. Better than new." He reached for her hand. "Whatever we come against, we'll face it together."

Sev smiled, the sun hitting her cheek and lighting her hair in a way that belied last night's turmoil. She turned, motioning for him to follow. Sev peered over her shoulder, catching his eyes. He smiled at her, his gaze soft, watching as she stepped onto the boardwalk.

"I'm right here, little mouse," he said as he followed her back into the house, leaving the storm and everything else behind them.

CHAPTER 17

There was much to do. The previous night's storm had left the yard windswept and full of debris. But first, he had to wake up a bit.

Phoenix ran a hand over his mussed hair. He was not wearing his prosthetic…he rarely put it on before midday, and it was nearing sunup. It was rare that he was up before Sev. He had never been a morning person, but he hadn't slept well, plagued by unsettling dreams.

He moved through the kitchen on autopilot, preparing his morning cup. Sev had tried to get him to stop drinking it, but it was an old vice, and he liked the taste.

He measured the water and then the grounds. He set it to brew and walked out to check the mail; the route was new, and checking the mail was one of Sev's new favorite things.

"It's so terrestrial," she had said to him, sounding much older than her years. She was thirteen now. He could scarcely believe it.

He opened the door to the mailbox. Inside, there was a single letter.

He took it without a glance and hurried inside to pour his cup. He sat by the big kitchen window and was three sips in before he flipped the letter over.

Sev's name was on the address.

Phoenix frowned. He wondered who would know Sev well enough to send her correspondence. Phoenix knew the names of all her friends and their parents besides. He was unfamiliar with the sender, and there was no return address.

With a momentary hesitation, he opened it.

He read a few lines, his morning cup forgotten. His throat constricted, and a terrible dread came over him. He hadn't known this type of dread for years, and it rattled him. With shaky hands, he folded the letter envelope and all and put it in his pocket.

He sat at the window in the kitchen, watching the morning sun shining over the sea, lost in thought.

Sev walked into the kitchen some time later. She was still in her pajamas. She walked straight to the refrigerator and poured herself some juice.

"You slept in," Phoenix said. His discontent from earlier was still present, though he tried to hide it.

Sev canted her head at him. "And you're up early." She narrowed her eyes, ever perceptive. "You ok Dad?"

He managed a small smile. "Right as rain, sweet mouse." Though he was far from it. He cleared his throat, gesturing out the window.

She walked up to stand beside him. "We've got a lot of work to do," she said as she glanced out over the yard.

Phoenix nodded, thankful for her changing the subject. "That we do. That felled palm will need cutting. The rest we'll tidy directly. We'll get it done."

Sev hummed. She patted his shoulder before finishing her juice, walked to the sink and deposited her empty glass. She stood there, both hands on the counter, looking at Phoenix.

"You sure you're ok?"

Phoenix's eyes sting. The letter burned in his pocket, an accusation of his deceit. He'd never lied to Sev; withheld information, yes, but never outright lied.

"Yes, dear heart," he told her before he could stop himself. "Couldn't be better."

They worked in the yard in companionable silence. Phoenix took care of the palm, chopping it into sections and stacking it to dry by the firepit for fuel. He gradually forgot about the letter.

Sev was gathering small branches and tossing them in a burn pile. She looked up, and a transport truck was rattling down the driveway. A man was driving, accompanied by a woman in the cab. There were several people standing in the truck bed.

Phoenix tensed, and Sev moved instinctively near her father. The driver got out of the truck and held up his hand in greeting.

"Hello, neighbor! I'm Jax. My wife and I live just down the beach. Quite a storm, huh? We're here to help with the clean-up."

Phoenix relaxed, releasing a breath he didn't realize he had been holding. He extended his left hand out of habit, and the man shook it enthusiastically. Jax motioned to the others in the back of the truck, and they climbed down. They all held rakes and other tools.

Phoenix ran a hand through his hair. "We're much obliged," Phoenix began. "It's not been much trouble...I hate to put you good folks out."

Jax waved him off. "Think nothing of it," he said amicably and wandered off to follow the others.

The last person climbed down from the truck. She seemed vaguely familiar, and Phoenix wondered where he'd seen her before.

The woman was carrying a toolbox and wearing coveralls. She had her blue hair up in a messy bun, but a few tendrils fell around her face. As she got closer, she winked at Phoenix. "Hello again, handsome."

Sev stifled a giggle, elbowing her father in the ribs. He swallowed nervously. "Excuse me, gentle lady, but have we met before?"

The woman offered her hand, and Phoenix took it. "I'm Pearla," she said. "You and your sweet daughter came into my store a while back...bought some clothes for the off-season." She flashed her eyes. They were kohl lined and as blue as her hair.

Phoenix blushed furiously. "Oh. You, uh...you live around here?"

Pearla smiled, her red lips glossy, and adjusted the tools in her hand. "The outskirts," she said. "But not far." She breezed by him to join the others already

183

in the middle of cleaning up, but not before patting Phoenix on the shoulder. It warmed him in a way he was wholly unfamiliar with.

Sev, Phoenix, and their helpful neighbors had their yard cleared and raked in no time, leaving the steppingstone path smooth, the stubby grasses and sandy surface once again visible and warmed by the sun. The carpenters among them were out on the beach, helping Phoenix rebuild Sev's shade. It would be better than before, as promised, with a little shake roof and driftwood benches to seat three people at least.

It was sunset before the work was done, but it was well and finished in half the time it would've taken for Sev and Phoenix to do it themselves. They all sat around the firepit, burning the last of the storm debris. Some neighbors played music on an instrument Sev had never seen before. Others sang along. There were drinks and snacks enough for everyone.

This feeling was unfamiliar to Sev. She had never had anyone other than Phoenix, not even Del, with whom she could feel safe and welcome. She suspected Phoenix felt the same. This feeling was community, she realized, and she and Phoenix had found it on Dobani.

Phoenix stood as the last song finished and raised his glass. "To our new friends," he declared, "who just happen to be excellent neighbors."

He glanced at Sev, her face reflected in the firelight, and realized she was thinking the same thing.

"I also propose, being that Celebration Day is just a month or so away, we all meet here again for some proper food. Sev's garden will have produced by then, and there will be plenty for all."

This announcement brought a smattering of applause and many toasts to their hosts, Sev and Phoenix. Sev moved closer to her father, the night growing chill. He put his arm around her. Music and laughter surrounded her. It made her feel full in a way she had never been before.

The days grew warmer. Sev dutifully tended her garden, checking on it every day before she went to school. One morning, Phoenix met her at their transport, dressed in his best shirt and pants and his hair gelled back.

She eyed him curiously. "You look fancy today. What gives?"

He feigned offense. "Do I need another excuse to look good other than escorting a fine, upstanding young lady such as yourself?"

She rolled her eyes, making him smile. "I suppose I am caught out," he said. "Today's my first day working in the office. I wanted to look my best."

Sev's eyes widened. "Really Dad? You mean you'll be at school today?"

He nodded and opened the door for her. "Nowhere else."

Sev could barely contain her excitement on the way to school. When it was time to walk into the building, she grabbed Phoenix's prosthetic hand, pleased when he squeezed back.

Several students glanced their way, but their eyes didn't linger. Sev waved to some of her friends before they pushed through the large double doors of the school.

It was warm within, the morning sun streaming through the skylight. Phoenix had not been here since they toured the school, but it was just as he remembered.

"I guess this is my stop, little mouse," Phoenix said as he paused outside the office entrance. "I'll see you at lunch?"

Sev reached up and hugged him. "You bet Dad," she promised. "Have a good day."

He stood there until she was out of sight, then he walked into the office to speak to the supervisor of volunteers.

Sev and her friends were already waiting for him when he made it to the dining hall. She waved him over, motioning for him to sit opposite her.

The cafeteria was bright and homey. Different food stations stood to the right. Drink choices to the left. Paintings by the art students adorned the walls, creating an inviting and comfortable atmosphere for students to have their lunch.

He settled at the table, nodding along as Sev introduced him to her friends. Her friends were polite, inquisitive, and very interested in his mechanical arm.

"How is working in the office?" Sev asked him once they'd finished eating. "Are you very busy?"

Phoenix considered. "A trifle," he replied. "There's mail to sort. Messages to deliver. Packages to receive, too." He canted his head, gesturing to Sev and her friends. "Did you have exams today?"

A girl with bright red hair chimed in. "We had critiques of our paintings. Mine got high marks. So did Sev's." She quieted, and Phoenix could almost hear the wheels in her mind turning.

"Did you lose your own arm on the green planet? Sev told me you were there."

"Jesse!" Sev interjected, looking scandalized. She blushed, unsure of what to say.

Phoenix smiled patiently. "Well, that's a fine question, Jesse," he began congenially. He tapped the tabletop with a mechanical finger, unconsciously making a point. "But I did not. Lose my arm on Terra Firma, that is."

"Oh," she replied in response to him, but Phoenix could tell she wanted to say more.

On the way home, it rained. Sev was uncharacteristically quiet, the heavy downpour creating a blanket of white noise between them.

"Phoenix? How *did* you lose your arm?"

Phoenix gripped the wheel a little tighter, considering his response. He wanted to be truthful, but he also considered his old life a dead thing. Something obsolete.

"I was dishonest," he said. "And I paid for it."

186

Sev seemed deeply troubled by that. "You lost your arm because you lied?"

He swallowed, suddenly very aware of the letter, of the secret he was keeping. "I cheated," he clarified. "At a game of tokens. I stood to lose a lot of money, so I cheated."

Sev frowned but said nothing. The rain beat down, the humid silence between them deafening.

"I'm not proud of it," he added. "And it was wrong. Do you understand?"

She sat quietly. "Yes Daddy," she said. "I'm sorry that happened, though."

The rain beat down on the roof of the transport, and he thought about what she'd said. "It's ok, mouse," he reassured her. Then, so quiet she barely heard him, "I deserved it."

CHAPTER 18

School was out for a time, and Sev had extra hours to fuss over her garden, to swim in the rapidly warming sea, and to read.

Phoenix had time to think.

Sev was growing up; not too many years from now, she would have a life of her own. One day, a family. And he would be alone.

It did not vex him being alone. He had spent most of his life as a loner, floating in the Black and drifting along on backwater worlds. But before Sev, he had never known the comfort of companionship. He had grown used to its warmth.

Sev scooted next to him on the couch; she was reading…finally getting to the other *Nautica* books she had ignored in favor of rereading her favorite. He put his artificial arm around her, still able to feel, through the miracle of Dobani medicine, when she shifted against him.

"Want me to read to you?" she asked. He did not respond directly…he was still rather somber from his earlier line of thought.

"What if I went back to school?" Phoenix asked her instead. If it surprised her, she did not show it.

She turned to him, neglecting her book for the moment. "I was wondering when you might," she said. "We've got the time." She smiled at him. "You can be anything you want to be, Phoenix," she encouraged, sounding every bit like he usually did. "You could find a job in the city. In the courts." She quirked her mouth. "Drek knows you love to talk enough."

He made a face, feigning insult. "I only want to be your dad," he replied. "For as long as you need me to be."

She furrowed her brow, her mouth turned down. She regarded him seriously. "I'll always need you, Phoenix."

She said nothing else. She turned back to her book, contemplative, now, as Phoenix was.

He thought about it for some time until Sev was heavy against him, her breathing slow and even, and the book open in her lap.

The garden was ready. After weeks of Sev watching the fledgling plants, after pulling weeds and watering and fertilizing and cultivating the soil, the branches of her plants were heavy with produce ripe for the taking.

She took the day off from school, with permission. She and Phoenix found themselves one dew-laden morning bent over the rows of vegetables, picking those that were ready and checking those that had a day or two of growing left. By midday, they had two baskets filled to the brim with colorful leafy greens and tubers, beans and root vegetables and herbs.

Sev and Phoenix washed the harvest carefully, refrigerating most and laying the herbs in the sun to dry. Phoenix reserved some greens and tubers for lunch, withdrawing some protein from the fridge that would pair nicely. He was in the middle of preparation when Sev walked back into the kitchen, changed from her soil-covered overalls and fresh from the shower.

"Were you serious about Celebration Day? About having everyone over for dinner?"

Phoenix stopped stirring and laid the spoon on the counter. "I was indeed, little mouse. Cook a big meal, have everyone over. It will be a grand time."

He turned the burner low and replaced the lid. "Tell you what; you make the calls. We'll do it this week…our own Celebration Day dinner. How about it?"

Sev nodded, eager to get to work. "Should we decorate?"

Phoenix inclined his head. "I'll leave it to your capable hands," he replied.

Sev busied herself with decorating their little house. She picked flowers from the field down the road and made garlands for the doors. She set the table in the kitchen with fruit and candles, and she boiled herbs and berries to fill the house with the sweet smell of the harvest.

Phoenix bought a roast at the butcher, and he and Sev pressed it with spices and herbs before setting it to stew in the oven.

The neighbors came bearing gifts, elixirs and desserts, some sweet treats Sev had never seen before.

Pearla arrived last in a cream-colored coat and a sweeping yellow dress, her hair coiled around her face. She handed Sev a basket of fruit and immediately complimented the décor.

"That's all Sev's doin'," Phoenix interrupted. "She's the mastermind behind all of this, to be true."

Pearla smiled. "Then thank you, Sev, for the wonderful invitation and for all the effort you've gone to. I haven't been to a party like this in quite a while."

Sev blushed, standing close to her father. She favored her with a small smile.

Phoenix straightened, remembering his manners. "May I take your coat?"

He helped Pearla shrug off her coat and left it on a hook by the door. They walked into the kitchen together where the rest of the guests were waiting, and Phoenix pulled out her chair. The kitchen was warm and vibrant, with the heady scent of roast and vegetables and the sweet spice of dessert and wine.

After their meal and plenty of laughter and conversation, their guests left under a clear and starry night, departing for home. They had helped tidy the dishes, so there was little to do but put away the leftovers.

191

Sev sank into the chair in the living room. She had kicked off her shoes but still wore the cotton dress she'd donned for dinner.

Phoenix walked by, passing behind her. He ruffled her hair from its careful style, and she scowled good-naturedly. "You did good, mouse. I think they'll remember tonight for a long time yet."

She sighed. "Thanks Daddy. Dinner was delicious. I'm glad we could share with our friends."

He hummed his agreement. He settled on the couch adjacent, working the fingers of his prosthetic.

"I think it needs adjusting," he remarked, a slight frown on his face. "You mind grabbing the tool for me? It's in the drawer of my bedside table."

Sev stood and padded into her father's bedroom. She was gone for a while. When she returned, she didn't have the tool.

"Dad?"

Phoenix looked up at the haunted sound of his daughter's voice. She was standing in the doorway holding the letter addressed to her. She had a stricken expression on her face.

Terror gripped him, and he floundered for words. He stood, holding his hands out to her.

"Sev, baby, listen—"

"Don't," she warned him, her voice hard. Her lips quivered, and tears spilled over her lashes. She held the letter out between them. "I can't believe you hid this. My mother's sister wants to meet me, and you didn't tell me?" She looked at him with something akin to disgust. "How could you?"

Phoenix approached her, and she took two steps back.

"I want to see her."

She sounded so broken, so betrayed, that he had to look away.

"How could you?" she repeated, this time with venom. She was trembling slightly, the letter still clutched in her hand.

Tears stung his eyes. "I only wanted to protect you, mouse. We—we don't even know her. She could be anybody. And you're so young. *Please.*"

She was listening with narrowed eyes, her body rigid. "That wasn't your decision to make," she said, softer now, but still angry.

192

Phoenix wiped his palm on his pants. He was sweating, and he was sick to his stomach. "I'm your father, Sev. I must do what's best for you. You know that."

She frowned, averting her eyes briefly before staring him down. "You're not my real father," she said, and it hit him squarely in the chest.

It was as if someone had knocked the breath from his lungs. He opened his mouth to rebuke her, to tell her to go to her room, but she had already walked away.

CHAPTER 19

Phoenix didn't sleep. The silence broadcasting from his daughter's bedroom was deafening, filling their home with the static of unspoken words. He'd never felt this way; he'd never been so bereft of someone who was under the same roof.

Sunrise came with Phoenix standing outside Sev's bedroom door, fist suspended in an aborted knock. He vacillated between announcing the vigil he'd kept outside her door for the past hour or turning the knob and going in anyway. He opted to knock.

There was no answer. In fact, the house seemed empty. His blood ran cold. When he opened the door, there was no resistance.

Sev was gone.

She'd made her bed, her stuffed sar-cat resting on her pillow. She'd packed a bag; there were missing clothes in her dresser. There was no note, no sign of her anywhere.

The cold grip of panic descended on him. He bolted from the room, calling for her in every corner of the house. He went out into the yard and down to the beach, fighting against the logical conclusion that Sev was gone...she had left him to meet someone she didn't even know. She was alone and angry with him.

He was sick. He made his way to Sev's shade and sat down on the driftwood bench. It was cool from the night air and from a season that was not yet blistered with constant heat. Phoenix pressed his palm against the handprints there, his and hers, just like on the skiff.

He needed to call someone. He went back into the house, driven by a renewed purpose. Phoenix grabbed the holopad and keyed in a few frequencies.

He would find her, he resolved. He would bring her back home. She could be mad at him…she could even hate him. But he was going to keep her safe.

Sev listened to her holopad trill yet again. Phoenix's face, tanned by the sun and delicately lined even in hologram, hovered above the pad until the notification stopped and it disappeared again. She couldn't answer him. She didn't know what to say.

The transport barge was large, larger than the one she and Del had taken to Terra Firma so long ago. The time she had met Phoenix, when her life had taken a dramatic turn.

She opened the last communication she had received from her Aunt Mara, re-reading it. Mara lived on Merren, a star system away. She had already told her so much about her mother…things Sev had lived her whole life craving to know. Stories about her growing up, how similar she was to Sev. Mara had sent her holograms of a fair-haired, lanky teenager not unlike herself, with kind eyes that held a mischievous glint.

Phoenix was wrong to hide this from her.

Knowledge of her mother was something she deserved. He had no right to deny her that. That he did it to protect her was a flimsy, vague excuse. Sev could take care of herself; she had done it her whole life.

But she missed him deeply. And beneath her anger and despite the newfound excitement of learning about her mother, she was ashamed of what she'd said to him.

Sev brushed her thumb over her father's contact information. His image popped up again, eyes crinkled and smiling, Drek's kiss standing up against the wind the day she'd taken the photo. She pressed her head against the view pane, letting the quiet of the transport lull her into an uneasy sleep. Her father's hologram winked out on its own, forgotten on the seat beside her.

Pearla knocked on the door of the little house, expecting Sev to come bounding out to answer it with all her usual enthusiasm. But when no one came, and there wasn't a sound except the crash of waves against the shore, she pushed her way inside.

The house was dark, not at all the cozy, inviting place it had been a few days before. There was no sign of anyone being home, despite the transport being parked outside.

She popped into the kitchen; it was dark there, too, and uncharacteristically unkempt. A dish towel lay discarded on the counter, and there were dirty bowls in the sink.

She found her way to the back bedroom, and it was black as pitch. Someone lay under the covers, though she couldn't tell who. She turned on the bedside lamp, casting the person in stark relief against the rest of the room.

It was Phoenix. He had pulled the blanket up to his chin, and his eyes were closed.

"Oh goodness," Pearla began. "If I had known you were sick, honey, I would've brought you something." She placed the back of her hand against his forehead, testing his temperature. "What can I do for you, Phoenix? How can I help?"

Phoenix opened his eyes, blinking slightly at the intrusion of light. They were red and puffy from crying. Pearla immediately knew something was very wrong.

"What is it, dear? And where is Sev?"

Phoenix frowned, squeezing his eyes shut. "She's gone," he rasped. "And it's all my fault."

Pearla patted his shoulder. He wasn't wearing his prosthetic. She had never seen him without it, but it did not bother her like she thought it might. "What do you mean 'gone'?" she asked. "How is she gone?"

He opened his eyes and met her gaze. She was so sincere, so genuinely trying to help, that he raised up on his elbow and maneuvered into a sitting position.

She waited for him to speak, sitting on the side of the bed while he found the words. He was in a disheveled state, hair uncombed and clothes in disarray.

Phoenix told her everything, even the circumstances of their meeting. He told her about Del and what happened on Terra Firma, about all they had been through.

He even told her about losing his arm, all that time ago, and what kind of person he used to be. When he finished talking, he was spent…rung out.

Pearla sat digesting it all. "And you've called Dobani authorities? What did they say?"

He wiped his hand over his face. "They're checking transport records," he answered. "But they want me to wait until she contacts me, besides." He sought her face, absolutely stricken. "I don't think I can do that, Pearla. I need to do something."

She placed her hand over his and gave it a squeeze. "We'll find her," she reassured him with a smile. "We'll get her back. Any idea where she went to meet this person?"

Phoenix shook his head. "There was no return address on the letter. Just a name. There was a comm channel listed, but I can't remember it."

She nodded. Eventually, Pearla coaxed him out of bed. She tidied the kitchen and living room while he showered. She prepared a light lunch; by the time he had showered and changed, she had their plates at the table.

Phoenix ducked his head, quite abashed. "You shouldn't have gone out of your way now."

She shook her head. "It was nothing, hon. I came here to thank you for such a lovely evening the other night. And it looks like I got to do that, after all."

Phoenix nodded, pressing his lips together. He was grateful for her kindness, even if he couldn't express it. Before he could say anything, there was a notification on the holopad.

He opened the message. It was from the authorities on Dobani.

He read for a few moments. His hand trembled, and he dropped the holopad with a clatter. He turned to Pearla, tears in his eyes.

"This woman is challenging the adoption," he stammered, his voice shaky. "She claims to be the rightful guardian."

CHAPTER 20

When Sev awoke, it was so dark outside she couldn't tell if it was day or night. Merren was a dark place with a short solar cycle, making the days brief and the nights eternal.

She walked into the living room where her Aunt Mara was smoking stim sticks and watching the holographs.

"I want to talk to my dad," Sev said. Her face was puffy, but to her surprise, her voice didn't tremble. "I need to. I left without saying goodbye, and I know he's worried."

Mara tapped the ash of her stim stick into a little dish, then brought it to her lips again. "You'll see him at the court date," she said, "when the courts absolve that fraudulent adoption and turn guardianship over to me."

Sev pulled her lip between her teeth. Her adoption was *not* fraudulent. She had asked Phoenix herself if he would be her father. They had gone to Dobani Proper. The papers hung over the fireplace in their little home. It was legal. It was *real*. Afterwards, he had taken her to the hot springs; she remembered it like it was yesterday.

She began to tear up. Mara had behaved harshly in the week she'd stayed with her. She told her less and less about her mother; in fact, she got angry when she mentioned it now. Aunt Mara wanted her to stay with her permanently. Sev couldn't fathom it.

Mara looked at her and tutted. "It's ok," she crooned, her voice saccharin. "Why don't you go into the kitchen and get yourself something to eat? You didn't have supper."

Sev sniffed, jamming her hands into her pockets. Mara had taken her holopad, claiming it would be a distraction for her and over-stimulating. She wished more than anything that she could talk to her dad. The ache to see his face again, to hear his voice, was worse than the hollow ache in her belly.

The kitchen had little to offer. It was not the cozy little alcove stocked full of fresh foods and yummy treats that Sev was accustomed to at home. There was no Phoenix there, cooking at the stove. There was nothing cooked at all.

The pantry held some prepackaged foods. She hadn't eaten them since she left Terra Firma. With a frown, she grabbed one of the most appetizing ones and tore open the foil pack. She didn't bother with a fork or water to rehydrate it. She shook the dry bits into her mouth and chewed.

Sev walked back through the living room to her bedroom, the food pack in hand. Mara sniffed, her eyes narrowed, and her mouth twisted in displeasure. "You eat like space trash, child. At least heat it first."

Sev frowned. She entered her bedroom and closed the door behind her. Before turning off the light, she threw the pack away, half-eaten.

As the court day approached, Phoenix and Pearla pored over the legal documents forwarded by the courts on Merren. The woman, Mara, had claimed blood guardianship of Sev and was petitioning to be the conservator of Sev's credits…her half of the calcet harvest.

250 credits. It was a substantial amount. Phoenix suspected this woman only wanted Sev for her newly accumulated wealth. It angered him. Phoenix would give up all his worldly goods to have his daughter back. He would do more than that.

Just who Mara was, though, was still a mystery to him. Sev's blood relative, maybe, but where had she been all this time?

When the court day arrived, Phoenix dressed in his best shirt and slacks and a new suit coat Pearla had chosen from her shop. She insisted on coming too, and since she was his only friend aside from Sev, he welcomed the company.

Phoenix stood by the transport, waiting for Pearla. She came out of the house wearing a simple green dress. Her blue hair was down along her shoulders, thin braids framing her face.

She stopped in front of him, canting her head in appraisal. "Your servos are still stiff," she intoned quietly, "that's why you couldn't tie your tie." She reached up to adjust the necktie he'd tried to knot for the occasion. He was not used to dressing up; indeed, he was completely out of his element.

She worked on his tie for a few moments, looping it and threading it through his collar until the knot was fashionably intricate.

"There," she announced, proud of her efforts. She straightened the lapels of his jacket. He'd never worn one before, and he was somewhat self-conscious.

"How do I look?" he asked. The days were warmer on Dobani; the tourist season was close at hand. He could feel himself sweating. He wished Sev was here, swimming in the sea. Phoenix felt her loss like another missing limb.

Pearla gazed at him, her eyes bright in the Dobani sun. "You look fetching," she said, giving him a wink. "And very professional." She patted his shoulder, her hand lingering. "You look like a capable father," she added. "Now let's go get your daughter back."

He nodded, determined. They drove off in the transport toward Dobani Proper. Getting to Merren required space travel; it would take half a day's journey to get there.

Phoenix didn't care. Every cell in his body vibrated with anticipation. He would see Sev again. He would talk to her. He could scarcely wait.

The courts building on Merren was an ancient, vaulted steel and stone building built in the old style. It was dark on Merren, and cold. Phoenix couldn't imagine his little girl happy here, with as much as she thrived in the sun.

They pushed through the tall wooden doors; the lobby of the courts was dusty and dated, with poor lighting and hard-looking chairs in the hall.

Phoenix and Pearla took a seat. Phoenix bounced his leg, anxious to see Sev after so long away from her. They sat in nervous anticipation for a long while until Mara walked in with Sev in tow.

Pearla placed a hand on Phoenix's arm, directing his attention down the hall where the two walked toward them.

Phoenix's breath caught in his throat. Sev was thinner; her hair was dull and brushed forward, partially hiding her face. She had her pack on her back and her hands jammed in her pockets.

He took one look at the woman he'd only known as Mara, and it suddenly all made sense.

"Jaden," he gritted out, loud enough for her to hear.

The woman stopped at the name, pushing Sev behind her with her hand. "Hello Phoenix," she purred. "You remember me after all."

He stalked forward, and Sev saw him. Her eyes lit, and she took a step toward him before Jaden pulled her back.

"Not so fast, little girl. Your dad and I have some unfinished business."

Phoenix clenched his teeth. "Let her go Jaden. This has nothing to do with Sev."

She smiled wickedly. "You're right, Phoenix. This is between me and you. But that doesn't change the fact that Sev here is my little niece." She flashed her eyes. "Blood is blood, after all."

Sev glanced up at her father. "Dad? What is she talking about?"

Phoenix regarded his daughter, his gaze softening. "It's ok sweet mouse. We'll work this out."

Jaden laughed harshly. "Never figured you for a softy," she said. "But it doesn't matter. Sev is with me now. Everything that's hers is mine. And there's nothing you can do about it, Phoenix."

She held up papers, and Pearla stood, moving to stand next to Phoenix. "Give me those," she said, her hand going out to grab them.

Jaden's mouth quirked, and she held them out of reach. "Don't think so."

She eyed Pearla, then Phoenix. "You didn't tell Sev and your little girlfriend how you owe me? How I was your partner, and you betrayed me and let me go to prison?" Jaden snarled. "Five long years of my life taken from me!" She squeezed Sev's shoulder possessively, eyeing Phoenix. "And now you're going to pay. You're going to suffer like I did."

Phoenix narrowed his eyes. "That was a long time ago. You are no relation to my daughter; therefore, your claim on her is forfeit."

Jaden sniffed once, leaving Sev in the hallway of the courts and pushing through the double doors to face the judge.

"You'll have to prove it first," she said. "And I know these courts better than you."

She disappeared into the courtroom and left Sev standing alone.

Phoenix rushed to her, wrapping his arms around her in a fierce hug.

"My mouse, I'm sorry. I'm so, so, sorry," he murmured. "Please forgive me?"

She pulled away from him, her hands braced on his shoulders. She was crying.

"I've missed you, Daddy. I want to go home. I want to go back to Dobani to live with you. I'll never run away again. Never."

He wiped her tears away with his thumbs, and Pearla came up to kneel beside them. "Your daddy's missed you," she reassured her. She tucked a strand of hair behind Sev's ear. "We're going to get this worked out. Don't you worry."

Sev managed a small smile and nodded. She remembered Pearla from the party. It was curious that she was here, but she didn't mind it. Her father deserved friends, too.

"Is what she said true?" she asked Phoenix. "You knew her before? And she's not my aunt?"

Phoenix swallowed, then nodded. "Yes, girl. I knew her a long time ago. Jaden's not your blood. She never knew Del. She never knew your mother."

Sev's lip quivered. "I thought as much. She isn't kind. I know my mom was nothing like her."

Phoenix caressed her face. "That's right, mouse. She's doing this to get back at me."

Pearla tugged at his sleeve. "It's time to go in. Let's go."

They walked into the courtroom together, letting the door close behind them. Sev joined Jaden begrudgingly at the table to the right. They settled in the chairs there, and the judge took the bench.

The judge leaned forward over his large desk and looked at Jaden. "May I have the documents proving this child is your niece?"

Jaden glanced at Phoenix and Pearla, a wicked smile on her face. She placed a possessive hand on Sev and handed the documents to the judge.

The judge flipped through the holopad. Phoenix held his breath; Jaden was a forgery expert, Phoenix knew, and the papers would be pristine.

He sat back in his chair, and the holopad winked out. "Phoenix, you claim to be this child's father. Is that correct?"

Phoenix stood. "I *am* her father, your honor. The adoption was on Dobani. I have the papers."

He passed the holopad to the court officer, who then handed it to the judge. Phoenix watched as the judge inspected the adoption papers.

"Indeed, you are Sev's adopted father by the authority of Dobani," he said briskly, "but the papers provided by Mara show that she shares a blood relation to the child. As her only living blood relative, this supersedes your claim."

He looked at Phoenix over his glasses, his face serious. "I'm sorry, Phoenix."

Phoenix felt his whole body go numb. Pearla grabbed his hand; it was only then he realized it was shaking.

The judge banged his gavel, and Phoenix flinched. "The child shall be remanded to the custody of her aunt on Merren. No review is scheduled. The courts will consider allowing visitation for the child's adopted father in six months' time."

Sev glanced at her father; he was looking down at the scarred desktop, his mouth a grim line. When he met her gaze, she gave him a weak smile. "I love you," she mouthed wordlessly. His eyes filled with tears.

Jaden motioned for Sev to rise, then led her by the elbow down a long hall. Sev took a last look at her father, then faded out of sight.

The judge and the officer left the courtroom. Phoenix sat frozen, unwilling to leave Merren without his daughter. He and Pearla sat there, alone, for a long time after.

CHAPTER 21

10 Years Prior

J aden sat on the corner of Central City Finance, the engine of the transport idling. They were burning precious fuel and credits were tight. She eyed the exit until up ahead she saw Phoenix, bag over his shoulder, hair slicked back, looking every bit the businessman.

She smiled; he played the part well. The businessman façade was only partially true.

He ducked inside the transport, settling in the front seat. Phoenix said nothing at first. He stowed the bag under the seat; it was just a prop, after all, and lit a stim stick.

"Well?"

He looked at her, a wry grin on his face. His hair had gotten long, and if he hadn't styled it so, it would be in his eyes. "Easy peasy," he said. "We can take it, no problem."

She narrowed her gaze. "Enforcers?"

He snorted. "Two, give or take their scheduled breaks. We'll wait for them to leave. And no alarms, besides."

Jaden's mouth fell open at that. "What do you mean, no alarms?"

He puffed on his stim stick and released a stream of blue smoke. "I mean, *no alarms*. They're broken, Drek be praised."

Jaden smiled. "Drek be praised." She drummed her fingers on the steering wheel before pulling out into the traffic flow of Central City. "When do we hit it? Like we planned?"

Phoenix nodded. "Just like we planned. I'll go in while you disengage the holocams. You'll follow. No air guns, no one gets hurt." He smiled, taking a last puff on his stim stick before tossing it out the view pane. "See? Easy peasy."

Jaden pursed her lips. Maybe it would be, she reassured herself. She pointed the beat-up transport south, toward their shared flat, and blended into the morning traffic.

The day of the heist came with little fanfare. Phoenix prepared what he would wear, confident in his plan and his ability to carry it out. Jaden served a sparse breakfast, but he did not eat. Call it nervous anticipation or just old-fashioned excitement, but his stomach was unsettled.

They arrived at the finance office in the mid-morning, leaving the engine running while Jaden worked on her holopad. She had a back channel open to the security cams in seconds. With a few decisive keystrokes, she'd disengaged them.

She gave him the all-clear, and Phoenix walked into the finance office with all the confidence of the part he was playing. Jaden could see him through the window, chatting with the clerks there. When he signaled her sometime later, she put away the holopad. Phoenix had forgotten his bag, and she shouldered it and walked toward the building. Upon entering, she headed across to join Phoenix at the clerk's desk. Two Enforcers stopped her at the entrance.

"May we see your bag, ma'am?"

Jaden paused, stricken. Both Enforcers were there, despite what Phoenix had said. She panicked, her heart beating double time. "Excuse me?" she asked in faux offense, trying desperately to buy some time.

One Enforcer took her by the arms and turned her around. The other stripped off the bag and opened it.

There was an air gun inside, along with a note.

The Enforcer held it up, disengaged the air gun, and gave it to his partner. He read the note aloud, but Jaden didn't hear it. Her ears rang. Phoenix stood by the clerk's desk, both hands in his pockets. He was smiling at her.

The Enforcers put binders on her and led her to a chair in the back room of the finance office. In the lobby, an alarm sounded.

After a while, the door opened, and Phoenix walked in. He stood in front of Jaden with a condescending smile on his face.

"I'm truly sorry, J, but the Cloze Family wants you." He winked, and her stomach churned. "I think you know why. They paid me more for you than this job ever could."

He lit a stim stick, puffed on it, and blew the smoke between them. "No hard feelings?"

With that, he grinned and turned his back on her.

Tears ran down her face. Jaden had always heard to never trust a cheater. She thought Phoenix was different. She'd been wrong. He had played her for a fool, and she silently vowed that one day, somehow, he would pay.

Present Day

Pearla scrolled through the holopad, occasionally taking notes. She had a cup of tea cooling on the table next to her, and her reading glasses pushed up on her nose.

The private investigator had sent over the latest brief. Their case was almost ready to present to the judge on Merren; she only wished Phoenix could help her.

She took her pad to the living room where Phoenix sat nursing his morning cup. He had declined in recent weeks. He had gone from the charming and loquacious man she had gotten to know to someone who ghosted the rooms of his own house, barely speaking.

She sat in the chair opposite him and regarded him with a small smile.

"Don't look at me like that, Pearla. Like I'm something to be pitied."

She turned her mouth down in a frown and tutted. "I don't pity you, love. I just wish you wouldn't be so hard on yourself."

211

He narrowed his eyes. He hadn't shaved in a few days, and silver flecked his stubble. "None of this would've happened if it wasn't for me. If it wasn't for what I did." He shook his head in despair, finally lowering it into his hands. "I've done a lot of bad things," he said miserably, "and my past has finally caught up to me." He looked up at Pearla, tears glittering in his eyes. "I'm just sorry Sev is stuck in the middle of it."

Pearla stood and moved to sit near him on the couch. She laid her hand on his arm. "Phoenix. Look at me, honey."

Reluctantly, he obeyed. His face was drawn, his usual tanned skin ashen. Pearla met his eyes.

"You may have done some bad things a long time ago, but you are not bad. Do you understand that?"

He sniffed and looked away. She held his face in her hands, forcing him to look at her. "You are a wonderful father, Phoenix. And you're a good man. You are."

She smiled at him, and he closed his eyes. He nodded softly, and when he finally looked up at her, there was more life there than before.

"I hate you're in the middle of this too," he said ruefully. "It's not your burden to bear." He swallowed, looking down. "You've been kind. Kinder than I deserve."

Pearla patted his cheek. "Go rest," she said. "Let me sort this out."

When he had gone, Pearla spread her materials over the couch and considered.

For Phoenix, Dobani was different without Sev. It was a desolate place. The sea held no beauty; the sun did not warm, its brutal eye scorching anyone falling beneath its gaze. Sev's garden fell to ruin, overrun by weeds.

Pearla had stayed. She was worried for Phoenix; she also refused to accept the judge's decision. Pearla had reached out to a private investigator in Dobani Proper, and together, they'd developed a plan.

When she explained her plans to Phoenix, he had initially dismissed them. "The judge believed Jaden," he said. "There's nothing for it."

But Pearla persisted. Sometimes, when no one else would believe you, you had to believe in yourself.

It was early the next day when Pearla received the transmission from the private investigator. The deep dive they had made into Jaden's past (and subsequently Phoenix's) had proved fruitful. She had the evidence she needed. Now she just needed to present it to the judge.

She left midday for Dobani Proper. The barge to Merren was slow and lumbering, but she settled into a seat near the view pane and watched the black of space slice into the pretty Dobani sky.

Pearla thought of Sev, of how excited she must've been on this journey. Phoenix had told her of how Sev yearned to know her mother…how she had never met her. This woman, Jaden, had promised Sev connection. To a young girl who lacked many touchstones in her life, that must've been nearly irresistible.

But Jaden was not who she claimed to be. She had been following Phoenix for some time, maybe even since she got out of prison. Jaden had been waiting to strike at the right moment, when it would hurt him the most. She aimed to cost Sev her inheritance and Phoenix his daughter, with no regard for what that might mean.

Pearla spent the entire trip going over things in her mind, weighing the words she would say to the judge. Before she realized it, the barge was breaching Merren's atmosphere.

Pearla had forgotten how dark Merren was. It was noon locally, and Merren's moon cast a silvery glow over the world outside the window. Beings walked by with headlamps as they made their way to lunch; children played games under the streetlights. She was used to the Dobani sun, the warmth of an almost year-round tourist season.

She checked her notes, making sure all was in order. The courts were in the center of the capital city of Merren. She hired a transport to take her there; she had scheduled an appointment with the judge, and she didn't want to be late.

The transport stopped outside of the courts building, and Pearla got out. She looked up at the magnificent structure, dark and foreboding, and memories of the court hearing came flooding back.

She walked inside and signed her name on the register. Others were in line to see the judge, and she realized the wait might be excessive. It didn't matter. Pearla had been working towards this moment since the original ruling, since the courts had taken Sev away from her father. She wasn't giving up.

Pearla had been waiting outside the judge's chambers for over an hour; despite her appointment, the judge was running late.

Sometime later, the door opened, and an older man walked in and sat down behind a large wooden desk. Pearla stood, extending her hand to him.

"Thank you for seeing me," she said. "I know you're a busy man."

He nodded and shook her hand. "What can I help you with, Pearla?" He flipped through some documents on his desk. "This custody matter you're talking about is settled."

Pearla presented the holopad. "There's evidence you were never privy to," she began. "Mara is not who you think she is. I know she's made a life for herself here on Merren, but her real name is Jaden. She served five years for attempting to rob a finance office in Central City."

The judge furrowed his brow and leaned forward, his elbows on his desk. "I'm aware of her time served. That has nothing to do with her being fit to raise a child. Especially one she's related to."

Pearla shook her head. "What you don't know is that Sev's adoptive father, Phoenix, is the reason she went to prison. Jaden hid that fact from the courts. She forged the paperwork. She is no relation to Sev at all. This custody claim is an act of revenge, not to mention Sev stands to inherit a large sum of credits."

The judge leaned back, looking over his glasses. "And you have evidence of this?"

Pearla pointed to the holopad. "It's all there. Punch cards from the Cloze family, given to Phoenix in payment for his part in the setup. Records of Phoenix and Jaden sharing a flat in Central City. Both their names are on the lease."

The judge scrolled through the information on the holopad for a tense few moments. He finally set it down, taking off his glasses and pinching the bridge of his nose.

"I see that the courts have made an error," he said. "Go get the child. Return her to her home on Dobani, with the court's apologies. I will contact the Enforcers and have Jaden handled myself."

Pearla could barely contain her excitement. She shook the judge's hand, thanking him profusely.

The transport ride to Jaden's house was a long one. Jaden lived on the outskirts of Merren in a small house between two mountains. The courts had provided Pearla with escorts to ensure a hopefully stress-free transition.

When they arrived, Sev was sitting in front of the house, reading by flashlight. She put her book down when the transport pulled up in the yard, squinting into the headlights to discern who the visitors were.

"Pearla?" she asked. "What are you doing here?"

Pearla walked up to the porch and knelt in front of her. "I'm here to take you home, Sev. Back to Dobani."

Sev's mouth dropped open, and she threw her arms around Pearla's neck. "You mean it? You really mean it?"

Pearla sighed, patting her back gently. "Yes dear. It's finally over."

Sev withdrew from Pearla's embrace, a new light in her eyes. Behind her, the Enforcers knocked on the door. When Jaden answered, they took her into custody.

Pearla and Sev called for another transport, eager to start their journey home.

Sev was quiet on the transport barge to Dobani. She and Pearla sat by each other, Sev in the window seat. Sev was looking at her holopad; she'd finally gotten it back from Jaden.

"So, you like my dad, huh?"

It took Pearla by surprise. Her cheeks pinked, and she gave Sev a small smile. "I do," she admitted.

Sev grinned. "Good. He must like you, too."

Pearla smiled. "I hope so," she said. She patted Sev's hand, and Sev laid her head back against the seat. Sev was tired, but also excited. Her wait for home was finally over.

When they arrived at the little house, Sev ran ahead, bursting through the door. Her father was nowhere to be found.

Pearla caught up with her and placed a finger over her lips. "Phoenix thinks I'm at my sister's," she whispered. "Let's surprise him."

Sev nodded. She dropped her pack, eager to see her room, her belongings. But most of all, eager to see her father.

Pearla walked to the bedroom door and called for Phoenix. After a few moments, he shuffled into the living room.

His face was gaunt, his clothes wrinkled. He had knotted the sleeve of his shirt below his stump; he rarely wore his prosthetic.

"Sev?" he asked. "Is that you mouse?" He walked a few steps toward her. "As I live and breathe. Is that really you?"

She fell into his arms. "Oh, Daddy," she said. "How I've missed you!"

Pearla stood apart from them, wiping tears from her eyes. She had her arms folded in front of her, a soft smile on her face. Above them, the skylight let in the morning sun, illuminating Sev and Phoenix in its warm light.

"I'm home," Sev said, burrowing her face in her father's shoulder. "Where I belong."

EPILOGUE

The water was clear and bright. Phoenix sat on the shore as Sev and Pearla swam, just a blip on the horizon as they sliced through the blue-green waters.

They'd laid a picnic among the sea grasses. Pearla had insisted; there were cold cuts and sweet cream fruit, and Sev's favorite sandwiches. Pearla still let Phoenix cook, but it was happening less and less. And Sev always wanted to help her.

Sev turned and waved to him, her blonde hair dark with water. He waved back with his prosthetic arm. He had his shirt off, and his skin was browning by the moment.

Near midday, Sev and Pearla walked across the beach to the blanket spread there. They settled, dripping wet, before Sev eagerly reached for the basket.

"Now, mouse. Have you worked up an appetite already?"

Sev made a face, squinting against the sun, and it pleased him. He handed her the straw hat she favored in the warm season, and she put it on.

They took their lunch, and Phoenix put up the umbrella. Sev and Pearla stretched out, letting the warm air dry their skin. They'd finished swimming for the day.

After she'd dried off, Sev fed the birds that flitted around the beach. Two hopped closer towards her, nipping at the bread in her hand, and she laughed. She stood, leading them away from the picnic and closer to the water's edge.

Pearla scooted back to sit by Phoenix. They both watched Sev as she teased the birds with bits of bread, throwing it in the air and watching as the gulls caught it in mid-flight.

Phoenix reached for Pearla's hand and gave it a gentle squeeze.

"I have all I ever wanted," he spoke into the wind. "More than I ever dared to dream."

Pearla smiled. She pressed her shoulder against Phoenix and relaxed against him. Near the shore, Sev walked back to join them, all out of bread.

About the Author

Jessahme Wren is an award-winning science fiction author who writes character-driven stories about resilience, hope, and found family. Her Terra series blends emotional depth with immersive worldbuilding, exploring what it means to heal, to belong, and to fight for the people we love.

A long-time educator, Brandi brings compassion and humanity to every story she creates. When she isn't writing, she enjoys reading, traveling, spending time with family, and relaxing with her two pets. She is currently working on future books in the Terra series.

Keep up to date on news and all my books here:

Thank you for purchasing this book.
If you enjoyed your read, please provide feedback in the
form of a review.

www.ingramcontent.com/pod-product-compliance
Lightning Source LLC
Chambersburg PA
CBHW060735180626
46819CB00001B/40